Her Country or His Lordship?

PAGE

Sensual, impulsive one moment; elegant, vulnerable the next. And on the eve of the bitter war of 1812, she was filled with heartfelt loyalty and rebellious need.

LORD HAZARD

His aristocratic charm gained him the key to private chambers and state secrets. His fiery countenance touched every woman's heart, his kiss their lips.

DAVID MASON

From the sultry tropical coves of Bermuda he pirated British gold and owed allegiance to neither land nor woman, until he took on the beautiful cargo that plunder his very soul!

Other Avon Books by
Jan Cox Speas

BRIDE OF THE MACHUGH	36152	$1.95
MY LORD MONLEIGH	36442	1.95

MY LOVE, MY ENEMY

JAN COX SPEAS

 AVON
PUBLISHERS OF BARD, CAMELOT AND DISCUS BOOKS

AVON BOOKS
A division of
The Hearst Corporation
959 Eighth Avenue
New York, New York 10019

Copyright © 1961 by Jan Cox Speas
Published by arrangement with the author.
Library of Congress Catalog Card Number: 78-54088
ISBN: 0-380-01869-1

First Avon Printing, May, 1978

AVON TRADEMARK REG. U.S. PAT. OFF. AND IN
OTHER COUNTRIES, MARCA REGISTRADA,
HECHO EN U.S.A.

Printed in Canada

1

It was not, from its beginning, an ordinary day.

Dawn came to Bradley's House on a quiet gray pause between dark and day, dripping wetly from trees and boxwood and eaves, holding to itself in the cool air all the sweet garden scents of white magnolia and moss rose and fragile mimosa. Beyond the land the Chesapeake slept silently, its surface rippled, like watered silk, by a faint breath of wind that trailed the haze behind it in tattered wisps across the water. To the west, where the woodland and tobacco fields bordered the roads leading from the Bay to Upper Marlboro, to Bladensburg, to Washington, the fog dissolved into mist and a drizzle of summer rain, laying the thick dust and cooling the oppressive heat of that summer of 1813.

On the Bay the fog showed signs of lifting before noon, and the inland rain was no more than a brief deliverance. But whatever its destiny, the day that dawned with cool mist and a gray silence, touched with the subtle cloudy beauty of an opal, was already set apart from the hot glittering days preceding it.

To Catherine Page Bradley, engaged in a small adventure of disobedience and misbehavior, the unique quality of the day seemed an extraordinary piece of good fortune.

Sitting quietly in the cockpit of the small sloop, she crossed her arms and held them tightly against her. In the hurry and stealth of leaving home she had forgotten to find a wrap, and her thin muslin gown with its narrow skirt and tiny sleeves seemed to leave an inordinate amount of her uncovered to the brisk morning chill. But if the fog was uncomfortably cold, she reminded herself sturdily that it also shrouded the world in an enormous cocoon; the British might be as thick on the Bay as forty thieves, but what they could not see they could not steal, or threaten, or shoot at the first sign of resistance.

She closed her eyes and breathed deeply of the damp air with its smells of brackish salt water, wet canvas sail, slippery decking that still gave off a faint resinous scent of white pine and hot yellow sun. Already she could distinguish an occasional warm feather of air from the land, hidden in the haze somewhere off the port bow. Soon the *Catherine*, slipping through the water with no more than a whisper of a sound, would round the point into the Severn.

Ahead, blurred and indistinct, would be the houses and steeples of Annapolis reaching upward through a canopy of dark wet green, and the sheltered harbor with ships reflecting their curved images across the glassy water while their masts raked the fog. Not to be immediately seen, but there as surely as the calm harbor and State House cupola, would be the noises and smells and infectious bustle of a port town, and the carriages and horses crowding the streets, and the town people who lived in the graceful brick houses and walked the tree-shaded lanes.

Inside her a slow delicious excitement stirred, warming her against the morning chill and the equally dampening disapproval in Duncan MacDougall's face.

For the past few minutes he had resorted to the final reproach of ignoring her, lifting his eyes to the sail or narrowing them to watch the drifting haze ahead, carefully centering his attention on the *Catherine* and her destination. But Page, looking from beneath her lashes at the fixed scowl on his plain stubborn face, was not misled.

"I thought you'd be pleased to have my company," she said at last. "Don't you ever find it lonely, sailing back and forth to town all alone?"

He could not ignore a direct question. But he made her wait a few minutes before he said pointedly, "It's one of the few pleasures of my life, getting away from the giggling and chattering."

"I don't chatter," Page said with dignity, "and I seldom giggle."

"You've six sisters who do," MacDougall said. "I've put up with a houseful of women for longer than I care to remember, and you're the worst of the lot." He regarded her with an ill-concealed exasperation. "One day you'll find yourself in one scrape too many, and when you look to me for help you'll not get it."

"You're as cross as an old bear," Page said cordially. "It isn't so terrible a crime, after all. Papa promised me a trip to town for my birthday."

"Not in the *Catherine*, he didn't. You know well enough you're not allowed on the Bay, and who's to explain to Samuel Bradley how it happened? It'll be me, no doubt, the way it's always been, but I can tell you now I've no hope of saving you from his temper."

Page sighed, obliged to admit that her father would indeed be in a tearing rage when he discovered that she had tricked MacDougall by the simple ruse of hiding below until the *Catherine* was well out into the channel. Samuel Bradley might send his small sloop wherever he pleased, satisfied that few enemy ships might outsail her; but he had not, since the beginning of the British blockade, cared to extend the same risk to his daughters.

She could not truly blame him. The British were guilty of the most heinous crimes, not the least of which was their very presence in the Chesapeake, keeping everyone in a constant state of turmoil. Since February, when Admiral Cockburn first brought his squadron to Lynhaven Bay, there had seldom been a week when one of his ships was not sighted from the steeple of the State House. And British captains, eager to line their own pockets with the spoils of war, were as likely to covet small civilian craft as men-of-war. In the wake of a dozen such mishaps to astonished neighbors up and down the shore, Samuel Bradley had declared positively that his daughters would either travel by horse or carriage, or they would stay at home. To the sociably-inclined Bradley daughters—as to anyone born and bred in a country where sensible people had always preferred the quick and pleasant waterways of the Chesapeake to the interminable and ill-made roads—the indignity of being forced off the Bay was one of the more irritating hardships of the war.

"If he promised," MacDougall said, "why didn't you wait and go with him? I heard him tell Bessie he'd take her in to shop one day next week."

"That isn't fair. I notice that you always have a number of pressing chores to keep you at home when it's time for Bessie to go to town."

He had the grace to grin faintly. "She's a fair nuisance, that one. I've stood on Fleet street for more than an hour, mind you, waiting for her to finish her chattering."

Page laughed. She was fond of MacDougall's sister

Bessie, a small Scots woman with an enormous motherly heart who had cherished the Bradley family as her own for years, reigning over the domestic life of Bradley's House as firmly as Duncan ruled the fields and stables. But no amount of fondness could ease the burden of a shopping trip with Bessie. The sisters drew straws to determine which would endure the long jolting carriage ride, the tiresome waiting while Bessie visited up and down the streets of Annapolis, and the strict surveillance that never faltered until Bessie had her chicks safely back home again.

"But that's nothing to do with you," MacDougall said. "At my age, I don't need a chaperon."

Page lifted her chin. "Nor do I."

"Aye, you need a keeper," he retorted, "and I've no mind to take on such a thankless position." He glanced at her briefly, his scowl returning. "You'd look more like a young lady if you'd bother yourself to put on that bonnet. There's no sense in going to town to buy fancy new clothes when you look like somebody's poor kin."

"Don't scold, Mac." Page slipped the bonnet behind her. "It's my very oldest one, and it was Martha's best and Emily's second-best before it came to me." She added, quite firmly, "I've made up my mind I'll never wear it again."

If she had dared she would have dropped the ugly thing in the water, but such profligacy would have done little to conciliate Duncan MacDougall. She consoled herself with the thought of the birthday money in her beaded reticule, and the letter she had written a month past to Madame Dorval, the French seamstress recently come to Annapolis.

She leaned forward, chin in her hands, trying to subdue her unruly excitement by ridiculing it. Surely it was absurdly childish, and ill-suited to the sober dignity one

5

should acquire on the occasion of one's eighteenth birthday, to feel so blithe and gay over an ordinary trip to town.

But somehow she could not summon up the smallest shred of sobriety, and her mouth curved into a smile against every measure of her will. It was not, after all, an ordinary matter to have escaped Bessie's vigilant eye and the dull isolation of Bradley's House; or to be dallying with the notion of buying new clothes when she had never before possessed a gown or a bonnet unworn by an older sister; or to have been given, by a kindly fate, this lovely hushed silver day of mist for her small adventure.

The *Catherine* had entered the river now and was approaching the town quay, but Page, forgetting the steeples and houses of Annapolis, stared at the two tall ocean-going schooners that had slipped through the blockade in the fog and were riding triumphantly to their anchors in the harbor.

Clustered around them and crowding the docks and quays were numerous smaller boats from landings on both shores of the Bay. Like Samuel Bradley, whose liking for good Madeira had sent MacDougall posthaste to town in the *Catherine*, the other Maryland planters had known of the approach of the schooners while their captains were still feeling a cautious course through the shoals and channels of the lower Bay. Now that they had come safely to port with their wines and molasses and coffee, despite the capricious Chesapeake and the scavenging British, most of the population seemed to be on hand to welcome them.

MacDougall's scowl deepened. "It'd suit me better if you'd stay on the *Catherine* and not go into town at all."

"No," Page said definitely.

"Then you'll come along with me to Andrew Barney's office and wait while I finish my business with him."

"I've nothing to say to Papa's agent," Page said. "You tend to your business, Mac, and I'll tend to mine."

"You're a nuisance," he said bitterly, "and I knew all along I shouldn't have let you come. It's no place for a proper young lady today."

"I'm not a proper young lady," Page said, and smiled at him.

He was not placated. "That's what Bessie will have you be, devil take the hindmost. But it's Mr. Bradley, not Bessie, you'd best be worrying about. Likely he'll keep you at home the rest of the summer, so there's little use in spending all your money on new clothes you'll never have a chance to wear."

"Papa would never be so cruel," Page said positively.

MacDougall sighed. Samuel Bradley, truth to tell, was not the man to be cruel to any of his seven motherless daughters, and least of all to this particular one, with her slanted smile and tawny hair so like that other Catherine, now dead these nine long years. But however much he indulged his daughters, when he happened to notice them, Samuel Bradley would undoubtedly have a great deal to say, and most of it unpleasant, to Duncan MacDougall.

"Besides," Page added, "I shall do as I please with the money. Papa made no conditions when he gave it to me."

"He didn't think you'd spend it higgledy-piggledy, like some backwoods wastrel come to town with his first dollar in his pocket. I'll wager Bessie expected you to lay it away for the day you'll go to Washington to visit your Aunt Hester."

7

Page's eyes slanted with amusement. "Papa doesn't care for Aunt Hester. He'd be more pleased if I didn't go to Washington at all."

MacDougall had nothing to say to that. As he brought the *Catherine* into the long narrow lane of the market dock, he admitted to himself that Hester Carroll was indeed a proud, disagreeable woman whose sense of duty caused an excessive amount of mischief. Bessie might have an abiding faith in ladies and Polite Society, but after one season in Washington Julia, the oldest Bradley daughter, had married a wealthy Virginia planter who kept the poor lass isolated on a Gloucester County plantation. Martha and Emily, the next two, were silly giggling girls who expected to go to Hester Carroll's in the autumn, and as a result talked of nothing but beaus and balls and Mrs. Madison's levees. Next would come Page, and then the three youngest; and before Hester Carroll had finished with the daughters of her dead sister, they would all be as different from that gay sweet Catherine as Aunt Hester and Polite Society could well make them.

It was an evil thing to contemplate, and it did not improve MacDougall's temper.

He watched Page as she scrambled over the side to the quay and paused there, swinging her bonnet by its ribbons, looking around her with eyes bluer than gentians, her slim body seeming to lift on tiptoes with eagerness.

"Hold on a minute," he said, less brusquely than he had intended, "and I'll walk with you as far as Mr. Barney's office."

Having won her point, Page waited with tolerable patience until he had tidied the *Catherine* and checked her lines for a final time. Then they walked together

across the crowded bustling market square, Mac-
Dougall leading the way by several steps. He was not a
tall man, yet Page reached only to his shoulder; and she
always found it difficult to keep up with his brisk no-
nonsense stride without resorting to an undignified
sprint.

"You're in a great hurry," she said. "Do you think
Mr. Barney will neglect Papa's interests and sell all the
good Madeira before you arrive?"

MacDougall didn't look around. "He'd not be such a
fool."

"Then you must be intending to leave for home
within the hour."

"I'll leave when I've tended to my business, and I'd
advise you to be ready."

"Would you really leave me behind? Only think,
Mac, what Papa would have to say if you treated me so
shabbily."

As she had confidently expected, such deliberate
provocation brought immediate results. MacDougall
stopped short and turned. Then, as he saw her face, the
anger in his own was replaced by a reluctant grin.

"You're a cheeky lass," he said. "Was I going too
fast for you?"

Catching her breath, she walked beside him for a few
steps. But before they had crossed the square he said,
"I see a friend I must speak to. Go on and I'll catch
you up."

Page sighed. "You're as bad as Bessie," she said, but
he had already gone, exchanging a cheerful greeting
with someone she could not see through the throng of
servants and housekeepers and farmers crowding
around the open market.

She took a deep breath, suddenly very hungry, giddy

with the sound and color scattered in gay brilliance across the old gray cobbles and rising about her like warm fragrant waves of scent.

There were vegetables spilling from their baskets in vivid splashes of red and yellow and green; barrels of fish and crabs, fresh from the Bay, piled in gray and silver splendor; golden balls of sweet butter wrapped in dark green rain-washed leaves; brown eggs in tawny straw baskets; fresh poultry and smoked hams and squealing piglets; fruit in rich glowing reds, plum-red, cherry-red, strawberry-red; great drifts of flowers, picked in summer rain that still glistened wetly on their blossoms of blue and lavender, moon-white and rose and primrose yellow.

Page went on slowly, reluctant to leave the vibrant singing color that seemed so extravagant, so beautiful, so surprising in the heart of staid old Annapolis town.

"Have you thought what you're to do if we're obliged to stay in town the night?"

MacDougall was at her elbow, his face scowling again, the small shred of good humor she had coaxed to life gone as if it had never been.

Puzzled, she said cautiously, "I can't imagine why we should be obliged to do anything of the kind."

"I've been talking to John Clement, captain of the Baltimore packet, and he advises me not to leave the harbor without a fair wind at my back."

Page looked down the harbor; the sky was still low-hanging and gray, but the mouth of the river was plainly visible. "The sun will burn off the fog before long," she said, "and we'll have as much wind as when we left home this morning."

"We didn't need much of a breeze at dawn, with the fog to hide us. But I'll not pussy-foot all the way home in broad daylight, not with some plaguey British frigate poking her nose into every creek along the way."

Page's eyes widened slightly. Surely not today, she thought despairingly, and surely not a frigate. "Mac," she said in a small voice, "are you sure?"

MacDougall turned and squinted his eyes at the tall masts of the West Indian schooners. "Clement says she chased those two up from the Capes. Her captain will be in the devil's own temper, having his game spoiled."

For a long silent moment, Page stared at MacDougall and he stared back with more than a hint of malice on his face.

"She's out there, right enough, playing cat-and-mouse, just waiting to snatch up some reckless fool for the admiral's pleasure. We must have missed her by less than a hair, and I've no intention of pressing my luck twice in a single day."

"If you're quizzing me, Mac, I'll make you regret it."

He shrugged. "You're the one will have regrets, my girl, before this day is over."

They walked along silently for an interval. Then Page said thoughtfully, "If it becomes a necessity, I have friends who will be kind enough to give me a night's lodging."

"With Mr. Bradley not knowing where you are or how you got there? Not likely, missy. I'll have to hire a horse and some poor lad to ride along, and send you home the long way."

The thought of being sent home in disgrace on a hired hack was not very pleasant. "You needn't be so odiously self-righteous," Page said, and added defiantly, "in any case, I may as well enjoy it while I'm here."

"Aye, you may as well," MacDougall retorted, "like the Queen of France eating her cake before going to the guillotine." Then he relented and grinned at her. "Go along and have your fun, and I'll come to fetch you when I've whistled up a respectable wind."

Page left him at the door to Andrew Barney's narrow brick office and walked slowly up the hill towards the State House.

Mr. Madison's war, she reflected, was an intolerable nuisance. In Washington the War Hawks had preached the necessity of fighting for free trade, and red-haired Henry Clay, who had never seen the sea, pleaded for sailors' rights. Nothing but war, they cried passionately, would avenge the insulting British habit of firing on American ships and impressing American seamen. A few out-spoken Federalists insisted that Napoleon had seized as many ships and seamen as the British, and American honor was equally in jeopardy if war was not declared against France. But Samuel Bradley had remarked, with some heat, that any fool could find a reason to fight another fool if he searched long enough, and Jamie Madison should steer his own cautious course and ignore all the fiery young western senators who wanted a war primarily to settle the Indian problem on the frontier and not, as they nobly avowed, to defend the rights of sailors who had never smelled an Indian or traveled beyond the Shenandoah.

But despite so many fierce and contradictory opinions, the Congress had finally declared war, willy-nilly as it were, on Great Britain. Page sympathized with Mr. Madison, who despite his hatred of war was obliged, as a man, to agree with those who deemed honor more important than life; but privately she thought anyone with a brain the size of a pea must see the folly of fighting a war with a navy of twenty-odd vessels, an army consisting mainly of paper regiments, and no money in the Treasury.

Certainly the British did not appear to be quaking in their boots. Aunt Hester had written that Dolley Madison was sadly offended when Admiral Cockburn sent word that he would soon make his bow at her drawing room, but even Samuel Bradley considered the admiral capable of announcing himself at the President's House at any given date. He had burned Havre de Grace and Frenchtown, after all, and had looted and pillaged towns and farmhouses at his pleasure, even stealing Commodore Rodger's sofa from Sion Hill, it was rumored, to sit upon while dining on stolen Maryland hens and country hams.

Nothing, however small and insignificant, was safe from the British; not even, Page thought bitterly, her own unimportant affairs.

She had almost reached the top of Cornhill Street. Pausing on the narrow sidewalk, she stared unseeingly at the riders on blooded Maryland horses, the occasional carriages splashing the muddy water left by the rain, the men passing in and out of the State House with their papers and preoccupied faces.

Sometimes it seemed to her that the British policy was simply to harass the people of the Chesapeake country into madness, much as a horde of pesky mosquitoes will drive the most sensible man to utter exasperation. Page could see the wisdom of such tactics; even the most ardent patriot must find it difficult to muster enthusiasm for a war involving, not glorious battles and waving flags, but pigs and poultry and the annoyance of having to stay always at home.

She stepped into the street, absently swinging her bonnet.

The next instant she found herself in immediate

peril, menaced by the rearing forelegs of an enormous raking chestnut so close above her that the frantic hoofs seemed to be pawing the air only inches away from her face.

For an endless moment she could not move, startled into immobility by the size of the horse and the frightening certainty that she was about to be trampled into the street.

Then it was all over. The horse was under control, brought down swiftly by his rider, and Page recovered enough presence of mind to step quietly back to the sidewalk, slipping the offending bonnet behind her.

She drew a deep unsteady breath and raised her head.

The man on the chestnut looked down at her without speaking. His dark face was expressionless and his eyes met Page's without a hint of anger in their cold gray depths, but for the length of that long silent moment she felt an inexplicable and childish urge to turn and run away.

She lifted her chin. "I'm very sorry," she said. "I was thinking of something else, you see, and I forgot to look."

If he thought the excuse a lame one he gave no indication of it. His eyes moved over her briefly and came back to her face, resting there for a thoughtful moment. Then he lifted his tall curly beaver and bowed from the saddle.

"My fault entirely, ma'am," he said politely.

Her face burned. It was only the barest civility, and so patently untrue that his hard clipped voice denied it the least pretense of courtesy and relegated her, instead, to that world of tiresome children and fools who cannot be held responsible for their stupidity.

Completely chastened, she stared wordlessly at him. She was certain she had never seen him in Annapolis before, for it would be difficult to forget that inscrutable face with its hard mouth and strange hooded eyes. With a flicker of curiosity she noted the way the exquisitely tailored coat stretched across the big shoulders without a crease, the intricate folds of his cravat, the shining topboots, the powerfully-muscled thighs in the pale yellow buckskins. Such elegance was not wholly alien to Annapolis, she thought with a quickening interest, but it was undeniably odd to meet it in Cornhill Street in the early morning of a wet dripping day.

She realized suddenly that he was waiting quietly for her to finish her rude scrutiny, and she felt her face flush painfully again.

"Don't look so distressed," he said, sounding somewhat amused. "It was not so easy to unseat me, as you see, and I acquit you of deliberately wishing to kill yourself in such an unpleasant fashion. Please do me the honor, however, of promising to be more careful in the future. It is always wise, you know, to look before you leap."

He bowed again, murmured, "Your servant," and rode on, followed by another man clad in sober black and mounted on a sober black horse. Plainly a gentleman's gentleman, the second man gave Page only a slight bow as he passed, but something in his face seemed to convey a friendly sympathy that took some of the sting from her embarrassment.

She turned and watched as they rode on down the hill. A small boy darted out of a house, shouting to a friend, and Page held her breath as the magnificent rawboned chestnut arched his head and danced uneasily; but his rider, sitting the saddle with a careless assurance, obviously had him well in hand again. Then the big shoulders and curly tilted beaver disappeared from sight, obscured by a carriage lumbering up the hill.

Page gave an imperceptible sigh. Nothing was going the way it should. It was really quite strange, she reflected with a swift amusement, how the day refused to fit into its normal ordinary pattern. She had been seeking an escape from boredom, but perhaps one should be wary of a boon so readily and generously granted.

She shrugged her shoulders and crossed the street, carefully looking both ways before she left the sidewalk.

2

Afterwards, Duncan MacDougall insisted that none of the incredible events of that day would have occurred had it not been for certain flaws in Page Bradley's character. He went on to explain that from her earliest days, when he had been obliged to fish her out of the Bay daily, she had possessed an untidy knack of attracting misfortune to herself as well as any unwary and innocent bystander.

Page thought it vastly unfair of him to dwell so persistently on the flaws in her character.

But when she looked back and pondered the exact moment when events began to rush together, hurtling from all directions to break over her head like a summer thunderstorm, she often sighed for herself as she had been that June morning, standing at the edge of the market square, dangling two new bandboxes by their strings and lifting her head to taste the wet mist still clouding the Bay and washing the rose-brick face of Annapolis town.

She was very happy, very gay, very heedless. For two hours she had wandered about town, doing all the things she had promised herself to do, and not even the prospect of the certain punishment awaiting her at Bradley's House could dim the glory of possessing a new chip bonnet tied with blue satin ribbons and a sprigged muslin dress with a blue pelisse. Besides these treasures, she had purchased from Madame Dorval a sprig of gauze flowers for Betsy, a striped velvet ribbon for Dolly, and an embroidered square to be worked into a sampler by Sarah, the baby.

She had visited the printer's to examine his new books, lingering so long over a narrow volume of *Don Quixote* that the printer had kindly suggested that she charge it against her father's account. She had seen Mr. Chase's elegant new London coach and admired its yellow and blue upholstering and enormous wheels, picked out in yellow, and with her last bit of money she had treated herself to one of the new ices, a delicious concoction of fruit liquid poured over shaved ice.

She had also, unfortunately, met several of her father's friends. The wife of one of them, a staid elderly lady in a calash bonnet pulled over its hoops like a large caterpillar to hide her face, reproached Page for walking in town alone and unescorted, and announced sternly that she would certainly ask Samuel Bradley what he was about, raising his daughters to be hoydens.

Page, knowing Papa's trenchant opinion of the simpering ladylike young girls who came to visit Martha and Emily, was not alarmed by this threat; but when she recalled how she had absently walked directly into the path of a highly-bred and sensitive chestnut, she shuddered to imagine what Papa would say of such wretched misconduct.

She knew very well what Duncan MacDougall would say if she did not stay away from the waterfront until he came to fetch her. But the sun was beginning to burn through the haze, striking the wet street with pale glints, and she could feel a freshening wind against her cheek. It would soon chase away the last vestige of fog and the

Bay would stretch in a wide blue glitter beneath the sun. If they left shortly, they might be home before Papa sat down to his luncheon of roast beef and potatoes.

Having made her decision, she went on across the market square. Dodging a loaded wagon, she came out on the edge of the quay. The *Catherine* was in sight at the far end of the narrow slip, but a shifting crowd of people, their attention fastened on something she could not see, blocked her way.

Mildly curious, Page stood on tiptoe to see what could be the object of such great attraction to the crowd of sweating men who had been unloading the ships, a horde of small boys, and a number of seamen off the schooners. But she was too small and their backs too broad, looming up like a mountain that haughtily cut off the view but offered no holds for climbing.

Whatever it was, the temper of the crowd was not pleasant. The men closest to Page were plainly angry; one, his seaman's pigtail of black hair pulled back from a sullen face marred by a livid scar, yelled something across the crowd, a malignant threat laced with obscenity, and the other men shifted their feet restlessly. Page, looking with longing at the *Catherine* out of reach down the quayside, realized that she was penned in on all sides, trapped in their midst. The man with the bitter scarred face was shouting again, the mutter of voices backing him up, and more people had joined the crowd behind Page.

A dirty boy, small and bright-eyed, darted past her. "A spy, we've catched us a spy!" he piped gleefully, and the rough sailor took up the words and yelled, "Damn him for a Limey spy! I say h'ist him at the end of a line and let him dangle!"

Page took a deep breath. Then, through a sudden break in the restless crowd, she saw the horse backed up almost to the quay edge, pale sun gleaming along the rich chestnut shoulders, proud head pulling impatiently against a tightly-held bridle.

A man just beside Page cleared his throat and spit on the cobbles. "Ask him how he left the bloody admiral," he demanded harshly, "and why he ain't wearing his fancy blue uniform!"

"He don't need no uniform," the seaman shrilled in a taunting voice, "it's writ all over his ugly Limey face! He's a spy off'n one of Cockburn's ships, damn his eyes, and I say string him up here and now!"

"Hanging's too good for him," another bitter voice called. "Take a look at me back, ye sneakin' coward, and see what two hundred lashes with the cat can do to pretty up a man. That's what I've got to show for three years of hell in His Majesty's Navy, by special invitation, ye might say, and me that's never set foot in England in me life!"

"A flogging," shrieked a young lad in blue jacket and nankeen trousers. "A flogging!"

"Aye, give him a flogging, lads, spread-eagled like they done it to me, and we'll see if His Majesty's officers are bloody heroes without a troop of marines to back 'em up!"

Page stood very still, remembering the hard clipped voice, the exceptional elegance, the faint air of arrogance as he looked down at her from the big chestnut. She had heard rumors that the British ships lying in the Bay received the Washington newspapers daily, and that a number of their officers went in and out of Washington at will, disguised by no more than a fine suit of clothes and a heavy purse. But she had never thought to meet a spy face to face in Cornhill Street, and surely the most alert of citizens would never suspect that any enemy agent would ride abroad with such a reckless unconcern for danger.

A clamor of voices broke out. Someone threw a stone. Page heard it strike the cobbles and hit twice with a distinct clatter, then splash into the water.

Her heart began to pump fiercely in her throat and her insides churned sickly. She put on her bonnet and tied the ribbons firmly. Putting out one hand to tap the backs of the men in front of her, she said in a clear cool voice, "Let me pass."

They turned, looking down at her with absent impatient faces. She moved ahead, never looking at them but repeating in the clear voice that seemed very high and boyish in the sudden silence, "Let me pass, if you please."

The broad backs moved aside for her. The men looked surprised, exasperated, even angry to be robbed of their sport; but the advantage of surprise would be no more than temporary, she suspected, and so the instant she caught sight of the man she ran forward, one hand outstretched, praying desperately that he would not look at her with the blank stare of a stranger and spoil everything.

"I've been searching all over town for you," she called across the space still separating them, hearing the words in her own ears as woefully inadequate, a mere sprinkle of rain dropping into the heavy sullen breathlessness before a storm.

"I thought I'd missed you," she went on hastily. "Did you come down to find the *Catherine*? Duncan MacDougall was convinced we should wait for you here on the quay, but Papa feared you might have been delayed in Washington and told me to inquire in town."

He stood with his back to the water, facing the hostile mob. His feet were well apart, planted firmly on the quay as if he had no intention of moving, and one hand flicked his riding crop lightly against his boot. Beyond that small movement he was motionless, but his stillness gave no indication of fear. The dark face was quite expressionless and the narrowed eyes moved dispassionately across the crowd, weighing his chances, judging the temper of the men and the explosive quality of their hostility, finally resting on Page with the same cool speculation.

"How long have you been in town?" she asked, wondering for one despairing moment if he thought her insane. "Aunt Hester wrote last week that you intended to arrive today, and Papa will be very angry that I missed being here to welcome you."

In that single instant before he spoke, stretching as long as the span of a lifetime while the clear bright voice that seemed to belong to someone else chattered on inanely, her mind stood calmly apart and noted the scene so distinctly that years afterwards she could still feel a cold sick chill when she remembered that gray morning with the pale sun glancing off the wet cobbles, and the haze tracing red brick and black shingles and white hulls and soaring yellow masts with muted and subtle fingers; while over all lay the scent of violence, heavy and pungent, frighteningly alien.

He took her hands. Then, without the slightest hesitation, he leaned down to kiss her cheek lightly.

"Your father, as always, is most obliging," he said, "but I can assure you that my welcome has been warmer than I expected." His glance went beyond her to the silent crowd, and came back to her face with a faint quizzical smile. "Farley and I have seldom been accorded so much attention. It seems to be a matter of mistaken identity."

Page, much struck by his cool poise, felt an overwhelming sense of relief; her hands trembled, and his own tightened briefly.

"I don't see how you could be mistaken for anyone but yourself," she said lightly. "Julia wrote that all the girls in Gloucester County went into melancholy declines when you left." Forcing herself to look around the ring of staring faces with an air of innocent curiosity, she went on, "Has there been some sort of trouble? That chestnut of yours, I daresay, and you deserve no better for riding such an uncivil brute in town."

He smiled. "Farley is in complete agreement," he said easily. "We have had a difficult time today on all counts, you see, and Farley's patience has been sorely tried."

Page looked at the sober-faced man holding the two horses. "Farley, how have you been?"

"Quite well, ma'am," he said. "If I may take the liberty to say so, however, I am extremely happy to see you again."

"I hope you noticed," she said unsteadily, her equanimity threatened, "that I took the precaution of putting on my bonnet."

There was an answering gleam of humor in his impassive face. "Just so, ma'am."

From the corner of her eye she saw a few of the men on the edge of the crowd break away and wander towards the market. But it was not over yet; the suspicious seaman behind her had not admitted defeat.

"I still say he's a Limey," he said loudly.

Another voice said, "Who's she? Is she in it, too?"

Page could only pretend she hadn't heard. She lifted her head to see the gray eyes looking down at her steadily, and realized he was still holding her hands reassuringly.

"We'll go home with MacDougall in the *Catherine*," she said evenly. "It's much quicker, and Papa will be expecting us. But the horses will have to be taken by the road."

A young man wearing a farmer's straw hat and heavy shoes stepped forward. "Miss, I'd be pleased to handle the horses for you."

"Thank you," Page said, wishing she could kiss his plain decent face. "Ask anyone and they'll tell you the way to Bradley's House. Samuel Bradley's, on the road south."

Farley, after one inscrutable glance at his master, quickly unstrapped two portmanteaus from his horse and surrendered the bridles to the eager farmer. Page took a step forward, then another; without looking, she knew that the two strangers had moved to stand one on either side of her. She hesitated, dreading the next step. Either the barrier of men would fall back or stand firm as a prison wall, and the *Catherine* was still a long hopeless way down the quay.

"Do you intend to stand gabbling all day? I've the tide and wind to consider, and if you don't hurry we'll be the night getting home."

When she heard the flat disagreeable voice and saw the sandy-red head, Page drew a small startled breath. But MacDougall did not give them away; he scowled at Page and nodded briefly to the man beside her.

"Good day to you," he said. "I see she found you. Now if you'll come this way, we'll start home before Mr. Bradley calls out the militia to look for us."

It may have been the use of Samuel Bradley's name again, suggesting even to those unacquainted with him all the weight and substance of an important man, or it may have been no more than MacDougall's blunt honest face. Whatever it was, it silenced the crowd, already unsure of itself, and dampened any lingering spark of the emotion necessary to enflame a group of ordinary men into a murdering mob. The men still watching stepped back, leaving an open path down the quay.

In the *Catherine*'s roomy cockpit, while MacDougall raised the sail and the gap between boat and quay slowly widened, Page looked back at the noisy crowded waterfront of Annapolis with bemused eyes.

She wondered what the two silent strangers were thinking. Here they were, on a strange boat with people unknown to them an hour before, sailing down the Severn towards an unfamiliar destination; and there were their horses, being led across the market square by a plodding farmer they had never seen before and could in no way be certain they would see again.

It occurred to her, rather belatedly, that she had been a trifle high-handed.

"But there was nothing else to do," she said into the silence.

No one spoke. Page, reminding herself that Papa would surely know how to straighten out such an incredible tangle, was somewhat less than consoled when she considered what Papa was likely to say when he discovered that she had brought home from town not only a new gown and a chip bonnet, but two British spies and a magnificent chestnut as well.

Bracing herself, she turned around. MacDougall, occupied with the business of getting the *Catherine* under way, paid no attention to her. The man named Farley had sat down, looking rather pale but still composed, his arms folded around the portmanteaus as if determined that they, at least, would not be taken from him without a struggle.

The other man, leaning his shoulders against the cabin hatch, looked up at the white sail filling slowly with the soft wind.

"I didn't want to see anyone hanged," she said in a small voice, "and they might have done it, you know, once they got out of hand. Only last summer a mob in Baltimore killed and wounded a number of people."

He looked down at her. "Yes, I know," he said. "Farley and I are greatly obliged to you."

But he did not appear at all shaken by the experience and Page, remembering her own bone-softening fear, stared at him curiously.

"Weren't you afraid?"

"Any man is afraid of a mob."

"Well, I must say you didn't show it."

"Nor did you."

Page sighed. "In another moment," she said candidly, "I would have swooned at your feet."

A brief smile touched his mouth. "When a man is forced to live by his wits," he said, "he learns to maintain an air of unconcern at all costs. In any game of chance, you see, one must contrive not to betray the turn of the cards."

Page considered him thoughtfully. He might wear his fashionable clothes and impeccable manners with the air of a gentleman; but his face, hard and tawny as a statue of carved wood, was shuttered and remote, while beneath the dark brows and lashes his eyes, a startling clear gray, gave back her image and no more, much as a pool of water will freely reflect the world gazing into it so that the depths may remain hidden.

She did not think she would care to play against him in a game of chance; moreover, she was inclined to feel that Mr. Madison, in the no less chancy game of war, had sadly underestimated his opponent.

"I daresay anyone in your profession grows accustomed to such harrowing affairs," she said doubtfully. "It seems very odd."

"I can assure you," he said gravely, "that I have not been faced with the prospect of hanging often enough to become indifferent to it."

"Once would be too often for me. I fear I'd be a miserable failure as a spy." She had not intended to say the ugly word and she added hastily, "It must require a great strength of character."

"I should think patience would be a more valuable asset," he said. "Think of all the mysterious plots that go awry and change the course of destiny."

The glint in the gray eyes was unmistakably amusement, and Page eyed him uncertainly. Then she turned to smile at Duncan MacDougall. "Mac, however did you manage to arrive at just the proper moment?"

"I saw a crowd and knew something was afoot. With you wandering about the town, it was easy enough to figure I'd find you in the thick of it." He regarded her sourly, and she knew that she had not been forgiven for her sins, which seemed to be increasing at an incredible speed. "Found a bit of trouble for yourself, didn't you? Do you never pause to consider the mischief you make for others?"

"How disagreeable of you," Page said. "Papa will say I was right to do what I did."

She sat down on the decking, her feet braced in the cockpit, and removed the forgotten bonnet.

"What Mr. Bradley might say is of little help at the moment," MacDougall said glumly. "I'd no intention of leaving for another hour. The wind's not steady, for one thing, and we may find ourselves becalmed somewhere out beyond the point."

He gave her a hard warning look, and suddenly Page

remembered the British frigate. Out beyond the point it might be waiting, like a cat at a mousehole, fat and sleek and eager to pounce.

"Aye," MacDougall said, "I see you've regained some of your senses. Just tell me what's to do then, missy, if this pesky wind dies."

Page, feeling slightly forlorn, glanced up at the sail. It was slatting gently in the fitful breeze, as if the *Catherine* wished to add her reproaches to MacDougall's.

"And if it doesn't," MacDougall continued, his eyes on the man standing on the steps of the hatchway, "I've still the problem of what to do with them."

"Do you mean to turn them over to the militia, Mac? I've been to no end of trouble, you know, to save them from one hanging."

"They're spies," he said flatly, "and if there's anything lower than a spy it's a cursed Englishman. The two together can turn a man's stomach, even without a war to consider. But you needn't fear, I don't relish a hanging for my worst enemy."

Page put her chin in her hands. "We might put them ashore across the river, and no one would be the wiser."

"They'd have a long walk. You sent their horses to Bradley's House. And we can't go back to town without them, not after the fancy tale you embroidered."

"May I interrupt this council of war?"

The man's voice was polite and faintly mocking. "Certainly," Page said, equally polite.

"Your problems are your own," he went on, "and I would hesitate to interfere. But since my presence is apparently adding to your discomfort, I might offer a simple suggestion. Would it be possible to intercept the Baltimore packet as it leaves the harbor?"

"Not a chance," MacDougall replied promptly. "I talked to the captain myself, less than an hour ago, and he didn't think to clear for Baltimore until after dark."

The man's eyes narrowed as he weighed the honesty in MacDougall's words. Then he shrugged. "A pity," he said. "Only this morning I paid for passage to the continent on a ship leaving Baltimore with the evening tide."

MacDougall laughed. "See what meddling will do for you?" he said to Page.

For an interminable moment she could think of nothing to say; there was no humiliation so lowering as the knowledge that one had blundered irretrievably.

But she lifted her chin. "It may be all for the best. After all, we could scarcely allow a spy to take information back to the enemy."

"Whatever spying he's done," MacDougall said, "it'd be of small use to him by the time he crosses the Atlantic."

"I don't believe he intended to cross the Atlantic at all," Page said stubbornly. "He's one of the admiral's naval officers, and his ship is probably just out of sight down the Bay."

The careless words dropped into the silence, disastrously clear and distinct, spreading like water ripples in the yellow washed sunlight. Shaken, Page stared at MacDougall and he stared back grimly.

3

The silence stretched thinly across several minutes, broken only by the small sounds of water moving gently against the hull, the whisper of the wind, a distant water bird crying exultantly in the sunshine.

"Don't distress yourself," the man said, sounding very amused. "There is really no cause for such despair."

Page lifted her eyes to meet cool gray ones.

"Please allow me to present myself," he said. "I am Jocelyn Trevor of London. I have spent the past two months in Gloucester County visiting a recently widowed sister, and my trip to America was for the purpose of offering her the comfort and assistance of her family."

Page considered him warily. He did not look like a man who traveled about on ordinary business and was concerned with nothing more dangerous than family affairs and a sister imprudent enough to marry a Virginian and be left a widow in a strange land. He had probably improvised the story on the spur of the moment; she had been the one to mention Gloucester County, back on the quay, and now he was using it to his own nefarious purpose.

"I don't think I would find it very comforting to be

visited by a spy in the middle of the war," she said, "brother or not."

"But then my sister does not share your suspicious nature," he said gravely. "She has always cherished a decided partiality for me, you see, and could never be persuaded that I have the black heart of a villain."

Page, meeting his eyes, felt it monstrously remiss of someone not to have designed a rule of etiquette governing the sort of conversation to hold with strangers whom one suspected to be enemy spies.

"Well, I daresay a spy is judged by the color of his coat," she said thoughtfully. "One is a villain or a hero, according to which country he owes his allegiance."

"A complicated question of ethics," he agreed promptly, "and since my country is at war with yours, I quite understand that I must assume the role of villain."

Page eyed him distrustfully. He was not at all handsome, that was certain, and he had the look of a villain with his dark face and hard mouth.

But then he said, "My dear child, I am not a spy. Nor am I a naval officer with a ship waiting for me down the Bay."

After a moment she said, "Only a gentleman from London? Truly?"

He bowed. "My apologies if I have disappointed you."

She smiled. "I think it most provoking of you. One doesn't meet a spy every day, you know. We've heard endless rumors about them, but they always seem to have just left for Washington or Baltimore."

"A kindly providence, Miss Bradley, trying to protect your romantic illusions. Imagine your grief if you were to meet a spy face to face and discover him to be an ordinary fellow, not at all bold and dashing."

Enemy or spy, her conscience warned her that it was all the same. But the war seemed far away and unreal at the moment, and one would have to be intolerably dull and tiresome not to be amused by a situation that did, after all, have its amusing aspects.

"It is most disheartening," she said gravely, "to realize that the world has grown too prosaic for romance and adventure. I shall be obliged to go back to reading novels."

"It would only make you long to go tilting at windmills," he said. "A fatiguing pastime, I assure you, and if you doubt my word you may ask Farley, who has proven himself an estimable Sancho."

The vision of Jocelyn Trevor in rusty armor and helmet tied with green ribbons, mounted on a melancholy swaybacked slug, was almost too much for Page's gravity. "Only today I found a new edition of *Don Quixote* for Papa. He isn't much of a reader, however, and I fear he would think the hero a miserable specimen."

Jocelyn Trevor laughed. "I have an uncomfortable presentment that he will demand satisfaction of me before turning his attention to anything so poor-spirited as reading."

"Papa would never do anything so ill-advised. But unless you are very cunning, he will certainly find a way to fleece you of that chestnut."

He laughed again. Farley, who had not spoken since he came aboard, looked amused, and even MacDougall was heard to chuckle. They might have been in perfect charity with one another, four old friends out for a pleasant afternoon sail. The wind had settled at last and the *Catherine* heeled contentedly. Soon they would swing around the jutting lower lip of the Severn and run for home, the little sloop skimming over the Bay like a sea bird, safe from any hand but the wind's.

A sudden thought struck Page. "Was it true, then," she asked Jocelyn Trevor, "that you intended to sail from Baltimore this evening?"

"It needn't concern us now. Farley and I must look around for another ship and another sailing date."

"But you paid for it," she protested. Impulsively she turned to MacDougall. "We could take the *Catherine* to Baltimore in an hour or two, Mac, and they would easily be in time."

"We could," MacDougall agreed, "but we won't. It's not for me to decide whether he's a spy or not. If Mr. Bradley thinks it proper for me to take him to Baltimore, there'll be plenty of time later in the day, but for now my duty is to see you safe to Bradley's House."

"A commendable attitude," Joycelyn Trevor said.

He stepped across Farley to settle himself in the cockpit, stretching out his long legs. He looked almost happy, his eyes hooded against the sun and his mouth relaxed. Page, wondering what her emotions might be at the moment were she sailing down the Thames with enemies all around, regarded him with admiration until he suddenly raised his eyes and smiled lazily at her. A little dismayed to be caught staring, she looked away quickly, focusing her eyes on the familiar reaches of the Bay.

She heard MacDougall's sharp intake of breath and knew he had seen the frigate at the same instant. Swallowing hard, she felt her heart thudding with a heavy painful beat in her throat.

"Ah, the devil's come to take his reckoning," MacDougall said softly. "A terrible sight for a God-fearing man."

Once they rounded the point they should have seen

her at once, but for the lingering veil of haze which blended all lines and colors into a soft monotone, distorting the vision as though one were looking through an opaque glass, obscuring the towering web of spars and rigging until the ship might have been a mirage there upon the distant swell of the Bay. But she was not a mirage or a distorted figment of the imagination and Page, swallowing again, could not take her eyes away from the sight.

"British?" Jocelyn Trevor asked calmly.

"Aye, British," MacDougall replied with heavy contempt, "as if you didn't know. Scavengers, more like, dirty, thieving scavengers. Robbers. Plunderers. Murderers." He added bitterly, "I can think of worse than that, if you care to listen."

Undisturbed, Jocelyn Trevor asked, "Are you going to turn back?"

"Not me. I've no idea of letting the British run me off the Bay."

"You have someone else to consider besides yourself."

"Aye, and it's me who knows best how to consider her."

There was a brief silence. Then Jocelyn Trevor said idly, "I trust so."

"You didn't leave anything in town," MacDougall said, "to go back for. I'd think you'd want to get closer to yon frigate, seeing as how she's full to the scuppers with Limey friends."

"Certainly," Jocelyn Trevor said smoothly. "You will pardon me if I admit I prefer a thieving Englishman to an obstinate Scotsman any day. My preferences, however, have nothing to do with your duty, which you have apparently forgotten, to get Miss Bradley safely home."

Despite the sarcasm, MacDougall looked mollified. "I know my duty, thank you all the same. As long as the wind holds, we've nothing to fear from them. Before they can lower a boat we'll be far past, and there's no British ship afloat can catch the *Catherine* when she's had a head start."

"And their guns?"

"The gunports are closed," MacDougall pointed out, "and I'll stay out of range of their small arms."

Jocelyn Trevor gave MacDougall an enigmatic look, but he said no more.

MacDougall was certainly obstinate, Page reflected, and it was plain that he disliked being told his business by an Englishman; but she knew him to be a cautious man on the whole, and well versed in the art of eluding enemy craft on the Bay.

Still, her heart continued to beat heavily as she looked ahead to the frigate, slightly to larboard. From the cockpit of the little sloop the frigate seemed very high out of water, her fat black flanks broken by the white band with its checkered row of gunports, sails smartly furled to show the massive complication of rigging and tall masts, an enormous vessel riding to her anchors like a dignified swan with folded wings.

Page's mouth tightened. The pride of His Majesty's Admiralty. The symbol of Britain's mighty navy that swept insolently over the seas of the world and forced all those of lesser strength to its will, that sailed arrogantly up the Chesapeake into the very heart of America, as if the British still owned it, and dared to anchor here almost at Samuel Bradley's doorstep with no one to say it nay.

"But surely you cannot hold me responsible," Jocelyn Trevor said quietly, "for all the sins of the Admiralty."

Until he spoke Page had not realized that she had turned her eyes from the frigate to stare fiercely at Jocelyn Trevor. But now she knew that all feelings of friendly charity had disappeared. He was the enemy, one of the same arrogant breed that walked the decks of the floating castle anchored ahead, and the war was no longer unreal and distant but here and now, a humiliation that ached in the heart and tasted bitter on the tongue.

She resented his perception. "You're an Englishman," she said coldly, as if no more damning evidence was needed. "It makes a pleasant sight for you, I daresay."

"But then I stood uncomfortably near to a hanging this morning," he said, his eyes glinting at her under their heavy lids. "You must agree that the sight is far more pleasing than if I suspected it to be an American warship."

"I can't imagine why I didn't leave you there on the quay," Page said, disliking him intensely. "It would have been no more than you deserved."

"Assuredly," he said promptly. "As you say, I am an Englishman."

Page turned her head and ignored him. The *Catherine* was near enough to the frigate for Page to see men moving on her decks. Perched in the rigging were uniformed marines, their scarlet tunics brilliant against the spidery yellow shrouds, muskets thin and black in their hands.

MacDougall, busy with his lines and watching his sails carefully to take every advantage of the wind, paid no attention to the swarms of sailors hanging over the railings of the frigate.

"Duck your heads," he said abruptly. "We'll come about now."

The boom swung over them with a vicious crack and for the length of that moment the *Catherine* trembled. Then her sails drew again and she raced away from the frigate, turning her heels to the staring seamen and marines and black muskets.

She found herself sailing directly into the path of a longboat loaded with marines. It had evidently been sent on an expedition up the wide inlet to the west while the frigate waited at anchor. Now, as an officer clipped out an order that sounded sharply across the water, the seamen at the oars sent the longboat directly for the *Catherine*.

Jocelyn Trevor spoke first, his voice cutting like the crack of a whip. "Put her about again, MacDougall. Head for the frigate and take her under their guns."

"And be blown out of the water?" MacDougall said between his teeth. "Not a chance!"

"Don't be a fool, man. They can't fire without running the risk of hitting their own men. Keep between them and you're safe enough."

"Then they'll pick us off with the muskets," MacDougall said furiously. "I can outsail any damned rowing boat!"

There was a sudden flash from the ship, a roar dwindling into a splash that dropped into the water ahead, and a round puff of smoke drifted leisurely from an open gunport aft.

"They're firing at us," Page said incredulously.

Jocelyn Trevor, his eyes on the approaching longboat, said, "Only a warning. They mean you to heave to, MacDougall." Then, in the same imperturbable voice, "The gentlemen in the longboat appear to have the same idea."

The longboat had altered course, heading at a sharp angle toward a point where the *Catherine*, on her present reach, might be intercepted. The oars flashed and dipped as the boat leapt across the water.

MacDougall muttered under his breath. "Watch your heads," he yelled, and the boom swept over their heads again with a violent whip. The *Catherine* went about, hesitated as if bewildered by such brutal treatment, and ran back toward the frigate.

Page, glancing astern, saw the oars glistening, water running in silver riverlets, as the longboat turned and came on rapidly on their starboard beam, narrowing the open gap through which the *Catherine* must run, slowly closing the trap. In the silence Page heard a peppery tattoo of sound, sharp and crisp, which was echoed in some strange manner against the *Catherine*'s mast and sails like a handful of pebbles thrown with a heavy hand.

Without warning she was pushed unceremoniously to her knees in the cockpit. Jocelyn Trevor's hand held her shoulder in a strong grip and his body shielded her so that she could see nothing but his face as he looked over her head at MacDougall, who was shaking an enraged fist and shouting, "Damn it, hold your fire! I've a woman aboard!"

"Put an end to it," Jocelyn Trevor said very quietly. "You did your best, but it's finished now."

She heard MacDougall say heavily, "Aye, it's done. I'd not risk having her harmed."

With a sort of horror Page watched the *Catherine*'s sails flutter and come down with a rush of canvas, and felt the gradual slackening of pace as the sloop lost way.

The creak of oarlocks was suddenly very near, as was an unfamiliar voice which spoke almost over her head.

"Have you struck, sir?"

MacDougall was silent. Jocelyn Trevor said, "Yes," and stood up; and Page, absently rubbing the shoulder where his hand had held her, raised her head.

The longboat was ranged alongside, held to the *Catherine* by several seamen whose oars pointed upright to the sky like a trim vertical line of spikes. The sun seemed brighter than before, glaring on the blue uniform and cocked hat of the officer, the brilliant scarlet and white marines, the sunburned faces and striped jerseys of the seamen. Page stared at them with a stunned disbelief and they stared back stolidly.

"I am Mr. Buckley, First Lieutenant of His Majesty's frigate *Antigone*," the officer said politely. "You are now His Majesty's prisoners, and if you will kindly step aboard we will proceed to the ship."

He gave a short order to one of his men, who scrambled across with a line. MacDougall and Farley stepped into the longboat and Jocelyn Trevor took Page's arm to help her. His hand was strong and warm, and oddly reassuring, but as soon as she stood beside MacDougall, Page pulled her arm away, thinking miserably that she wanted neither his touch nor his reassurance.

"Please sit down, ma'am," the officer said at her elbow.

She obeyed wordlessly. He spoke again and the oars moved in unison; shortly the frigate loomed over them like a massive precipice. Something cold and frightening settled in Page's stomach like a sodden lump, but whatever happened it seemed imperative that she hide her apprehension at the awful prospect of being taken aboard a British man-of-war as a prisoner. Even Cockburn's naval officers had not yet been reported to have harmed women and children, and surely she belonged to one or the other category. In any case, she could not allow the staring British seamen, or Jocelyn Trevor, to see an American behave in a timid and cowardly manner.

She went through the entry port, and Jocelyn Trevor, just behind her, said quietly, "Keep a stout heart," and smiled down at her.

The young officer opened his mouth to speak, but Jocelyn Trevor's voice cut into the silence, clipped and emphatic.

"Be kind enough to tell your captain that I wish to speak with him immediately."

Mr. Buckley, who had a brief instant before been prepared to issue orders rather than receive them, stared in momentary astonishment. Then he glanced automatically toward the quarterdeck, obviously expecting to find his captain there; he looked taken aback to see only a staring midshipman on his way down the steps.

"By the way," Jocelyn Trevor said, "what is his name?"

As if fascinated, Mr. Buckley said, "Kincaid. Somerset Kincaid."

"It would be," Trevor said. "His brother and I were up at Oxford at the same time, but I can't say that I recall the connection with particular relish."

Mr. Buckley stared. The midshipman reached his side and said, "The captain's compliments, sir, and would you bring the prisoners to his cabin."

Mr. Buckley looked relieved. But Trevor said, "I will see him alone. You may tell him, if you please, that Lord Hazard awaits his pleasure."

There was utter silence on the deck. Only Farley, Page noticed, was too preoccupied with his precious portmanteaus to stare, but it might be, she reflected, that he had long since grown accustomed to his master's chicanery.

"Lord Hazard, did you say?" Mr. Buckley said incredulously.

"I trust, sir, that you do not intend to question my credentials," Trevor said gently. "Yes, I did indeed say Lord Hazard."

Mr. Buckley was plainly suffering an agony of indecision. Afraid to believe and afraid of the consequences were he to mistakenly disbelieve, and deploring the fact that most of his crew was on deck to witness his dilemma, he could only glare wordlessly at Jocelyn Trevor.

Page began to feel sorry for him. So, apparently, did Trevor. "I understand your predicament, Mr. Buckley. If your duty prevents you from leaving the deck, by all means send someone else."

The color faded from Mr. Buckley's face. "I'll take you to the captain at once," he said nervously, adding as a definite sop to fate, "my lord."

Page felt her lips quiver and repressed them sternly. Trevor was doing an excellent piece of acting; his portrayal of a British lord was so skillfully done that anyone might readily believe the faint but unmistakable arrogance, the superb assurance, the crested air to be his own by natural right.

"Stay close by Miss Bradley, Farley," he said. "After all, we owe her a rescue of sorts."

Mr. Buckley, still staring at Jocelyn Trevor as if he found it basely unfair for a British lord to be wandering about the Chesapeake in a small sloop, barked an order to his marines and disappeared with Trevor down a companionway. The marines moved back a pace or two, leaving MacDougall and Farley in an open space with Page.

"I can't imagine why he thought it necessary to affect

a disguise," Page said admiringly to Farley, "but I must say I've never seen anyone lie so convincingly."

Farley seemed about to speak, but in the end he only gave her a quick smile. Page looked curiously about her, at the masts towering above her, the bleached-white deck, the polished brasswork, the busy activity of a routine that undoubtedly went forward, as stated in the Regulations, regardless of war or pestilence or catastrophe.

"Mac," she said abruptly, "they're taking Papa's Madeira!"

"The thieving devils," MacDougall said, his face an alarming mixture of rage and hopelessness.

The Madeira was now on the deck of the *Antigone*, handed up from the *Catherine* by a line of burly seamen, but in a trice it had disappeared down a hatchway. On the verge of following it were two bright new bandboxes.

Page flew across the deck. "You shall not steal my boxes," she said coldly.

The seaman, with brawny tattooed arms, paused to look down at her and grin. Then he opened one of the boxes and held up a corner of sprigged muslin with an enormous dirty hand.

"Cor, I 'ad it in mind to save 'em for me old lady. A mite larger than you, she'll be, but she always 'ad an eye for pretties."

"Give them to me," Page demanded, not retreating an inch.

"Give the lady her boxes," another man said in a low voice. "Here comes the bloody bo's'n."

A harsh voice shouted, "Back to work there. No more talking or I'll give you a taste of the cat for your dinner." The seaman dropped the boxes as if they had been live coals.

The next incident happened so quickly that later, when she was able to laugh about it, Page could remember nothing but a great deal of noise on the part of the British navy and a frenzied fury on hers.

The boatswain had orders to sink the *Catherine*, and MacDougall, goaded by blind rage into protesting, sprung across the deck to grapple with two brawny sailors and was given a hard clout which felled him on the spot. Page, incensed by such brutality, immediately began to upbraid the boatswain who, beset by an angry young lady and an irate man protecting the young lady by brandishing a portmanteau, retired in exasperated disarray and ordered his grinning men to set the boat adrift without knocking a hole in her bottom. This concession, unfortunately, fell far short of pacifying anyone, and if Mr. Buckley had not suddenly appeared on the quarterdeck to restore order, the unbounded confusion on the deck of the *Antigone* would have reached proportions unheard of in His Majesty's Regulations.

"All hands on deck," shouted Mr. Buckley, quite forgetting to relay his orders properly down the chain of command. "Weigh anchor and make sail!"

The drums rattled, the pipes twittered shrilly, and the few men remaining below tumbled on deck with a patter of bare horny feet. They paid no attention to Page, drawn by Farley into the protection afforded by one of the deck carronades, and none to a prostrate MacDougall other than pulling him out of the way.

"Farley, we must see to MacDougall," Page insisted. "He may be badly hurt."

"I doubt it, ma'am. It would be wiser to stay out of the way for the moment."

"Hands to the capstan, there!"

There was now a new confusion aboard the frigate, but it was safely covered by Regulations and every man of the crew had his appointed task. There was no sound except the thud of feet and the lively piping, and the grunting of the men bending their weight upon the bars of the capstan, encouraged by the boatswain with his cane.

"Farley," Page whispered, "they're sailing away with us!"

"Just so," Farley said. "I believe you may rest assured, however, that his lordship will see to your safety."

"But I don't see him," Page said despairingly. "Why doesn't he do something?"

It would soon be too late to do anything. The cable snaked slowly through the hawseholes and the men above in the rigging fell to with vigor, but there was no sign of the ship's captain or of Jocelyn Trevor.

Page looked at Farley. "What did you call him?" she asked very carefully. "His lordship, Farley?"

"Just so, ma'am," Farley said, his face expressionless.

Beyond words, Page stared at him. Above her head the topsails broke from the yards and the great courses tumbled loose and were sheeted home, and the fair wind MacDougall had whistled up to take them safely home to Bradley's House blew steadily against her face.

4

Captain Somerset Kincaid stood before his desk, hands behind his back, and stared angrily at the papers there. He would have preferred to vent his anger at Jocelyn Edward Trevor, fourth Viscount Hazard, but an instinctive sense of self-preservation restrained him from addressing a viscount as if he had been one of the ship's junior officers.

"I regret I cannot grant your request, my lord," he said, "but surely you must understand my predicament."

"You have my sympathy," Hazard said. "I had allowed myself to hope, however, that you would also understand mine."

The cool, faintly mocking voice gave Kincaid a painful stab of indigestion. He should not have eaten the greasy American pork, he thought bitterly, or washed it down with so much sour red wine; foreign food, as any decent Englishman should know, was no more to be trusted than foreigners.

"You have had a difficult time, I'm sure," he said shortly. "America is a barbarous place at best, my lord, and you cannot have been aware of the dangers of traveling in an enemy country in time of war."

"On the contrary," Hazard said, "I was treated with

every consideration." He looked amused. "Except for a brief interval when I was almost hanged."

Kincaid scowled. "That would have been unfortunate, sir."

Hazard smiled. "I appreciate your solicitude, Captain." He was leaning his shoulders against a bulkhead, boots negligently crossed. "But I was rescued by a heroic young lady, who certainly deserves payment of a better sort than this from His Majesty's Navy."

Kincaid's cravat felt uncomfortably hot. Damn it all, the fellow was an arrogant wretch, detaining the captain of a frigate as if he were no more than a lackey. Above his head he could hear the pad of feet, the twittering pipes, the creak and clatter as the anchor was swung into place and stowed. He should be on his quarterdeck, where he could show this insolent lord that here on the sea Somerset Kincaid ruled with absolute power every inch of his ship, from mastcap to keel, and every man jack aboard.

"My orders leave me no alternative, sir," he said stiffly. "My ship must be placed at Admiral Cockburn's disposal immediately, and the tide and wind will not wait."

"But you kept the admiral waiting long enough to intercept Miss Bradley's sloop," Hazard said casually. "You also fired a gun, I seem to recall, to emphasize your intentions."

"But I could not possibly know that you were aboard, my lord."

Kincaid still felt a cold chill of relief that he had not, as he was sorely tempted, blown the miserable boat out of the water. The Trevor family was an old one of considerable wealth and impeccable lineage, and the present viscount was one of the most eligible and notorious young peers in England. Kincaid's younger brother had once said that Hazard was a dangerous man to cross, and had added, with some exasperation, that the Viscount had an unerring eye with a pistol, an uncanny luck at the gaming tables, and an undeserved appeal for beautiful women. But Kincaid was not concerned with an old piece of brotherly gossip; he needed only a single look at the man to know that Viscount Hazard, whatever his reasons for leaving the sophisticated diversions of London to mix with common vulgar Americans, could not be lightly dismissed even by a frigate captain.

"As for the sloop, my lord, I have captured more than a dozen small vessels this past month. My orders were to take any enemy ship afloat, of whatever size."

Lord Hazard raised a dark brow. "That must be rather poor sport," he said idly. "A fifth-rate frigate, my dear Kincaid, and nothing to show for her thirty-eight guns but a few tiny coastal vessels?"

Kincaid flushed. "We are engaged in a war, my lord."

Hazard said, "I seem to recall something about it." He regarded Kincaid with narrowed, depthless eyes. Then he said gently, "I have only a passing acquaintance with such matters myself, but I would not have thought His Majesty's invincible navy would find it necessary to make war on unarmed sailboats and young ladies."

Kincaid stiffened, on the verge of making a withering comment on feather-headed civilians who meddled in the serious business of fighting wars; but he remembered suddenly that Hazard's reputation as a cavalry officer had led Lord Wellington to request his services through several of the more dangerous campaigns in the Peninsula. Not that army service meant a great deal, Kincaid reflected with some condescension; Wellington's staff officers, it was rumored, did not like to spoil their splendid uniforms in the rain and often fought their battles from the shelter of umbrellas.

"I have my orders, sir," he said finally. "You should know that I cannot question them."

Hazard looked slightly bored. "I am not asking you to neglect your duty, Captain. But orders or not, I shall expect you to extend every consideration to Miss Bradley."

"Certainly," Kincaid said coldly. "I must impress the man, but as soon as possible I will try to find suitable transportation for the young lady."

It was a damned nuisance, he thought angrily. No one but a chivalrous fool would care what happened to the girl, and he could have used the man. Most of his crew had been impressed against their will and were miserable landsmen, the lot of them, rogues and criminals, the sweepings of His Majesty's gaols and the press gang. He had not been surprised when five of them deserted the week before, swimming ashore while the *Antigone* lay off Tangier Island. But the two admirals, Cockburn and Warren, had hinted at plans for revenging the embarrassing failure of their late expedition against Norfolk. Kincaid was quite certain that they would expect him to be on hand, with a full complement of crew and marines, when they went into action again.

Instead he was some hundred-odd miles to the north, delayed by a Bay fog and a difficult viscount, and without the two merchantmen whose capture, and additional seamen, might have softened the admirals' wrath at his tardiness.

"If you will excuse me, my lord," he said testily, "I must see to my ship."

"By all means," Hazard said. "Do not let me detain you."

Kincaid bowed and flung open the door, only to find himself confronting the young American girl and a sober individual in a black suit. His cravat choking him dangerously, the captain said, "Your servant," and pushed past them toward the open deck.

Hazard straightened, his head almost touching the beams, and watched the girl as she entered. She gazed briefly after the captain and then turned her attention to the cabin, the big table still littered with the remains of the officers' luncheon, the wide stern windows, the transom with its cushioned locker, the canvas carpet checkered in black and white, the black eighteen-pounders lashed fore-and-aft on either side, and finally to Hazard himself.

She considered him in silence for a long moment. "And to think," she said at last, "that none of this might have happened if I had not spoken to you on the quay."

With difficulty he restrained a smile. "It is unfortunate," he said, "that your kindness should be rewarded so disagreeably." He gave her a swift glance and pulled a chair from the table. "Please sit down."

She obeyed him without protest. Behind her Farley put down the portmanteaus and two battered bandboxes, straightened his neckpiece, smoothed his sleeve carefully, and began to clear the table with the comfortable air of one whose duty is always plain before him.

"Can you tell me," Page asked in a clear polite voice, "where they are taking us?"

"The captain is in some haste, I understand, to join two admirals whose squadrons are gathered in Hampton Roads. He left them yesterday to sail up the Bay on an errand which proved somewhat disappointing, and now he must repair to Hampton with all speed."

"Hampton," Page repeated, her face going pale. Then she said, "Mac has been taken below and they refuse to allow me to speak to him. They also stole Papa's Madeira, and set the *Catherine* adrift . . ."

"I am sorry about the *Catherine*."

She considered him thoughtfully, seeming to weigh the sincerity of his words by some secret inner scale of her own.

Then she said slowly, "I keep thinking of Papa's feelings when we don't come home. Or if the *Catherine* drifts ashore, all empty, and someone takes her back to Bradley's House."

"I regret that there is no way to lessen his apprehension at the moment," Hazard said, "but you may well be home before he receives any news of the *Catherine*."

She looked up quickly. "Do you mean that the captain intends to set us free, after all? It seems unreasonable, when he refused to allow us to leave in the *Catherine*."

Hazard said gravely, "I believe the captain suffers from a digestive disorder, brought on by an excess of bad luck, bad temper, and uncooperative Americans. Two rich prizes slipped through his fingers, he is overdue at an important rendezvous with his admirals, and his first lieutenant was routed by a few irate farmers who declined the honor of supplying the British navy with fresh water and food. You must agree that such irritations would try the patience of a saintlier man than our captain."

Farley, disappearing through the door with an armload of dirty dishes, could be heard speaking to the marine standing guard outside the cabin. When his voice died away there was no sound but the sibilant rush of water beneath the frigate's keel, widening to a white wake that could be seen through the stern windows as it spread across the gray water behind them.

"It was very strange," Page Bradley said abruptly, with an undertone of incredulity, "to stand on deck and watch Papa's land go by, and realize that no one would ever believe that I was sailing past Bradley's House on a British ship."

She was sitting very straight in the chair, holding on to her composure with the obstinacy of desperation. Hazard suspected that she would not accept pity or sympathy if they were offered; pity she would consider an insult, and sympathy a threat to that uncertain poise, balanced so precariously between apprehension and despair. He wanted to smile, but at the same time he felt oddly moved and not a little proud. She sat there looking absurdly young and forlorn in her plain old-fashioned dress, her face pale and her mouth on the edge of trembling, resolved to hold her head high whatever the price.

"You'll be sailing back shortly," he said quietly.

But she said sadly, "Without the *Catherine*, however, and I doubt if MacDougall will ever forgive me."

Leaning against the table, Hazard put his hands in his pockets and studied his boots. He would have to tell her sooner or later that Kincaid was stubbornly determined to impress MacDougall, and that even if transportation for her could be found immediately, an improbable piece of optimism at best, the chances were that she would return to Bradley's House alone while MacDougall pursued an unwilling tour of the Atlantic with the British navy. It would not be easy to tell her, and even more difficult to explain why such a thing could happen; the Admiralty and His Majesty's ministers, after all, had so signally failed to explain the virtues of impressment that the Americans had gone to war about it.

"Never mind. It will all come right in the end, I'm sure."

He realized belatedly that he was scowling blackly at his boots. Looking up to find her watching him, he thought he saw a hint of a smile in her blue eyes, but it disappeared at once behind the thick fringe of lashes.

"It is kind of you to be so concerned," she went on in a small shy voice, "but you mustn't feel responsible. None of it was your fault."

"If you were better acquainted with me, you would know that I seldom indulge in kindness," he said. "But I can assuredly recognize a responsibility when I see one. However it began, the mischief has been done."

"I expect there will be worse to come. Misfortune always comes in three's."

"A foolish superstition," he remarked. "In any case, fate should already be satisfied. You left home, you met me, and you ran afoul the British navy."

This time he was certain of the smile. Then Farley came back into the cabin, carrying a steaming mug and wearing the expression of one who has fought a battle against great odds and won.

"I have taken the liberty, ma'am, of procuring a cup of tea for you."

Page took the mug in both hands. "Thank you," she said gratefully. "I don't know how you managed, but it's precisely what I need."

"Never ask him how he manages," Hazard said. "It is entirely possible that you might discover him guilty of enormous crimes, not excluding murder."

Farley's face relaxed into something very close to a smile. But he said quite soberly, "Mr. MacDougall has been taken to the berth deck, ma'am. I was unable to reach him, but one of the midshipmen assured me that he was put to bed. In a seaman's hammock, so I understood."

Page sighed. "They gave him a fierce blow. I fear he'll have a wretched headache when he comes to his senses."

Hazard frowned slightly. "You didn't tell me they had handled him roughly. Did he give them any provocation?"

"He only objected to their mistreatment of the *Catherine*."

"I see," Hazard said dryly.

"Well, I objected, too," Page said, "but they didn't strike me."

"Naturally not," Hazard said coolly.

"Because they thought me a lady?" Page shook her head. "I assure you that had nothing to do with it. It was Farley, coming to my rescue with a portmanteau."

"Sancho again," Hazard said, and laughed. "I think I'll have a stroll on deck to see how matters stand with our captain. If you need anything, Miss Bradley, I'm sure you will find Farley a fellow of infinite resource and tact."

When he had gone, the cabin seemed very quiet and empty. After a long moment Page said absently, "Are all Englishmen like him?"

"If I may say so, ma'am, there is no man like his lordship."

Page looked at Farley thoughtfully. "He does not seem very concerned about the war."

"As to that," Farley said, "his lordship is not a member of the Opposition, but it is my understanding that he did not approve of the war from the beginning."

"He is still an enemy," Page said, "and will surely do all he can to see us defeated."

"That's as may be," Farley said with a mild reproach, "but he will also see you safely home to Annapolis." Then, as if seeing in her face that she despaired of ever seeing Annapolis again, regardless of his lordship, he added tactfully, "Would you care for another cup of tea, ma'am?"

By the end of an interminable afternoon in the cabin, which seemed to grow smaller and more like a prison with every moment, Page was so weary of tea and impatient of tact that Farley went away with an inscrutable face and came back with Hazard, who apologized for staying away so long and immediately took her on deck for a breath of air.

"I have seen MacDougall," he said. "He has an aching head and a bitter heart, but Farley tells me that he was persuaded to take some food. If he can only restrain his appetite for knocking English heads together, we may yet be able to save him."

"Save him from what?"

Hazard declined to answer. Instead he suggested that she make the most of her time on deck by strolling back and forth with him in the narrow area encompassed by the starboard guns, the big boats with smaller ones nestled within and the companionway leading down to the berth deck below. But the high gunwales shut off any view, and Page wished that she might change places with the seamen moving on the gangways above them, who at least had a glimpse of the Bay.

Then she noticed that they seldom looked up from the business at hand; their faces were sullen and guarded, and there was no laughter or casual talk as they worked. Page, whose experience of ships was limited to the West Indian schooners, whose dark-skinned seamen with flashing white grins and bright clothing were a familiar sight in Annapolis since the war, and the raking Baltimore clippers with their brawny crews that walked-up the anchors with lively chanties and cheered as the sails broke free, was suspicious of a ship so silent and withdrawn and of hostile sailors who never raised their eyes.

Hazard, when she commented upon it, only said, "It would be a remarkable thing if any of them were satisfied with their lot. It is a miserable life, even with the best of officers, and most of the sailors you see here were the unwilling victims of a press gang."

"Do you approve of that wretched custom?"

"I doubt if any Englishman approves," he said coolly. "But so long as Bonaparte remains at large, the navy stands between him and an invasion of England. And since a navy must be manned by men, it is sometimes necessary to obtain them by any method that comes to hand."

"I never heard anything so cold-hearted and cynical!"

"A nation fighting for its life cannot afford sentimentality."

"You would feel differently, I daresay," Page said indignantly, "if there was the slightest possibility that you might have to fight in England's army, or suffer impressment."

"You are probably right," he said casually. "The very thought unnerves me."

She glanced at him warily, suspicious of the amusement in his voice, but he said no more, taking her back to the after cabin and a hot meal presided over by Farley and Captain Kincaid's body servant.

In a few minutes the captain entered the cabin, followed by Mr. Buckley and an older man with a melancholy face who was introduced as Mr. Wilkins the Sailing Master. The five of them sat down to dinner. The captain bolted his food without looking up from his plate, the flushed red of his face becoming a dangerous magenta as the meal progressed and Hazard's occasional civilities, spoken in a bland amused voice, demanded that he answer in kind. The other two officers were completely silent, Mr. Buckley with a fixed expression of blankness and Mr. Wilkins unhappily aware that each bit of food he chewed sounded embarrassingly loud in the silence.

But when the captain finished his meal, nodded in Hazard's general direction, scowled heavily at his officers and quitted the cabin by slamming the door behind him, the atmosphere around the table lightened perceptibly.

Mr. Buckley, before he left, was even emboldened to say to Page, "I deeply regret the inconvenience we have caused you, ma'am," and he looked so young and shy that she could not help smiling at him. She was glad that she had when she learned later that he had offered his cabin for her use and had already moved his possessions so that she could retire at will. But despite his kindness, she did not think that she would be able to sleep. Mr. Wilkins had mentioned that a Baltimore pilot was still aboard, and the captain did not intend to anchor for the night. It brought an odd catch to Page's throat to realize that Bradley's House was falling farther behind with each moment that the frigate dropped down the Bay toward Hampton Roads.

Pushing away such dismal thoughts, she asked Hazard, "Where will you sleep?"

"I suggested that I join Farley below," he said, "and share with him the diversion of sleeping in a hammock. But Mr. Buckley's sense of propriety deemed it necessary to evict the unfortunate Mr. Wilkins."

"Sleeping in a hammock would be disastrous to your consequence," Page said, and suddenly remembered that she had never once accorded his consequence the proper respect. "Should I call you 'my lord'?" she asked, pausing at the door to Mr. Buckley's cabin. "I hadn't thought of it before, so you mustn't think me deliberately rude."

"Would you prefer it?" he countered gravely.

She considered it. "I don't want to be thought improper," she said at last, "but the thing is, we aren't accustomed to titles in America. We did away with all that, you know, when we won our war for independence."

"By all means," he said, "let us disregard such unnecessary civility. I wouldn't like to offend the delicate sensibilities of a revolutionary."

Page had a pang of guilty embarrassment. She was on a British ship, after all, and when in Rome, even as a prisoner, one should not behave like a narrow and churlish provincial; she owed him, if nothing else, the courtesy of good manners.

She looked up to see that his eyes were narrowed against laughter. "My family and friends call me Joss. I think you might also adopt it, under the circumstances, with perfect propriety."

"It is very obliging of you," she said, and added before she closed the door, "my lord."

The cabin was very small, crowded by a large black gun, a swinging cot on which rested her bandboxes, and a large sea chest. Overhead an oil lantern swung lazily with the motion of the ship, issuing an unpleasant smell of oil in the hot stuffy air.

Page sat down on the cot and stared bleakly around her. Then, with resolution, she curled up on the cot, back to the gun, and listened to the silence that was not, when the ear grew accustomed to it, in the least silent but filled with a medley of ship's noises that went on unceasingly: the heavy patter of bare feet on the deck above her as some seaman went about his duties; the ship's bell striking two bells in the first watch; the creaking of the wooden timbers and the murmur of water against the hull; and above it all the steady faint singing of the Bay breeze in the rigging.

She was asleep before the ship's bell struck again.

5

When she opened her eyes the oil lamp was still smoking above her. Sitting up to look around her with drowsy bewilderment, she suddenly remembered all that had happened and closed her eyes again. After a moment she opened them slowly, seeing with cold clarity the ugly gun, the closed door, the cot, her rumpled gown. A thin gray edge of light filtered through the tiny port as if in meager promise of daylight to come, but the cabin was dark and gloomy as a dungeon cell. As the first sight to greet one's eyes on awakening, at a moment of awful loneliness and hunger, it was enough to make a stone weep.

But her attention was caught by the shrilling of pipes and thumping of feet on the deck above her head. Almost immediately, she recognized the grumble of the cable as it roared through the hawsehole, and with a slight jerk the ship swung to her anchor. Then someone knocked at the door, and Page was very glad that she had not, after all, succumbed to the weakness of tears.

It was Farley, bearing a tray of hot food and a steaming mug of coffee.

"I trust you passed a satisfactory night, ma'am."

Page said faintly, "Yes, thank you."

"I thought you might be glad of a bite to eat. If it

Jan Cox Speas

will not distress you, ma'am, I might mention that the ham is from southern Virginia and quite succulent indeed. The eggs, I believe, were fresh only yesterday from a Maryland farm."

Farley looked exactly as he had the day before, his dark suit unwrinkled and his equanimity unimpaired by a night of swinging in a hammock on the berth deck, and he seemed to think it nothing out of the way that he should appear, like a kindly angel, with hot food and the comfort of his presence at a moment when she desperately needed both.

He placed the tray on the chest and handed Page a white linen napkin. "Mr. Buckley sends his compliments and begs to inform you that the eggs, in a manner of speaking, were not stolen. One of his seamen took them without permission, but he was sent back at once with sufficient payment."

Page felt her melancholy fade away, replaced by an irrepressible sense of well-being that had to do with the oddities of the British character, yellow eggs and brown-and-pink Virginia ham and hot black coffee, and, not least of these splendid luxuries, the existence in the world of someone like Farley.

"Just so, ma'am," he said with a glimmer of a smile.

He bowed and left her, and she turned to her breakfast with greedy pleasure, dispatching the last crumb before he returned with a basin of hot water, a towel and a gilt hand mirror.

"His lordship sends his compliments," he said, "and asks that you take particular pains not to break the mirror or he will be unable to tie his cravats."

She sensibly refused to answer what was plainly a deliberately provoking message. But when Farley had gone she looked at herself with dismay in the mirror and immediately went about the business of freshening her hair and face.

When her cheeks were pink from scrubbing and her hair tied back with the striped velvet ribbon she had purchased, surely a hundred years ago, for Dolly, she exchanged her wrinkled gown for the lovely sprigged muslin with its blue pelisse. It fastened down the back with a long line of tiny buttons, and Page, for the first time in her life having no sisters at hand, was still struggling with the thorny problem when Farley knocked again.

He perceived the situation at once and said, "In London, ma'am, I was often called upon to aid his lordship's younger sisters when they were still in the schoolroom and not yet allowed an abigail. If you will allow me, I would be pleased to give you my assistance."

Page was not certain she cared to be relegated to the world of younger sisters and schoolrooms, but under the circumstances she could not deny Farley's exquisite tact.

"Thank you," she said. "It would be most obliging of you."

"If I may say so, ma'am," he said, buttoning the unreachable buttons with impersonal deftness, "you look most fetching today."

Later, when she knew him better, Page would have recognized this as a compliment of the highest order, coming from a man so sparing of admiration for anyone but his master. At the moment she only said ruefully, "It isn't precisely the fashion for a ship-of-war, do you think? I should be more the thing in rags and tatters, and perhaps clanking irons."

This reminded her of poor MacDougall, languishing miserably below, but Farley reported him to be in excellent spirits, if still somewhat bitter, and although he was ordered to stay below he was in no way restrained.

Page gave a sigh of relief. "Where are we?" she asked curiously. "Surely we can't have reached the lower Bay already, and dawn only just come."

But it appeared that dawn had long since passed and the morning was well advanced. It was a bright sunny day, according to Farley, although apparently no sun could penetrate the dark gloom of Mr. Buckley's cabin.

"We are anchored in Hampton Roads, I understand, and the last time I ventured a look we seemed to have joined the other British ships."

Farley went on calmly to say that there had been a furious battle the day before, that the British had carried the day and captured the town of Hampton, and that Captain Kincaid had gone by barge to the admiral's flagship to report the arrival of the *Antigone* and, Farley did not doubt, to tender his apologies for his tardiness.

It was not cheerful news. "Do you think MacDougall and I will be able to leave soon?"

"I'm afraid I couldn't say, ma'am. His lordship suggests that you remain in your cabin until the situation has been clarified."

So Page sat back down to wait. Her patience, however, was severely strained by the dismal gray half-light of the tiny cabin and the malevolent air of the squat black gun which soon began to take on a strange life of its own, seemingly determined to crowd everything in the cabin, including Page, against the bulkheads.

As if the sense of being suffocated was not torment enough, she could hear a faint rattle of guns, fired sporadically and at some distance, and now and then a wild burst of shouting. Whatever was happening in

Hampton, it would surely be better to know the truth than to be kept there in the gloom, imagining all sorts of horrors going on outside in the bright sun.

Hazard appeared at her door suddenly, looking so splendid in elegant buckskins and gray tailored coat, his top boots polished brightly and his cravat spotlessly white, that she doubted if Farley had been spared any time for the hammock on the berth deck.

"Captain Kincaid has gone in search of his admirals," he said without preamble. "They have established their headquarters in Hampton, and the captain intends to report to them at once. But since I place no great dependence on the captain's good word, I think it advisable to go ashore myself."

Page's eyes widened. "Do you think you should?"

He raised a dark brow. "Is there any reason why I should not? You will remain in your cabin, if you please, until I return. The first lieutenant has stationed two marines just outside the wardroom and Farley will be within call at all times, so you need feel no apprehension."

"But I don't please to stay here," Page said, lifting her chin. "This is a dark dreary place and I have had quite enough of it."

"You will do as you are told," he said coolly.

He looked very tall and forbidding, his big shoulders looming above her, his voice sounding very different with no smooth overlay of charm or amusement, possessing a peculiar hard ring as if his words struck upon cold metal.

She wanted to protest, to inform him with icy dignity that she would do as she pleased no matter what he said. But to her amazement she heard herself saying, "Are you going alone, and unarmed? What if someone shoots at you?"

"Then there will be one Englishman less, and that should please any number of people."

"It will be very dangerous, I'm sure," she said dubiously. "I wish you will be careful."

His smile was so unexpected, so warm and brilliant, that she caught her breath.

"Thank you for your solicitude," he said. "I promise I will be very careful."

He had his hand on the door when the pipes twittered over their heads, followed by the slow rolling of a drum; after a brief interval of tramping feet, all sounds died away into silence.

Page looked at Hazard. "What is it?"

"We are to be treated to a flogging," he said curtly. "One of the seamen made an impertinent remark to an officer. I heard the captain order the punishment, but I believed I had persuaded him to delay it."

"A flogging?" Page repeated, and was glad that her voice betrayed no tremor.

Then she heard the unmistakable whine of the cat-o'-nine-tails as it cut through the air. A man screamed the high unnatural scream of pain. Then the cat whined again, and the scream came simultaneously. Page swallowed, hearing the rolling drum in her temples like the pounding of her blood.

Hazard took a stride toward her. "Three dozen," he said, "but I wouldn't advise you to count them."

She kept her eyes on Hazard's, as a drowning person will cling desperately to anything within reach. Without a word he put a hand on either side of her face, covering her ears. Pulling her to him, so that her face was hidden against his coat, he held her there firmly, saying something over her head. She never afterwards remembered what he said, but his voice went on and on, hard

64

and ringing, so close to her that she could hear nothing else; and the world was shut away by the strength of his hands over her ears and the steady beat of his heart somewhere just under her face.

Then, mercifully, it was over. He took his hands down and put her away from him, not ungently. On the deck the drum had ceased and there was another shuffling of feet as the crew went back to their duties.

Hazard said casually, as if nothing had happened, "My apologies for keeping you so long in such a 'dark dreary' place. But before the day is over I fear we will all have gone beyond apologies."

Then he was gone. Page sat with her chin in her hands, turning his words and manner of behavior over in her mind. But she knew so little about him that it was impossible to come to any conclusion; and it was not until midday, when the afternoon watch had just begun and Farley appeared with a tray of food, that she had any hint of the day of terror reigning in Hampton.

"I didn't wish to be the one to tell you," Farley said soberly, "but his lordship felt that you should know. It is rumored that the officers lost control of their men after the town was taken. A disgraceful occurrence, ma'am, and small wonder his lordship is displeased."

Page drew a deep breath. So that was what he meant about the British going beyond apologies, and why he looked so remote and preoccupied, speaking in that hard implacable voice. She imagined, for a dreadful moment, the things that could happen when troops ran wild in a captured town, and her skin went cold and clammy.

She managed to look back at Farley steadily. "Are you sure? Perhaps it is only a rumor, after all."

"I would like to think so, ma'am."

But he did not sound as though he thought it only a rumor, and Page said numbly, "Why did he go in to Hampton, then?"

"To speak his mind to an admiral or two, if I know his lordship. I've seen him in a temper before, and I don't envy the man who stands in his way."

Page reflected that it was unlikely he would be able to find any sort of transportation for her and Mac-Dougall when Hampton doubtless lay in ruins, but to speak of her own problems, or even to be unduly concerned, when others were in far more wretched straits, would be a sad piece of selfishness.

The day dragged on at an interminable pace. Mr. Buckley came to her door once and suggested that it might be more tolerable for her to wait in the officers' wardroom. Page thanked him civilly, for he had been very kind, and when he assured her that none of the officers would disturb her, she accepted his invitation gratefully.

Seated at the table in the wardroom with a dingy deck of cards left behind by one of the officers, she was toying with the grossly improper idea of asking Farley to join her in a game of piquet when she felt a subtle change in the silence and looked up to see Hazard standing in the door.

"Don't look so stricken," he said immediately. "It isn't as bad as it might have been. Bad enough, God knows, with the admirals hiding behind closed doors and General Beckwith nowhere to be found. But a few of the officers have been trying to gain some control over their men, and when I left, the town was fairly calm." He gave her a hard straight look, neither compromising with the truth nor attempting to hide it. "There has been a great deal of looting and some unpleasantness, but so far only one civilian death has been discovered. Regrettable, but under the circumstances the town is fortunate to have only one."

It was not quite so horrible as she had been imagining all that long hot day; bad enough, as he had said, but it could have been far worse. "We have learned to expect unpleasantness," she said, "from British soldiers."

He sat on the far edge of the table, swinging one boot. "In a war," he said coolly, "you can expect a great deal more than unpleasantness. Cockburn, however, insists that the British troops under his command had nothing to do with it. The culprits, so he told me, were a detachment of French prisoners who volunteered for duty as an alternative to Dartmoor prison." He added, his voice edged, "I am not persuaded, after seeing Hampton, that the townspeople will appreciate the difference between French and English soldiers as readily as the admiral."

Page found it difficult to believe that he honestly disapproved of English admirals, English soldiers or English behavior on American soil. "What do you care?" she asked, picking up the cards and arranging them in a neat pyramid. "Why should it matter to you whether they were English or French?"

His eyes regarded her thoughtfully for a moment. Then he said, "For the past three years I have been fighting in Spain and Portugal with an army that knows its commander-in-chief would not hesitate to hang the first soldier guilty of turning his rage upon a civilian. It has given me a taste for a disciplined method of warfare, and a strong dislike of admirals trying to fight out of their element."

She stared at him. "If you are truly in the army, what were you doing in America?"

"Visiting my sister," he said. "I thought I told you."

He had told her, but it seemed very odd. "The British army in Spain is no different from any other," she said. "I've heard of the dreadful things that have happened there, and the towns that were sacked."

"War has a way of being dreadful," he said flatly, "and so do armies. In Europe the method of warfare has been the same for centuries; when a town refuses to surrender and can be taken only with a great loss of lives, few officers can prevent their men from sacking it in retaliation. But it is not the same as plundering and murdering helpless civilians who have had nothing to do with the battle."

Page studied his hard grim face with a fleeting apprehension. But she said, "I can't see any difference. There must be any number of civilians who live in towns and yet have nothing to do with the fighting."

"There is a difference," he said curtly. "There is also a great difference between fortress towns in Europe and small undefended American villages, as I should think George Cockburn would have the good sense to know." He changed the subject abruptly. "As to the matter of sending you back to Annapolis, I have the admiral's permission to do whatever I think best. Captain Kincaid, I am sure, will be delighted to have the problem taken out of his hands."

The cards she had so carefully built into a pyramid collapsed, and she picked them up slowly, one by one.

"I found a young lad who promised to take a message to your father as soon as possible," Hazard went on. "You may be at Bradley's House before him, but I thought it would do no harm to send him."

She had no chance to thank him. Outside the wardroom someone called, "Joss, where the devil did you go?" and the next moment an officer stepped through the door, talking cheerfully to Mr. Buckley over his shoulder.

"I'm sure you have the best of intentions, my dear fellow, but I'll reserve my opinion until I've seen her. In my experience, young ladies in need of being rescued are seldom beautiful, but on the contrary are far more likely to be squint-eyed and abominably disagreeable."

Page, blinking a little at his grandeur, saw a tall thin young man with receding fair hair, a long hooked nose and bright blue eyes. He was wearing a blue coat with brilliant gold trim, thick silk cravat and breeches of a dazzling white, and under his arm he carried a cocked hat.

Apparently his eyes were not yet used to the gloom of the wardroom, for he did not appear to notice Page in the shadows at the end of the table.

"Joss, have you hidden the poor girl in the cockpit? There, Mr. Buckley, you see I was right. She has a wretched squint and a shocking disposition, not to mention an angry mother who will chase us across the seven seas and a brother who can plug a wafer at twenty paces and will demand satisfaction at once. The devil take it, Mr. Buckley, it's the story of my life."

Mr. Buckley stared fixedly at the young officer, as if by not looking at Page he might by some miracle erase the fact of her presence.

But Hazard only looked amused and said, "Noel, you fool, stop chattering." He turned to Page and added, "I have known him a number of years and can vouch for his amiability, if not his tact. Miss Bradley, may I present Commander, the Honourable Noel Stuart, of His Majesty's brig *Falcon*."

Stuart, catching sight of Page, was not in the least disconcerted. "This is the little American? It isn't possible. Not a sign of a squint, and the most charming face I've seen since I left London." He gave Page an elegant bow, cocked hat over his heart, and when he straightened his bright blue eyes laughed into hers. "I beg your forgiveness, ma'am, and hasten to assure you that I am entirely at your service."

She could not help smiling back at him. Then Hazard said, "I think we must abandon any idea of arranging transportation from Hampton, Miss Bradley. No boats or carriages are available at the moment, and no accommodations where you might wait."

Farley still hovered unnoticed in the background, his face showing a sober concern. Mr. Buckley, solemn and anxious, stood stiffly by the door. Commander Stuart watched Page with a lively interest, and Hazard, studying the tip of one boot, was obviously choosing his words with care.

It seemed to Page a most ridiculous and ironic twist of fate that the British, ashore in the little town of Hampton, were wreaking all the brutality of war on any hapless American in sight; while here, in the wardroom of a British ship-of-war, four Englishmen were directing all their attention to the problem of restoring one unimportant American to her home.

Hazard asked, "Do you know anyone in Norfolk?"

Page shook her head. There were Bradley relatives in every corner of Virginia, but at the moment she could think of no one, friend or kin, closer than her sister Julia in Gloucester County.

"It is just across the river," Hazard said slowly, "but I am told it is now crowded to the rafters with American militia, preparing against the possibility of another British attack. Under the circumstances I doubt if suitable lodging could be found for you."

"I will gladly try it, if you like," Stuart said, "but I

feel I should mention the small difficulty of landing anyone from a British ship."

Hazard, his eyes on Page's face, said nothing.

"MacDougall will find lodging for me," she said. "If you could only find a way to put us ashore, I'm sure we can manage the rest."

No one spoke for a moment. Then Hazard said quietly, "Unfortunately, it isn't that simple. MacDougall has been impressed, and is now a seaman in the service of His Majesty's Navy."

Page said, on a note of disbelief, "You must be jesting, sir."

Mr. Buckley cleared his throat uncomfortably. "According to his orders, ma'am, the captain is acting within his rights."

"Whose rights?" Page asked incredulously. "No one has any right to impress Duncan MacDougall. You must set him free at once."

Mr. Buckley said unhappily, "I deeply regret the whole affair."

"Unless I mistake the matter, Miss Bradley," Hazard said, "your country is fighting a war to settle such matters. But at the moment, since the outcome is still in doubt, MacDougall has most certainly been impressed by Captain Kincaid."

"Can't you do something about it?" Page asked, but she reminded herself that he had no reason, after all, to care what happened to MacDougall. Or to her, when it came to that, and it was unfair to expect miracles of him.

But he said, "Yes, I can do something about it. However, I have no desire to see Mr. Buckley hauled before the admirals and court-martialed, which is precisely what will happen if MacDougall is allowed to go ashore in Norfolk."

Stuart, somewhat apologetically, interrupted to say, "My dear fellow, I'll go along with any devious scheme you have in mind, but we haven't a great deal of time."

Hazard ignored him. "The *Falcon* is clearing for Halifax within the hour," he said to Page. "Since Captain Stuart is carrying dispatches, he has the admiral's permission to see that his ship is adequately manned. Being short a few topmen, he is borrowing, shall we say, from all available sources." He added, with the flicker of a smile, "Fortunately for Mr. Buckley's future in the navy, he is outranked and has no choice in the matter."

"Do you mean that MacDougall will be taken to Halifax?" Page said with misgiving. "What on earth will he do there?"

"Once the *Falcon* has cleared the Capes, no one will be the wiser if she discharges a passenger somewhere along the coast."

"And you will go to Halifax with the *Falcon*?"

"Yes," he said briefly.

Page was silent. The thought of being put ashore in Norfolk, which loomed in her mind as a strange town filled with indifferent strangers, separated from home by all the endless miles of the Bay, while MacDougall sailed away on a British ship, was suddenly intolerable.

"Then why not two passengers?" she asked. "I won't stay in Norfolk without MacDougall, and if we were put ashore anywhere along the coast we would be as close to Annapolis as we are now."

"I would be delighted," Stuart said promptly.

Hazard stood up. "Get her things, Farley." He gave Page a faint smile. "I would not have left you alone in Norfolk in any event," he said coolly, "but I wanted you to make the choice for yourself." When she said nothing he added, "I have a number of faults, but the vice of abducting young ladies is not among them."

Noel Stuart grinned and looked as if he might make a pertinent comment, but after meeting Hazard's cool gaze he only said, with a cheerful shrug, "We had better take our leave of this pest ship, old fellow, unless you intend to be on hand when her captain returns."

He and Mr. Buckley left the wardroom. Farley, loaded with the portmanteaus and bandboxes, managed to hand Page the chip bonnet with blue satin ribbons, and gave her a reassuring smile.

Hazard, searching her face, said lightly, "The adventure is not yet ended, I'm afraid."

Page, with a furious determination not to betray her uncertainty or allow him to suspect the near panic that had settled once again, like a great lump, inside her, said as lightly as she could manage, "I can't think why you should describe all this as an adventure. It gives me a very odd notion of your character."

"But," he said, "my character is quite odd, so it isn't surprising that you've noticed it." Then he added, as he had done once before, "Keep a stout heart."

When they came up into the June sunlight, blindingly bright after the gloom below, the first face she saw was MacDougall's, dear and familiar against a backdrop of the ship's black and white and yellow, and her heart slowed to its normal pace again.

Whatever happened, she reflected soberly, she was more fortunate than the poor people of Hampton, and there were worse fates than to be alive in a world where Lord Hazard walked beside her with his strong hand under her arm, and Farley followed close behind, and Duncan MacDougall still scowled severely at her for her sins.

6

To the west the sun disappeared behind the land, leaving a crimson glow in the sky which gradually ghosted away before the clear dark blue of approaching night. The *Falcon*, with everything aloft unfurled and pulling, stood out to sea in the fading light, her bow lifting to the long fetch of the Atlantic swells, the fair wind humming a song up all the long height of her rigging.

Aft, leaning against the taffrail, Hazard whistled idly under his breath as he watched the activity on the deck. The master stood with his hands behind his back, head tilted to observe the trim of his sails. Close beside him was Noel Stuart, speaking first to the master and then to the helmsman, as if reluctant to leave his ship in any hands but his own while the land still loomed on the horizon. Forward the watch moved silently about its duties, an occasional seaman raising his head, like the master and captain, to look approvingly at the billowing sails aloft. By the break in the quarterdeck Page Bradley and Duncan MacDougall were talking, their conversation carrying across the deck to Hazard each time MacDougall's voice rose angrily.

Hazard had been watching them for some time, his face remote and eyes hidden behind their heavy lids. Now, as a ship's boy came aft in the dusk to light the binnacle lamps, Noel Stuart crossed the deck to the taffrail.

"The fellow has been at it for an hour or more," he said to Hazard. "Shouldn't one of us be gallant enough to rescue Miss Bradley?"

"Leave him alone," Hazard said. "He's had a difficult time of it, and the end is not yet in sight."

"It would be useless, I suppose, to assure him that the entire ship's company shares his solicitude."

"He's a Scot, my friend, and a Yankee."

"Surely," Stuart said ruefully. "The only good Englishman is a dead one, and even then not to be trusted. Has he threatened you yet?"

"Not yet, but I imagine he will." Hazard's voice was unperturbed. "I would do the same if I stood in the unenviable position of having to answer to Samuel Bradley."

"The child's father?"

"And a gentleman, I understand, who likes his daughter as much as he dislikes the British."

"Well, she's a taking little thing, and far too young and pretty to be chasing about an ocean in the midst of a war with only you, my good fellow, in attendance."

"You are forgetting the scowling Scotsman."

"So I was. Do you think him an acceptable chaperon? I own I would not, were I an angry father, but then I've known you for a long time and it is to be devoutly hoped that Mr. Bradley will look upon you as a complete stranger."

"Go to the devil," Hazard said amiably.

Stuart laughed. "I admit I've been at sea so long that I've lost touch with the world, but the last time I saw you in London you were keeping a lovely lady in barbaric luxury, and rumor had it that she was costing you no less than a small fortune. Worth every guinea of it,

I'm sure, but I shouldn't have thought she would have left you with a taste for schoolgirls."

"Take care," Hazard said coolly.

"I hope Miss Bradley will do so, old boy."

"She is little more than a schoolgirl, as you say," Hazard said slowly, "and thus far she has seen nothing amiss in the situation beyond the unpleasant circumstance of being captured by the enemy." After a moment he added, his voice still pleasant but holding a faint undertone of steel, "I would prefer that she retain that happy innocence as long as possible."

"My lips are sealed," Stuart said promptly. "No offense intended. Not that I'm a coward, you understand, but I've seen you too many times with the pistols. And one cold dawn at Brighton, of all places, when you proved somewhat deadly with the sword."

Hazard grinned. "If you weren't such a worthless fribble, Noel, you'd have been called out long since."

"I trust that I have your assurance that you will do no such thing, at least aboard my own ship, because I have every intention of asking why the young lady wasn't left in Norfolk."

Hazard was silent, his eyes on Page Bradley's white gown, now blurred in the growing darkness. Then he said briefly, "I didn't care to have it on my conscience that I had left her alone in a town mobbed with untrained militia and camp followers."

"Lord, and all these years I never suspected you had a conscience," Stuart said. Then, suddenly grave, he went on, "You had better tell me what you've planned, Joss. We both know that it will be difficult, if not impossible, to put anyone ashore. Not to mention the sad truth that the coastline up from the Capes is a desolate stretch of sandy beach unsuitable for the most resourceful of Robinson Crusoes."

"I don't intend to put her ashore on a sandy beach."

"I thought not. New England, then?"

"Didn't you say you were carrying dispatches there?"

"To the blockading squadron, and Boston wouldn't be far out of my way."

"Any difficulty in getting ashore?"

"We'll hoist a flag of truce and sail straight into the harbor. Boston is full of Federalists who think they're fighting the wrong country, you know. When war was declared they called it a terrible calamity and flew their flags at half-mast." Stuart shrugged. "It's a risky business for those New Englanders, I should think, stopping only this side of treason, but we've a sporting agreement that affairs shall go forward in as reasonable a manner as possible."

"Treason, perhaps," Hazard said thoughtfully. "But a Yankee shipowner with his ship confiscated by French Decrees and his crew kept in French prisons for years isn't going to embrace the Republic simply because Washington tells him that Bonaparte is a sincere and misunderstood gentleman."

"And every Englishman an arrogant tyrant," Stuart said. "But mind you, Joss, they hate us in New England. It's only that Bonaparte seems the greater of two evils."

Hazard said, almost absently, "Half the ships supplying Wellington sail from New England ports."

Stuart laughed. "Precisely. The British are not so intolerable as the strain on the Yankee purse. The Admiralty, I suspect, would like to see all America bankrupt, but the poor sods marching with Wellington need their supplies, and so we blockade with the greatest of tact and Warren hands out licenses to the Yank traders."

"A circumstance which must cause Mr. Madison

some mild concern," Hazard remarked. "A general with a divided command is unlikely to win battles."

Stuart stared at Hazard in the deepening dusk. "From the beginning our orders from the Admiralty were to encourage that division," he said slowly, "but I suppose you wouldn't know anything about that."

"Only what I read in the newspapers. The Admiralty doesn't confide in army staff officers, my friend."

But Stuart looked thoughtful. "Now that I remember, you left the Peninsula when everyone thought Wellington would keep you in headquarters until the thing was ended, and here you turn up in America, cool as you please, putting it about that you're only visiting." His grin flashed white in the darkness. "Go ahead, tell me that his lordship gave you a special leave to go jaunting about the world on family affairs. You might tell me he's handed his sword over to Boney and I'd believe it sooner."

"He certainly didn't give me leave to get myself strung up as a spy," Hazard said lightly. "I could have used a bit of Federalist sympathy in Annapolis."

"You had Miss Bradley," Stuart said, "and I can assure you she is far more charming than any dour New Englander. Very well, no more awkward questions. But tell me this, Joss. Do you mean to abandon the child in Boston?"

"I promised I would see her safely home," Hazard said idly.

"You seem to have a taste for nooses," Stuart said. "However, I daresay you know what you're about; you always did. But have a care."

"I intend to."

MacDougall had finally disappeared and Page Bradley walked toward them slowly, swinging her bonnet. The wind blew her hair across her face and she pushed it back absently as she glanced up at the sails. Pausing a moment to study the binnacle and the brawny size of the helmsman standing his trick at the wheel, she tilted her head as if to listen to the high steady roar of the wind in the rigging. Then, briefly, she looked back toward the land, dropping behind them in the night.

Stuart bowed and said, "I hope you found your quarters comfortable, Miss Bradley?"

"Yes, thank you. But I'm sorry to have taken your cabin."

"A trifling service, believe me."

He left them to speak to the officer of the watch. The wind had shifted and the watch was called, the men running to trim the sails and then disappearing below, leaving the ship quiet again. Stuart remained on the weather side of the deck, looking out into the darkness, then up at the straining curve of the sails. Finally he turned and paced back to the helmsman.

"He feels the wind in his bones tonight," Hazard said. Then, "Was MacDougall very unpleasant?"

"He gave me a thundering scold," she said. She turned to look out across the foaming wake. "He thinks I should have remained in Norfolk, whatever happened to him. He is right, I daresay, but sometimes it is difficult to see how matters will go until it is too late, and then one is obliged to go on doing one foolish thing after another."

"Did you tell him that I refused to put you ashore?"

After a moment she said with a troubled honesty, "If I had insisted, wouldn't you have left me in Norfolk?"

"Emphatically not."

"Even if I had pleaded," she asked curiously, "and perhaps wept?"

"Was there the slightest chance that you might have done either?"

She was silent. Then she sighed and said, "No," and added, "So you see that I must share the blame."

"I see that you have very little trust in my ability to return you to Annapolis," Hazard said coolly, "or you would not be so concerned about MacDougall's opinions."

"I have enough to concern me," she said bleakly, "even without that."

"Doubtless," he said. "You are on an enemy ship, surrounded by desperate and violent men who quite obviously intend to harm your person or, at the very least, to shackle you below in irons and feed you nothing but wormy ship's biscuit. It is precisely what a young lady should expect, after all, from Englishmen."

"How absurd you are," she said. "Whatever I'm afraid of, it isn't that."

He could tell from her voice, with its hint of a smile, that he had succeeded in diverting her for a moment.

"Are you afraid of being landed on the coast and left to make your way home with MacDougall?" After an instant's pause Hazard went on, almost gently, "I'm afraid I was obliged to deceive you, Miss Bradley. It will be impossible to land either of you on the coast."

She stood quite still. Finally she said slowly, "Did you know that before we left Hampton?"

"Yes."

"So did I," she said, so low that he had to bend his head to catch the words. "I was quite certain of it, but I hated so badly to be left behind in Norfolk that I wouldn't let myself think of it." She swallowed audibly. "The Delaware, then? It isn't such a great distance from Philadelphia to Baltimore."

"Not the Delaware," he said bluntly. "Nor New York. The *Falcon* is carrying dispatches north, so it will have to be Boston."

She lifted her face to him, but he could not see it. She said nothing at all.

Beyond the rail the seas mounted, curled into white spray, raced past, and the deck slanted even further to leeward. The pipes shrilled suddenly and the watch came on deck, scrambling up the weather rigging to send down the topgallants, while at the wheel there were now two helmsmen to hold the *Falcon* on her course. A shower of spray came over the side and rattled along the deck, and a gust of wind whipped Page Bradley's muslin gown against her. Even in the darkness she looked small and slight, scarcely reaching to his shoulder, and somehow, in that wild world of wind and straining canvas and surging waves, touchingly forlorn.

"You had better go below," he said, and took her arm.

She did not protest, seeming grateful for his assistance across the slanting deck. When they paused at the door leading to the after cabin he looked down at her in the flickering light; but the blue eyes were slanted and lowered, hidden behind the fringe of lashes, and if her face was pale and her mouth uncertain, she managed to keep her voice steady.

"Good night," she said.

He did not move. "Don't be distressed," he said quietly. "Boston is a long way from the Chesapeake, but I hope the journey will not be intolerable. I intend to hire a chaise, and MacDougall and I will escort you to Bradley's House."

Her eyes lifted swiftly and he saw their surprise. But she said only, "Thank you," and turned away, gazing down at the bonnet in her hand so that he could see only the curve of her cheek and her bent head, showing the childish fragility of her shoulders.

He looked at her with an amused exasperation, and for a brief moment considered taking her in his arms to comfort her. It was an instinctive impulse springing from such an impersonal compassion that he had almost stepped toward her before he came to his senses.

In the end he only said, gently, "Sleep well, little one," and closed the door.

Page lay on the cot in the small sleeping room, bulkheaded away from the after cabin, and stared above her, eyes wide open in the darkness. A sliver of light from the lantern in the after cabin moved across her face and the door swung restlessly back and forth until she finally got up and hooked it back. The cot, however, was equally unquiet, swinging up, hovering, then soaring down again as the *Falcon* pressed on her way.

She had removed the muslin gown and, clad only in her thin shift, wrapped a blanket around her. The air had cooled excessively since sunset and the blanket was pleasantly warm. She kept her mind carefully blank, refusing to surrender to the insidious panic that swept through her, receded, then slyly returned, as impervious to reason or pride as sea waves eating away at a sandy beach. With resolution she fastened her eyes on the swinging oil lantern, visible through the open door, until it blurred and faded away into a soft impenetrable darkness.

She awoke with a sudden jolt and a slap of pain that brought tears to her eyes. For a long dazed moment she did not remember where she was and could not imagine why her forehead ached so amazingly. There was nothing but a wavering light that hurt her eyes and a wild din that crashed, roared, shrieked and thundered about her ears. She had a momentary sense of having awakened from a nightmare to find herself in an unfamiliar world more terrifying that the dream.

She had fallen from the cot. First she felt the deck under her hands and face, then recognized the light from the lantern. But when she tried to sit up the cabin seemed tilted at such an impossible angle that she immediately tumbled against a bulkhead and banged her head again.

Exasperated, she finally managed to get to her feet, wavering like someone quite disguised with wine. Reaching for her gown, she wrapped the blanket tightly around her and began the difficult climb up the slanting deck. By the time she reached the big table she felt as if she had climbed a mountain; the ship pitched and rolled, staggered, then rolled again, making it a marvelous feat simply to keep on her feet.

She had some idea of putting on her gown. If the ship foundered one might as easily drown in a shift as not, but some dimly remembered maxim urged her to meet her fate fully clothed. A very small effort, however, convinced her that she could not hold on with one hand and manage her gown with the other so long as the ship pitched about so remorselessly.

She heard the rattling which must be rain deluging the deck above her, the roar of waves against the side, and the thundering shock as mountains of water came over the bow and swept down the deck. Every timber in the ship protested, with such a creaking and groaning that the very decks might have been breaking apart. Above it all, bringing her heart to her throat, was the high keening scream of the wind as it hurtled out of the night.

The door was flung open, then slammed closed. Hazard stood there in dripping tarpaulin coat and sou'wester, his dark face running wet with rain.

"Don't be alarmed," he said swiftly. "I only came below to see if I might be of service to you."

But her first thought had not been that the ship was in danger and he had come to warn her, but that his face had a strange look of unguarded happiness and his eyes glittered with the same exultancy that must grip the gulls soaring in excitement down the high wild corridors of the wind. He had been on deck in the storm and it had taken possession of him, and for once he was neither remote nor impassive.

"The worst of it has passed," he said. "The gale freshened since midnight and the *Falcon* has been beating to windward. With the coast under his lee the captain preferred more seaway, but now we are hove to and she should ride more easily."

The ship shuddered and lurched, and Page grabbed the table. Hazard grinned and said, "She has a devilish roll, doesn't she?"

"Yes," Page said faintly, beset by the problem of keeping her balance and, when she suddenly remembered that she was not dressed, clutching the blanket around her. She put her gown hastily behind her and immediately regretted letting go of the table; with the next roll of the ship she staggered, lost her hold on both the blanket and the table, and went headlong across the cabin toward Hazard.

He caught her and held her steady. Then, as if the touch of her bare arms had only just brought the fact of her disarray to his attention, he gave her a cursory glance and said, matter-of-factly, "You'll freeze with no more clothes than that. Give me your gown."

There was nothing else to do. She had gone beyond embarrassment, feeling only a stunned and bemused gratitude. Without a word she handed it to him, and he braced her against the table and pulled it over her head, turning her to button it down the back.

"I'm surprised that you haven't already had consumption," he said severely, "wearing no more than this ridiculous muslin."

Startled, Page said, "It isn't ridiculous. It's the very latest fashion."

"What a scatterbrained reason for giving yourself lung fever. I'll wager a guinea that everything you're wearing, including your slippers, would hardly weigh eight ounces. Women can be the most damnable fools."

"You seem to forget," Page said with what dignity she could muster while he was buttoning her dress and scolding her as he might a tiresome child in the nursery, "that I wasn't allowed a choice of clothes to bring with me on my journey."

"So you weren't." He turned her around and she saw the laughter flickering in his eyes. "Stay where you are and don't leave go of the table."

She stood where he left her and in a moment he was back, balancing easily to the pitch of the deck, carrying one of his coats over his arm.

Tailored to fit across his big shoulders without a crease, it hung loosely on Page and the sleeves dangled below her hands. Hazard grinned unfeelingly.

"Not quite so fashionable, but confess you've fewer goose-pimples."

A wave roared over the bow and along the deck, and the ship labored unsteadily before rolling again.

"You should try to sleep. It's a long time yet until dawn."

"I can't seem to stay in one place long enough to sleep."

"Well, you can't stand here the rest of the night," Hazard said reasonably.

He removed the sou'wester and tarpaulin coat and threw them across a chair. He wore no coat and his white shirt, undone at the neck, was sticking to him damply. He did not look like the impeccable viscount she had first seen in Annapolis, but he seemed far more approachable.

"Please don't feel obliged to stay with me. I'm not afraid to be alone."

His eyes flickered to her face. "Don't lie," he said. Then, with a quick smile, "At least you're not seasick, which is nothing short of miraculous in these seas."

Bracing one of the chairs against a bulkhead, he said, "Come here," and without waiting for her to obey, picked her up and sat down with her in his arms, propping his feet against the cushioned transom. "Unusual circumstances," he said, "call for unusual measures."

She was quite sure that she should protest, however unusual the circumstances. But she was not at all sure that he would respond in the accepted gentlemanly way; it would be more like him to tell her not to be a silly fool. In any case, he would certainly recognize any protest for the lie it was; impropriety, however dangerous, did not at the moment seem as important to her as the comforting assurance of his presence.

"Take a deep breath and close your eyes. I promise I won't let you fall."

She obeyed him wordlessly. The voice of the gale enveloped the ship, screeching, roaring, hammering, keening, a tumult of sound more frightening than the violent pitching of the ship; but her face was against his shirt, warmed by the hard flesh beneath and the beat of his heart, and his arms held her so firmly that the panic gradually faded away and she was lulled into a drowsy indifference.

When she next opened her eyes the cabin was filled with a dull gray light.

"Good morning," Hazard said.

Her eyes widened and she raised her head to meet his lazy smile.

"Have I been asleep?"

"For hours." His eyes were hooded by the heavy lids as he looked down at her and his face was unreadable, but he seemed so wide-awake that she did not believe he had closed his eyes at all. "As peacefully as a babe, too, which speaks well for your conscience."

"And you?" It was discomfitting to find herself in his arms in the cold light of day and she looked away. Then, refusing to bargain with embarrassment, she raised her eyes to his. "I hope you weren't too uncomfortable."

"Quite comfortable," he said, sounding amused, "but I fear my conscience isn't as innocent as yours."

A knock startled her, but Hazard said easily, "Yes?"

A voice beyond the door answered, "The captain's compliments, sir, and would you please join him on deck?"

"I'll be there at once." Hazard stood up, putting Page on her feet. The ship was still rolling, but the force of the gale seemed to have subsided somewhat with daylight, and Hazard, shrugging into the tarpaulin coat, said, "If Farley managed to survive the night, I'll send him along with breakfast," smiled at her and was gone.

At once the cabin was not a comforting refuge but an alien and unfamiliar place where she was a stranger among enemies, and suddenly so cold and lonely that her very bones ached with wretchedness.

Wrapping his lordship's exquisitely tailored coat around her, she sat in the chair he had vacated and stared out bleakly at the storm-lashed expanse of sea heaving past the stern windows.

7

The *Falcon*, no longer hove to, but clawing her way, close-hauled, to the northward, had sustained a good deal of damage aloft during the night. But repairs were going forward as rapidly as possible, what with the wind and seas still buffeting the ship, and Stuart did not think it necessary to turn and run for the shelter of the Chesapeake.

"But I don't mind telling you that I doubted, once or twice, that we'd survive the night." His voice was hoarse from shouting orders all night into the gale. "We're damned lucky, you know, that the masts are still with us."

"And our captain," Hazard said, with a brief glance at Stuart's face, encrusted with salt and pale with weariness. "Why don't you go below and breakfast? You look as if you could use some hot coffee, liberally laced with brandy."

"Sorry, old fellow, but we can't risk a galley fire in this weather. It'll have to be cold food, but by God, I relish the thought of brandy. Let us see to the matter at once." Stuart turned to the officer of the watch. "I am going below, Mr. Webster. You will call me, if you please, if you feel that anything needs my attention."

They were just leaving the quarterdeck when the lookout, clinging to his swaying perch high above the deck, sang out, "Sail ho!"

Stuart, hands on the barricade, put back his head and shouted, "Where away?"

"Off the port bow, sir," the answer came, shredded by the wind.

Stuart took the telescope handed him by the first lieutenant. Going fore, he swung into the shrouds and went up the mainmast like a cat. At the maintopmast-cap he held his glass to his eyes, while below him every man on deck raised their faces in expectant silence.

When Stuart stood on the quarterdeck again he looked first at the sailing master. "Steady as she goes, Mr. Reynolds. Keep her as near the wind as she'll lie." Then, to his first officer, "We'll let her come down to us. Break out the Spanish colors, Mr. Webster, until we can be certain of her flag."

"Shall I beat to quarters, sir?"

"Not yet. I sent the watch down to breakfast, and it may be they'll need a good meal under their belts."

The first lieutenant took his glass to the tops and remained there for some time. When he returned he said, "A sloop-of-war, sir, from the looks of her. She's running straight down for us, but she's flying no colors yet that I could see."

Stuart turned to Hazard, the weariness gone from his face and his eyes very bright and blue. He said gravely, "I'm sorry, Joss. She may be one of ours, but if she's a Yankee I haven't a choice. Even with passengers and dispatches aboard, I'll have to stand and fight."

"Don't apologize," Hazard said. "It's a devil of a war." Then, abruptly, "I'm more a soldier than a sailor, but for what it's worth, I'm at your service."

Stuart grinned. "Worth a regiment, if we can board

her. But damn it all, Joss, I wish the child were not aboard."

For a moment Hazard said nothing. Then he gave Stuart a level direct look and said, "The responsibility is mine."

"MacDougall will have to be locked up, I'm afraid, and Miss Bradley should be sent to the hold."

"I'll see to it," Hazard said curtly.

It was apparent, in a very short while, that the *Falcon* had a fight on her hands. The officers, swarming up the shrouds, looked through their telescopes to see the red-and-white American flag break from the stranger's mast and stand straight out in the stiff wind. She was a fast sloop, coming down rapidly, her gun ports open and guns run out. Her commander was obviously not misled by the red and yellow colors of Spain at the *Falcon*'s masthead.

"Eighteen guns," Stuart said. "We carry the same number, and I doubt if hers are heavier in so light a vessel. But I'd lay a monkey she'll be easier to maneuver in this sea, and that may make a difference. Mr. Webster, you may beat to quarters, if you please, and clear the ship for action."

Hazard swung down the ladder to the waist. His mind coldly assessed the things that could befall Page Bradley in the fury and confusion of a sea battle. The hold below the waterline might be safe from enemy shot, but the danger of a fire was always present, as well as the possibility that the ship could sink without warning to those below. Farley, of course, would do all within his power to keep her safe, and Noel Stuart would fight to the death for his ship; but Hazard, who was accustomed to being the master of his fate and who for a lifetime had met any challenge with the reassuring knowledge that he would stand or fall on his own abil-

ity and intelligence, felt a bitter sense of impotency to
realize that not he, but a number of uncertain and
problematical factors, would determine Page Bradley's
safety in the next few hours.

He found her in the cabin with Farley, finishing a
tray of cold meat and wine. She looked up to meet
Hazard's silent regard from the door.

"What is it?" she asked in a quiet little voice. "Is
something wrong?"

He wondered how she knew, when he was certain
that his face was too well-trained to give him away.
Then the drum began to roll from the deck above, its
staccato notes of alarm sounding clearly throughout the
ship.

"Only a strange sail on the horizon," he said calmly,
"which has turned out to be an American one."

The color left her face for a moment and then came
back, a delicate flush of pink beneath the skin. But she
did not speak.

"Farley, you will conduct Miss Bradley to the hold
and remain with her until you hear from me." When
Farley looked as if he might protest, Hazard said with
cold emphasis, "I depend on you to stay by her, whatever happens."

Farley met his master's hard steady gaze and, with a
perceptible effort, swallowed the words he had been
about to say. "I will do my best, sir."

Then, because he had so little of comfort to offer her
for the harrowing hours that might lie ahead, Hazard
smiled at Page and said, "It might be more cheerful
below if you carry the wine with you. And don't forget
that you can't possibly be the loser, whatever the outcome."

He turned away and went back on deck at a run.
Stuart handed him a heavy belt and two boarding pis-

tols, lethal weapons boasting small cutlasses to be snapped into position as needed, and on second thought added a sword. Hazard, strapping them on, looked about him with narrowed eyes, carefully noting the differences between a battle before the gates of a forted Spanish town and one on the slanting, rolling deck of a gun brig.

The men had poured up through the hatches with the first beat of the drum, and for several minutes the ship had been a turmoil of disciplined activity. The decks were cleared of all movable gear and strewn with sand, ports hauled up, lashings cast off and the guns run out, and all hands were ready at their stations. On the quarterdeck all eyes were on the approaching vessel, now easily seen from the deck, and in the expectant silence, broken only by the whistle of the wind, the ship's bell clearly sounded four bells of the forenoon watch.

Hazard knew that the sloop had the weather gauge to her advantage. Coming down from windward, plunging with the heavy seas and heeling before the gale, she might maneuver at will; while short of wearing round and running, the *Falcon* could do little but wait, thrashing slowly under shortened sail and rolling so heavily that her gun muzzles were sometimes under water.

"Break out our colors, Mr. Webster," Stuart ordered, and shortly the Union Jack and the British ensign fluttered aloft. The men let go a rousing cheer and Stuart, in the same calm voice, said, "See that the men are kept quiet. I want no demonstration of any kind."

The sloop was almost within hailing distance when she suddenly altered her course, hauling to the wind. The hands manning her aloft could be plainly seen, while behind her open ports the lighted matches of her gunners flickered ominously.

"She's going to close," Mr. Webster said excitedly.

"She wants to fight," Stuart said, "and it is my duty and pleasure to oblige her." He raised his voice. "Stand to your guns, men!" Then, to the lieutenant in charge of the port side gun battery, "Fire as your guns bear, sir!"

As the ships came abreast, running side by side at a distance of not more than fifty yards, Hazard felt the deck beneath him shudder and leap as the *Falcon*'s guns discharged, and through the smoke that was instantly scattered by the wind he saw the rippling fire along the American's flanks and heard the thunder of her answer. There could not have been more than half a second between the broadsides, and the *Falcon*, still reeling from the recoil of her guns, shook to her keel from the impact. Grape whined overhead and sent a tangle of rigging to the deck, and an enormous splinter from the rail flew past Hazard's head. Beside him Stuart said calmly to the quartermaster at the wheel, "Keep her as she is," and received an equally calm, "Aye, aye, sir."

At the guns the orders could be plainly heard. "Stop your vent. Sponge your gun. Prepare to load." Then, "Take your aim. Fire!"

The carronades crashed again. Somewhat tardy, the American broadside blasted away and the *Falcon* shuddered as the shot struck home. One of the guns tore across the deck and crashed into the starboard railing, crushing two men beneath it.

Stuart shouted, "Get that gun lashed!"

Several men jumped to the task, impeded by a jumble of cut rigging and a jagged piece of yard that fell on their heads. Hazard swung down the ladder, taking an axe from a man who fell against him, and helped to cut the wreckage away until they could get lines around the gun, finally subduing its maddened lunges across the deck.

"Keep at it, lads," Stuart yelled. "Fire as you will!"

The answering roar of the American guns thundered against the ship. The first lieutenant went down in a bloody heap at Hazard's feet. The screams of agony in the waist grew in number; the dead were piled at the masts, out of the way, while the wounded were dragged below. A block fell, then another, and a sail ripped and slatted overhead.

But the broadsides went on, the British crew drilled to such iron discipline that when one man fell another quickly took his place, firing with such speed that their shots outnumbered the American's three to two. The two ships were close together, blasting away at point blank range, drenched with spray as they rolled toward each other with so little leeway that the men loading their guns were hitting their rammers against the other ship.

Even in the din and confusion, it was plain to Hazard that the *Falcon*'s fire was not so accurate as the enemy's. Their deadly hail of fire swept the deck from end to end. A jagged piece of spar whistled by his head, so close that he was surprised to find it had missed him and hit the sailing master by the binnacle. With a splintering crash the mainmast gave way, trailing rigging and sails across the deck. Then the foremast came down, sweeping men off the deck like ninepins, and the masts and yards and rigging dragged to larboard and silenced at least half the port guns in the wreckage.

It was possible to see that the sloop had also suffered so much damage in her rigging that she could not maneuver away from the *Falcon*. She had gained slightly, her bows ahead of the *Falcon*'s; when the two ships fouled, the *Falcon*'s bowsprit tore through the sloop's fore shrouds. Hazard, reaching for his pistols, was almost knocked off his feet by the impact. Then, with a great roar, the sloop raked the helpless *Falcon* with a final broadside.

The cry "Away boarders!" sounded so clear and near at hand in the sudden silence that Stuart's voice was by comparison faint and painfully weak.

"All hands on deck to repel boarders!"

But there was only one seaman on the quarterdeck to relay the order, the quartermaster, who still stood at the helm, rigid and unmoving, staring ahead with expressionless face. In the waist no more than a dozen men still stood, seeming dazed with the turn of events.

Hazard, without waiting for Stuart, ran for the ladder leading down to the waist, a pistol in each hand, thinking to rouse the men out of their lethargy and lead them on to the forecastle to try and stop the horde of Americans, swinging across the heavy bowsprit with cutlasses and pikes and pistols.

Behind him Stuart said, "Leave it, Joss. It's no use."

Turning, Hazard saw that Stuart was leaning against the binnacle head for support, one hand clasped to his shoulder where the blood slowly drained through his fingers and down his arm. The other hand still held his sword, but the point touched the deck.

Turning back, Hazard saw the American officer on the foredeck, pausing a moment with his pistol at the ready, his men barely held in check behind him.

"Have you struck, sir?" he called across the deck.

"Yes," Stuart said in a quiet dead voice. "Lower the colors."

No one moved. Then the American officer came aft, his face a study of emotions as he saw the bloody havoc in the waist, and the silence stretched across the *Falcon* to the sloop, broken only by the wind and the moans of the wounded.

"I am Lieutenant Robert Biddle, sir, of the United States sloop-of-war *Worthy*."

Stuart looked up wearily. He lifted his sword with an effort and held it out, hilt first.

Beside him Hazard stood motionless, and the helmsman at the wrecked binnacle seemed chained to the wheel.

"A gallant fight, sir," the American officer said quietly. "I will have a surgeon's mate come across at once to help with your wounded."

Stuart looked at the lieutenant silently, as if gathering himself for the effort to speak. "Thank you, but I should think you would have need of his services yourself. Weren't your damages heavy?"

"We have only five dead, sir, and no more than that wounded."

Stuart stared at him incredulously, and below them, at the companionway in the waist, Page stood very still and wordless. A protesting Farley was just behind her, but once they reached the daylight his voice died away into the same stunned silence that ruled the deck.

She had meant to stay below until someone came for her. But when the guns had ceased so abruptly, she could no longer endure the suspense of not knowing what had happened, or stay another minute in the dark hold, where she and Farley had tried to talk cheerfully despite the stench of the bilge, the thunder of the guns, the unexplained crashes and shuddering as the ship rolled, and worst of all, the rats that scampered over her feet until she was on the verge of screaming.

Now, in the bright windy morning, her eyes moved over the terrible carnage in the waste and flickered away, her face going as white as her gown. Moving her head slowly, as if it hurt painfully, she looked toward the quarterdeck and saw the little cluster of men standing there: Noel Stuart, his face grown old and wan in the sunlight, blood still seeping through his fingers and dripping to the deck; the American officer in his blue uniform, the seaman holding the ragged pieces of the Union Jack; and last of all, Hazard, still holding his pistols in his hands, his shirt torn to the waist and splattered with blood.

She kept her eyes on him, while drawing a deep agonizing breath, and knew that he had seen her when he said, "Lieutenant Biddle, we have aboard two American prisoners, Miss Page Bradley and Duncan MacDougall. I ask your consideration on their behalf."

He did not look at her again, and it was the American officer, his youthful face shocked to see her standing in the midst of the dead and wounded in the waist, who came hurriedly down the ladder toward her.

The battle had lasted three quarters of an hour. Broken and battered, the *Falcon* wallowed in the sea, her masts gone, her decks a tangle of men and rigging and wreckage, more than half her crew dead or wounded.

After the survivors had been transferred to the victorious *Worthy*, her captain, Master Commandant James Jacobs, ordered the prisoners taken below and a surgeon's mate sent immediately to Noel Stuart. Then he put a prize crew into the *Falcon* and stood by while they made an effort to re-rig her. Despite the damage her hull was still seaworthy, and Captain Jacobs announced his intention of taking his prize into Charleston.

A tall spare man, middle-aged, with gray at the

temples and a pleasant smile, he politely took time in the midst of the industrious activity whirling about him to listen with surprise to MacDougall's story. Page, who said nothing at all, was assured that the *Worthy* would see her to Charleston, where she and MacDougall could stay until her father had been notified of her whereabouts and could make arrangements for her journey back to Annapolis.

"And when I get you there," MacDougall said, "you needn't expect me to go past the front door with you again. When I think of all that's happened, and what Samuel Bradley will have to say about it, my blood runs cold."

Page listened obediently to his reproaches, but she could not summon enough interest to care about any of it. Standing on the *Worthy* in the bright sunlight, with Hazard's coat still around her shoulders, she felt so cold and weary that she was perilously close to trembling. She looked around her with the calmness of unreality, seeing everything from an indifferent and remote distance: MacDougall's blunt concerned face, the gay red-and-white striped flag fluttering aloft against the blue sky, Captain Jacobs across the deck from her, the American officers and crew who laughed as they worked and regarded her with such friendly interest.

She should, she told herself numbly, feel a great pride and reassurance to be an American on the deck of an American ship such as the *Worthy*, battered and worn from her victory but still every inch a fighting ship. But pride could not warm her inside or erase the memory of the past few hours, and the reassurance of being among the victorious was an empty comfort when she thought of Noel Stuart, who had lost his ship and his men and whose eyes, tired and strained in defeat, vere the same that had laughed so brightly into hers, offering help when she badly needed it.

"How is Captain Stuart?" she asked MacDougall.

"He'll live. The captain put him in his own cabin, and the rest of them have the run of the ship."

She already knew that, seeing Hazard with Captain Jacobs by the forecastle. He still wore the torn and bloody shirt, open at the neck without a cravat, and his buckskins were somewhat the worse for wear; he was not even, at the moment, very clean. But no stranger, watching him as he talked with Captain Jacobs, the two of them studying the *Falcon* as she rolled in the water, would ever have guessed him a prisoner.

"He's got the devil of a nerve," MacDougall muttered. "Ought to be in irons, the lot of them."

Page said nothing. But like everyone on deck, she watched Hazard, noting thoughtfully the air of confidence, the careless assurance, the way he held his dark head and shoulders with a pride so unconscious that it was close to arrogance.

Without warning, he turned and looked directly at Page. For a brief moment his gray eyes searched her face, then they flickered away; for the length of that moment she felt herself coming alive again, so abruptly and painfully that she wanted to weep.

"You'd best go below," MacDougall said. "This is no place for you, with the men staring and work going forward. Where did you leave your bonnet?"

Suddenly, above them, a voice cried down from the masthead, "Sail ho!" A moment later the cry was, "Two points on the starboard bow!"

The work of repairs went on without interruption while Captain Jacobs climbed the shrouds, his glass under his arm. Page and MacDougall stood as if carved from stone, faces lifted to watch Jacobs, and when

Hazard came up behind them he, too, put back his dark head and looked aloft.

But they did not have to wait for word from the captain. The officers on the quarterdeck were staring to windward, crowding along the weather rail, and a seaman atop the hammocks lining the gunwale muttered in disbelief, "Christ, what a piece of luck!"

Hazard went up the ladder to the quarterdeck in a single lunge, MacDougall just behind him. Page, somewhat slower, reached the upper level just as Jacobs jumped to the deck, his face graver than ever, his mouth held as stiffly as his shoulders. His officers waited in utter silence for him to speak.

"It would be useless to try to escape her," he said heavily. "We are too badly damaged to get away, and to stand against her would be suicide."

Page, like the others, stared to the northward. Running down toward the two small ships so close together on the heaving sea was a massive ship-of-the-line, all sail set and pulling taut in the wind, her bows throwing a great white wave. Her gun ports bristled ominously, her enormous flanks showing checkered rows of menacing black muzzles, and at her masthead the British colors floated with an arrogant flourish.

Page's throat suddenly choked with a sob. She turned abruptly to Hazard, but if his eyes held a suspicion of ironic amusement, his face was carefully without expression of any kind.

"Damn it all," MacDougall whispered incredulously "Damn it all."

Captain Jacobs gave a brief sigh, then stifled it.

"Strike the colors," he said.

8

The drawing room was cool and dim, shut away from the bright day by tightly closed shutters. It smelled faintly of stale air and dampness and the strong flower scent, ordered frequently from London, that hung like a visible aura in the immediate vicinity of Mrs. Charlotte Chudleigh.

Page Bradley sat in a stiff chair beside the tall windows, hands docilely in her lap, and listened with patient courtesy as Mrs. Chudleigh's sweet fluttery voice droned interminably.

Bermuda was a hot fatiguing place, crowded with minor colonial officials, native blacks, navy men, and the Bermuda gentry whose families were clannish, inbred, and boring to an extreme. "No one of any consequence, my dear, and yet they give themselves such airs. To one accustomed to the best circles of London, such a society seems excessively tedious."

Moreover, the hot winds blew unceasingly, ruining one's digestion and complexion, or else it rained for days and the entire world grew wretchedly damp and mildewed; no woman, said Mrs. Chudleigh plaintively, could endure such a climate without losing both looks and health. As if such mortification were not enough, most of the islanders had turned to piracy and had

become odiously wealthy, while more law-abiding citi
zens were forced to pay fantastic prices for even the
most necessary items of existence. If it had not been fo
the late Mr. Chudleigh, who had left Mrs. Chudleigh an
adequate competence to support her widowhood, she
was quite certain she would soon be destitute.

"I would prefer to return to London, but with thi
dreadful war, you know, and the delicate state of my
nerves, I have been advised not to undertake the haz
ards of an ocean voyage."

Page, who might have told Mrs. Chudleigh a grea
deal about the hazards of ocean travel, nodded dutifully
and said nothing.

"One can only trust that Bonaparte will soon be de
feated, but how England can hope to be victorious
when her ships wander about the Atlantic so far from
France, is quite beyond my comprehension."

"England is also at war with America, Charlotte,"
Miss Eliza Wyndham said gently from the doorway.

"Yes, of course," Mrs. Chudleigh said, looking at her
sister rather blankly, "although why England should
desire another war is more than I can see. Prices go out
of sight, and everything must be convoyed back and
forth, and ships are always being sunk just when one
has ordered something quite important from London."
She paused a moment to sigh. "The naval tradition isn't
what it used to be. His Highness Prince Clarence was
stationed in St. George's Town, you know, and we had
him once to dine. But now any number of the officers
seem to have quite ordinary origins."

"I thought you liked Captain Stuart," Miss Eliza
said.

"But such a dear boy, Eliza. Mr. Chudleigh knew his
father, and no one could possibly say that an earl is
ordinary." Mrs. Chudleigh searched for her shawl and

found it, as usual, trailing on the floor. "And I found Captain Jacobs delightful when he called. So distinguished, and such perfect manners. Yes, I must admit that the navy still has its gentlemen."

"But Captain Jacobs is an American officer," Miss Eliza said with only the faintest hint of humor in her voice.

"Oh, dear, shouldn't we have received him? I never thought, Eliza, and he seemed so amiable."

"I'm sure he is," Miss Eliza said. "He is Miss Bradley's countryman, after all."

Mrs. Chudleigh smiled warmly at Page. "Men can make life so difficult," she said, "with their wars and affectations. But in my house, my dear, I assure you that we shall disregard such foolishness completely."

Page regarded the two sisters with a grateful affection. Mrs. Chudleigh was small and wispy and faded, like a rose drooping on the stem, and her continual state of confusion was reflected not only in the artless patter of her voice but in her obvious delusion that she was still the same pretty young Charlotte who had adventured half-way across the world with an adoring Mr. Chudleigh. But it would have been impossible to dislike her, nor could one be so rude as to smile at the sight of her satin turban, invariably crooked above the wrinkled but still heart-shaped face, and her old-fashioned gowns, trailing boas, feathers and lace shawls.

Miss Eliza, on the other hand, was a tranquil monochrome in gray and black, her face contained and quiet, her dark eyes looking out at the world with a calm serenity. She wore her hair pulled back plainly across her ears, and her gray gowns were fastened under her chin with a black horsehair brooch. She looked like a parson's daughter, which indeed she was, and she had an uncomfortable way of seeing straight to the truth.

But no one who had noticed how often her words were laced with dry humor or had heard the quiet, "I've brought you a glass of hot milk, love, to help you sleep," could long stand in awe of her.

"But men can also be very charming when they choose," Mrs. Chudleigh said with another sigh, "and no one can deny that a dinner without them is a deadly affair. Eliza, did you send word to Government House that we shall expect Lord Hazard at eight?"

"I did," said Miss Eliza, "and his lordship sent his compliments and deepest regrets that he had already accepted another engagement elsewhere."

"How tedious," Mrs. Chudleigh said, disappointed. "I make no doubt he is overwhelmed with invitations, but surely common civility would remind him that he came to dinner only once, and then took his leave so suddenly that I was left in the middle of a sentence."

Page, remembering that disastrous night, stared down at her hands and wished unhappily that Mrs. Chudleigh would talk of something else.

But she would not.

"It puts me out of all patience," she said. "But it isn't my affair if they wish to make fools of themselves. Titled bachelors, especially one so handsome and wealthy as Lord Hazard, are scarce as diamonds in Bermuda, and all the mamas with eligible daughters are fighting like dogs over a marrow bone. But depend upon it, his lordship is past an age to be impressed by such antics."

"Don't worry your head over it," said Miss Eliza. "I'm sure he can take care of himself."

She went to the window and pulled back the heavy silk curtains, and the sun slanted through the shutters and fell across the Wilton carpet in bright streamers of yellow.

"You look a little pale today," she said to Page. "Would you like a walk in the garden?"

"It's that wretched wind," Mrs. Chudleigh said, "blowing from the south for days on end. Don't take her outside, Eliza, the heat will make her ill."

But Page, who was beginning to feel stifled by the dim room with its heavy rosewood furniture and rows of dark portraits, all of Chudleigh ancestors who affected beards and armor and solemn expressions, went willingly with Miss Eliza.

"It will rain soon," Miss Eliza said, "and Bermuda will seem a different place. Charlotte's flowers are fading, I fear, but a little rain will set them to rights again." She talked on easily and quietly, never requiring an answer. "We will have full cisterns, too, and the world always seems brighter when there is enough water to bathe as often as one chooses."

Page considered the shortage of water, inevitable on an island where all water came from the sky and ran down white rooftops to be caught in wooden cisterns, and wondered fleetingly if Farley, at Government House, was finding it a difficult problem to keep his master's shirts and cravats the required degree of snowy whiteness.

"The oleanders came from Charleston," Miss Eliza said. "Mr. Chudleigh ordered them especially for Charlotte's birthday one year, but she preferred an English garden."

The walled garden had precise narrow walks and a profusion of hollyhocks and larkspur and scented roses, but the brilliant oleander and the incredibly turquoise and emerald sea beyond the wall could never, like the elegant house, be disguised as anything English.

It was the house, Page reflected, that had precipitated her foolish behavior the night Hazard came to dine. "I'm not surprised that he won't come again," she said. "I don't know what possessed me to behave so oddly."

"I'm sure that couldn't be his reason, love," Miss Eliza said gently.

Page was not so sure. He had been at his most charming, captivating Mrs. Chudleigh with his light-hearted London gossip, teasing Miss Eliza into smiling, treating Page with an impersonal cordiality, and looking so dark and elegant in his white Bermuda linen that Page was obliged to admire his gallantry. Not many London gentlemen, she was convinced, would exert themselves to please three people who mattered so little to them, and she had been so disarmed that she even admitted to herself how glad she was to see him again.

On the enormous British ship-of-the-line she had stayed close in the cabin assigned to her. But Hazard and Noel Stuart, despite his wound, had spent hours with Captain Jacobs and his officers, fighting the battle over again and again, debating the causes and results of the war, winning and losing a great deal of money at cards, making vast inroads on the ship's store of wine, and becoming, in the inexplicable way of men, the best of friends. Page had been relieved to be left alone, and when they reached St. George's harbor and Hazard went off to Government House to straighten out the confusion as best he could, Page had found herself almost hoping, with a bleak despair, that no one would believe her innocent of any devious plots against the British and she would soon find herself in a small bare cell, completely alone and locked away from the rest of the world.

But instead he had taken her to Mrs. Chudleigh's, and whatever explanation he had made, it had apparently satisfied the two sisters. From the moment Page arrived she had been treated as a long-awaited guest; no questions were asked, no mention was made of sloops or frigates or ships-of-war, and for almost two weeks she had been cosseted and spoiled, and made to rest in a huge canopied bed draped in mosquito netting.

"I thought I wanted to see him," Page said, picking a yellow rose. "He had been so kind to me, from the very beginning, and I wanted to tell him how greatly I appreciated it."

"Of course, love," Miss Eliza said sympathetically.

But there had been that moment in the drawing room when suddenly, without warning, she had looked around her with the growing panic of feeling herself walking and talking in a nightmare. There was the English furniture, the row of English ancestors staring down from the walls, the English hunting prints and the engravings of London scenes, even a packet of London mail on the sideboard. And there were Mrs. Chudleigh and Miss Eliza and Hazard, two very British ladies and a British lord.

Page stared at them silently while the panic caught her by the throat. Then, just as she thought she could not sit still another instant, Hazard turned unexpectedly. His eyes flickered to her face, then narrowed slightly; without saying a word, he took a single swift step toward her.

Page stood up and backed away. "Don't come near me," she whispered. Then, looking at him despairingly, she flew across the room and wrenched open the door and fled up the stairs.

Even now, it embarrassed her to remember it.

"One would have thought all the Furies were pursuing me," she said ruefully to Miss Eliza.

"I expect they were, in a manner of speaking," said Miss Eliza. "I thought, perhaps, that you had suddenly remembered the war, and were amazed to find yourself sitting among your enemies."

Page nodded, looking out at the cool blue horizon above the sea. "At home," she said slowly, "one thinks of war in terms of ships sailing up and down the Bay, and men fighting so far away that the news doesn't arrive until weeks after a battle is won or lost. But it is a vastly different thing to see a war with one's own eyes."

"I daresay it will always be so for a woman," Miss Eliza said. "But have you noticed, love, that men seemed to thrive on wars?"

Page thought of Noel Stuart, who had called on Page as soon as his wound permitted, to assure her that MacDougall was safe at Government House, where he must remain until he could be sent back to America. She had expected Stuart to be the same tired defeated man she had last seen, but while the lines in his face and a certain gravity in his voice betrayed that he had not forgotten that terrible morning, neither had he forgotten how to laugh. He was like a steel spring, coiling back to life with a snap; his eagerness for a new ship and new battles was so evident that Captain Jacobs, who had been present, remarked with some amusement that he hoped the Admiralty would see to first things first and send him safely back to New York before giving Stuart a new command.

"Never fear," Stuart said. "I must stand my court-martial first."

"A pity," Jacobs said. "Surely they cannot question either your courage or resolution in the action."

Stuart shrugged. "It's the usual thing. The honor of the navy, and my own as well, must be clearly established." Then he said, more cheerfully, "The Admiralty, understandably, does not look with favor on a captain who loses his ship. But if I'm acquitted honorably, they may be kind enough to give me the opportunity of meeting you again."

"I'd be delighted," Jacobs said promptly.

Despite their friendship, the two men had not, Page knew, been speaking of a social encounter.

She looked at Miss Eliza thoughtfully. "Have you ever asked a man to explain his honor, and the things he must do to uphold it?"

Miss Eliza's dark eyes held a glint of humor. "No. Have you?"

"Frequently," Page said, "and it seems to me a great piece of nonsense."

"Indeed it is," Miss Eliza agreed mildly. "There is a great deal of nonsense in almost everything, if one cares to look for it."

They smiled at each other. In the silence a cardinal sang blithely from a cedar tree, and the wind tossed the oleander blossoms banked against the wall. From the kitchen could be heard the giggling chatter of the native house servants that swarmed over the house, and on the road beyond the hedge a solitary horseman stirred up clouds of dust. The day was hot and fragrant and brilliant with color, and permeated with such peace that the grimmer realities of life seemed remote and distant.

"You have been very kind to me," Page said quietly.

"Another piece of nonsense. You know we've been delighted to have you. And now, love, if you're feeling more the thing, the seamstress is waiting to finish fitting the last gown."

"But I don't need another gown," Page hesitated, wishing she could make it plain to Miss Eliza, at least, that she had only a few pennies in her reticule. She had tried to explain only to have her protests waved aside by Mrs. Chudleigh. "My dear, one cannot go about in a wrinkled muslin forever, and some of the most enchanting patterns have just arrived from London." So the seamstresses came, bringing their copies of *La Belle Assemblee*, and the shopkeepers began to deliver chip hats, bonnets, slippers, and, at Mrs. Chudleigh's command, scented rice powder. "You're dreadfully brown, dear child, and this is just the thing to make you fashionably pale again."

Even Miss Eliza, who was not ordinarily in the least dense, ignored Page's protest. "This new one will become you," she said now. "The French cambric is lovely, and the pelisse is as yellow as a buttercup."

"But I have no money," Page said for the hundredth time.

"I can't imagine why you would need money, love."

"I am already too much indebted to you and Mrs. Chudleigh."

Miss Eliza stooped and picked a faded larkspur and murmured, "There, that's better," as if she had been removing a piece of lint from her gown. Then she said thoughtfully, "Charlotte would disagree with me, I fancy, but I think I should tell you that you are in no way indebted to us. The bills are being sent to Lord Hazard, love, by his own request."

Page's eyes widened. "The bills for everything?"

"For everything except our great good fortune in having you with us."

Page took a deep breath. "Why didn't you tell me before? It can't be at all proper for him to do such a thing, and how will I ever repay him?"

"He assured us," Miss Eliza said calmly, "that he was responsible for all your misfortunes, as well as the loss of your luggage, and therefore felt obliged to take your affairs in hand."

"I had no luggage," Page said, "and he is not in the least obligated to me."

"Don't let it upset you, love. I feel sure his lordship would do nothing to place you in an awkward situation."

"Then you don't know him very well," Page said emphatically.

"I know that he charged us both to take every care of you, and to let him know from day to day precisely how you go on. It was his idea that you should have sufficient time to rest, with no visitors to plague you, and when you still seemed in low spirits, he suggested having some new clothes made to divert you."

"I should have guessed it," Page said with growing indignation. "From the beginning he has behaved as if I belonged in the nursery."

"So he has," Miss Eliza agreed amiably. "The fresh fruit and eggs for your breakfast come each morning from Government House, and Charlotte has strict orders to see that you eat and sleep properly. He could not be more solicitous of you, love, were you his own sister."

"He is arrogant and high-handed," Page said, unimpressed by his lordship's notion of solicitude, and added, "And I am not his sister."

"No, but surely needful of his protection?"

Page's eyes slanted ominously. "He has taken an unfair advantage, and so I shall tell him."

"Do, love," said Miss Eliza cordially. "You are far braver than I, but be assured I will stand behind you to the end. In any case, the servants are within call, and perhaps he will do nothing so terrible here in the garden. Do tell me, since you know him so well, does he look to be in a tolerable good humor?"

Page whirled around. He was coming toward them across the lawn with long easy strides, impeccably dressed, entirely at his ease, and somehow bigger than life. In one hand he carried, of all things, a beruffled parasol and a bonnet.

"Your servant," he said to Miss Eliza, bowing over her hand. Then he handed Page the parasol and bonnet. "These belong to you, I believe. Mrs. Chudleigh asked me to give them to you, along with a request that you will please, if you wish to retain your looks and health, not stand so long in the hot sun."

His gray eyes, light and hard as stone in the bright sunlight, looked down at her gravely.

"Thank you," she said faintly.

"Come along," he said, "we're going for a drive in Mrs. Chudleigh's curricle." He took Page's arm and said to Miss Eliza, "I'll have her back in time for dinner."

Page searched her mind for a suitably courteous excuse. But when none occurred to her she said baldly, "No."

"Craven," he said, and his eyes laughed down at her. "Shall we take one of the maids to assure your safety?"

Page gave Miss Eliza a pleading look, but she received no aid. "I'm sure that won't be necessary. One can drive out with a gentleman in an open carriage with perfect propriety, even in Bermuda. But do, my lord, remember that she isn't yet accustomed to the heat. And, my love, keep your head covered and your spirits serene, and do not chafe at trifles."

They were hand-in-glove, two of a kind, Hazard with his quirked eyebrow and Miss Eliza with her dark eyes glinting humorously.

"Do your sisters always mind everything you say?" she asked, tying on her bonnet.

"By no means," he said. "In my experience, all young ladies are sadly muddle-headed, and must be ordered about for their own salvation."

"I knew you would have an excuse for it," Page retorted, "when anyone only slightly acquainted with you must know you to be excessively presumptuous."

"Go on," Miss Eliza said. "What was that about his lordship taking advantage of you? Do point out his faults, my dear, while you have the opportunity."

"She needs no encouragement, ma'am," Hazard said, "to find fault with an Englishman."

"I understand it to be an old American custom," Miss Eliza said. "One must make allowances, my lord."

Mrs. Chudleigh's curricle was an old-fashioned one and the two grays between the shafts had seen better days. But as they drove down the narrow rutted road winding between stands of tall cedars, Page drew a deep breath of hot flower-scented air and felt very glad to be away from the oppressively English house with its prim English garden, walled so carefully to keep out any foreign taint.

"Such a lovely day," she said, "and such a lovely island."

"Now say you're sorry you were so rude," Hazard said, "and I was right to insist on bringing you out."

"I'm sorry, my lord, and you are always tiresomely right."

"Thank you," he said gravely. "May I consider that we have made a fresh start, or is it impossible for you to ignore, even for one afternoon, all of those tedious faults of mine?"

Page looked pensively at a wild plum tree leaning its branches across the road.

"Unfortunately, I can do nothing about my nationality, but we might avoid one irritating reminder if you would call me Joss instead of 'my lord'."

After the wild plum they passed under a tall tree with oddly-shaped yellow fruit, and Page studied it with deep interest.

"A pawpaw tree," Hazard said politely. "As for the rest, I shall endeavor to be a model of humility and modesty for the length of our drive."

"Don't be absurd," Page said.

"Well, I admit it sounds rather boring," Hazard said, "but after our last meeting I resolved to take the greatest care not to frighten you into running away again."

The pawpaw tree gave way to cedars, then to a brief view of the sea, very blue and cool beneath a sun-filled sky. Beside the road the sharp spikes of yucca glittered like swords and a blue bird flashed from a thicket of flowers and chattered angrily at the horses.

"It wasn't that," Page said at last. "I wasn't afraid of you."

"I know," he said quietly.

For a time they rode in silence; and Page, who had waited uneasily for the strange wave of panic to sweep through her once she was with him again, realized with an aching relief that it had not returned. There was no place for it in the bright hot day and the dusty brilliant landscape that was unfamiliar but not in the least frightening.

"A truce, then?"

She hesitated. "Not until we've discussed a matter of importance."

"I am at your service."

"It isn't proper for you to pay my bills. And however it is done elsewhere, in America a gentleman does not provide clothes for a lady at his expense."

"Nor in London, little one."

"I cannot repay you now," she said, a little awkwardly, "but you must keep a strict accounting for my father."

"Must I? But I have long since acquired the habit of discharging my own obligations, you see, and I cannot change now merely to solace your pride."

Page lifted her chin. "I don't want to be anyone's obligation."

He turned the curricle along a narrow sandy lane, overgrown with foliage and shaded by tall cedars, that led down toward the sea.

"But in England I am the head of my house," he said lightly, "a circumstance which holds it my duty to be responsible for my land and estates, my tenants, a large payroll of servants, and a family numbering three sisters, two brothers, my mother, and countless cousins and uncles and maiden aunts. Surely you can understand how I might have acquired a taste for having everything my own way."

"They must think you the worst sort of dictator," Page remarked. "Do they never accuse you of being disagreeable, and selfish, and a tyrant?"

"Frequently."

"It doesn't seem to have helped," Page said. After a moment she added, "I might remind you that the head of my house is Samuel Bradley."

"Who is not here," Hazard said promptly, "and therefore I stand to you in his stead."

"I can't imagine anyone thinking you in the least fatherly."

He laughed. "That is the only kind thing you've said to me today."

The curricle stopped at the end of the lane and Hazard jumped to the ground. Beyond him, down the slope of the hill, sea curved in a gentle cove bounded with pale pink sand and guarded by coral rocks standing sentinel on either side. There was no one in sight, and no sound but the sigh of the wind and the surge of waves against the shore.

Instead of politely holding his arm to assist her, Hazard put his hands on her waist and swung her down to the ground.

"Why don't you take off that bonnet?"

"Mrs. Chudleigh says the sun is dangerous."

"If Mrs. Chudleigh had ever been in the Chesapeake country in the summer, she wouldn't be so concerned about you."

"She says all ladies of fashion must have a lily-white complexion and look as fragile as a piece of porcelain."

"Then I'm afraid your chances are ruined. You already have six unfashionable freckles."

She couldn't help laughing. Removing the offending bonnet, she left it in the curricle, and they walked down the hill to the beach, a curving half-moon of white and pale pink sand. The tide was low and the shallows curling lazily about the rocks were tinged with mauve and lavender, but as the land shelved away, the water became a translucent emerald and shaded into an intense peacock-blue that stretched all the long shimmering way to the horizon.

Entranced, Page drew a deep breath of the sweet salty air and held her face up to the sun.

"For this," she said, "I forgive you all your faults."

"A clever piece of strategy on my part," he said, smiling at her. "I know you better than you think."

He spread his coat on the sand for her to sit on, and stretched out full length beside her, hands behind his head. The silence lengthened, an easy companionable silence broken only by the sound of birds in the cedars and the lazy froth of surf. Above the water enormous white clouds rolled out of the south, piling up into great towering peaks that reached to the very arc of the blue sky.

"Has it been difficult for you," Hazard asked suddenly, "staying at Mrs. Chudleigh's?"

"Oh, no," Page said quickly. "They've been kind to me, and I shall miss them when I go." Then she added, hesitantly, "But my conscience pains me, all the same. It is hard to think of them as enemies."

"Doubtless because they aren't," Hazard said. She turned her head to look down at him, but his eyes were narrowed against the sun, leaving only a thin glittering line of gray. "Nor am I," he said deliberately, "despite Mr. Madison and the King's ministers and all the patriots in America."

"You cannot dismiss a war so lightly."

"I can do what I please with it," he said carelessly, "and so can you." He rolled over on one elbow, his eyes searching her face. "Your heart and mind are your own, Page, and they aren't easily controlled by Orders in Council and Decrees made by capricious men halfway across the world."

"But they should be loyal," she said, "to my own country and my own people."

"No one has asked you to be disloyal," he said coolly. After a moment he added, almost absently, "A declaration of war may be binding upon the men sworn to uphold it, but it cannot force them to hatred."

Page drew a pattern in the sand with one finger. "It seems even more reprehensible," she said slowly, "for men to kill without hatred."

"I can't tell you why men kill," he said quietly, "or why they die for a cause or a man or a country. If we all lived by reason, my sweet, there would be no wars." The words were slightly mocking, but his voice was gentle. "But it is one thing to hate in the heat of battle, and another to hate a gallant enemy when the battle is done."

Page sighed. "And what of those who have no battles to fight? A man uses his honor to explain everything, but women have no such convenient code to follow."

"Then you must leave wars to men and their honor," he said, "and walk the middle road."

"Do you?"

"When I am with you, which is all that matters."

"And when you aren't?"

"A delicate point of honor," he said, and smiled at her.

She caught up a handful of silky sand and trickled it through her fingers. "How did it all begin?" she asked wearily.

It was a foolish and naive question, perhaps, but she had noticed that however provocative and surprising his answers, he never turned a question aside with an evasive half-truth, or pretended not to understand, or laughed at one's ignorance.

Nor did he now. "Like all wars," he said, "with stupidity and misunderstanding. A few insolent naval officers too far from the Admiralty to be reprimanded, faulty communication between London and Washington, an excess of short-sightedness on both sides. Not to mention an ingenious gentleman named Bonaparte, who is a past master at playing both ends against the middle."

"Papa dislikes the British," Page said, "but he thinks only a fool would trust a Frenchman."

"Such ingratitude. Didn't Papa fight in the American rebellion?"

"Our war for independence," Page corrected. "He

fought with the Sixth Maryland from the day it was first mustered."

"Then he should know that the French had a great deal to do with the American victory."

"But only to spite the British."

"Well, there you have it. Given enough time, history usually repeats itself."

She considered it gravely. "But a Bonaparte is not precisely the same as a Lafayette."

"Granted. And if England had been capable of Bonaparte's duplicity, Mr. Madison would still be debating with Congress whether France or England was the villain and you would be safely at home, sighing at the boredom of July in Annapolis."

Inexplicably, she felt as if a heavy burden had slipped from her shoulders. She wished that she could have spoken to him sooner, if only to ease the confusion inside her, but perhaps it was just as well. She had needed to be alone with it, to worry it and turn it over in her mind until she had worn away some of the aching numbness that had settled in her bones that morning when she came up out of the *Falcon*'s hold to the aftermath of battle.

The thought suddenly occurred to her that he knew very well how she felt, had known from the beginning, and that was why he had stayed away from Mrs. Chudleigh's for so long; he was as bad as Miss Eliza for seeing straight into one's mind.

"In any event," she said, "I'm grateful you aren't a Frenchman."

"That's because you've never met one. You'd like the French charm, I think. They kiss your hand at every turn, and sigh over your beauty, and politely agree with everything you say."

"How dull," Page said without thinking. Then her cheeks burned and she said quickly, "The sun is gone."

The towering clouds had met overhead, darkening the day and giving a crinkled metallic look to the water beyond the rocks, and the wind tasted wet on her face.

"It's going to rain," Hazard said, pulling her to her feet. "You'll get a wetting, I'm afraid, and I'll get a rare scolding from Mrs. Chudleigh."

He put his linen coat around her and they ran for the curricle, but before they had turned into the main road the rain began to patter on the sand in wet circles. In a matter of minutes it had become a hard downpour, even beneath the cedars, and when the road became more exposed the wind lashed at them in gray slanting sheets of water.

Page was soon soaked through to the skin, her face and hair running water as if someone had poured a bucket over her head, her dress and Hazard's coat so dripping wet that it no longer mattered that she was sitting in a huge puddle. But the rain was not uncomfortably cold, and Page, crinkling her eyes against the stinging force of the wind, thought it vastly pleasant; she was wet from head to toe, and all at the same time, for the first time since she arrived in Bermuda.

When they turned into Mrs. Chudleigh's gates and swept up to the drive, a groom ran out to the horses. Hazard jumped down, shouting something to the boy, and lifted Page to the ground. They ran for the shelter of the doorway and stood there, dripping pools of water. Page, when she had caught her breath, could not stop laughing, although she suspected that it sounded like a gurgle from under a fathom of sea.

"I trust you enjoyed your afternoon drive, ma'am," Hazard said, "and that you won't suffer any ill effects from the sun."

"Nothing ever goes the way it should when I'm with you," she said unsteadily. "I don't know what it is about you, but you turn the most ordinary things into something extraordinary."

There was, in truth, much that was extraordinary about him even at the most conventional moments. Now, his face running with rain and very dark against the white shirt plastered wetly to his wide shoulders, hands on his hips as he laughed down at her, he had an undeniably rakish air. Against Mrs. Chudleigh's prim door he looked a pirate who needed only a knife at his belt and a dangling gold earring; with a backdrop of angels and seraphim he would be a black Lucifer, shamelessly pleased by his fall from grace. Only the quality of evil was lacking, but she had to admit that it might easily be hidden behind the narrowed gaze and the infuriating habit he had of keeping his face as guarded as an Indian's.

Then he said, "You'd better dry off at once and change your clothes," and she had to laugh at her foolish fancies.

"Farley will look at you in complete dismay," she said. "Nothing you are wearing will ever be the same again."

"Farley will be delighted to learn that you have recovered from your melancholy decline."

"Give him my regards," she said fondly. She started to give him his sodden coat, but when she glanced down at her muslin gown, clinging so wetly to her body that she might have been wearing nothing at all, she held the coat tightly around her with a startled embarrassment.

But he paid no more attention to her disreputable condition than he had the night he helped her to dress in the cabin of the *Falcon*. "Before you go in," he said, "I have a piece of cheerful news for you."

She waited, thinking that he did not look very cheerful.

"You will be leaving for America within the week. An exchange has been arranged for the American officers and crew of the *Worthy*, and the Royal Navy has agreed to send you and MacDougall to New York with them."

She stared at him, unable to say anything. She had been waiting for such news for so long that it was difficult, caught so by surprise, to take it in.

"The ship has a Yankee captain," he went on, "sailing under a British license to trade between the West Indies and Portugal. Whatever his political convictions, however, I am advised that his ship is sound and his seamanship admirable. It should be a safe voyage, and not unduly long."

After a moment she said, "And you?"

"As soon as it can be arranged," he said, "I'll take passage for London."

She looked up at him silently, pushing a wet curl out of her eyes, and thought it odd that she should suddenly feel so cold and clammy, as shivery as if the wind had laid an icy hand on the back of her neck.

"I've received new orders," he said, almost curtly, "else I would go with you. But Captain Jacobs has promised to escort you all the way to Annapolis."

She nodded. There was nothing to say, except to thank him, but somehow she could find no words for that, either. She felt very queer and hoped he wouldn't notice; but his eyes were on her face, searching out the words she didn't say, seeing everything, missing nothing.

The groom came up in the rain, leading Hazard's

horse. He must have called for it when they first drove up; he was anxious to get away, doubtless, and congratulate himself on arranging her affairs so neatly.

"I'll see you again before you sail," he said. "Thank you for a pleasant afternoon."

He had pleaded another dinner engagement, Page remembered, and now he must be in a hurry to get back to Government House to change; she'd warrant he was dining with some fashionable Bermuda mama and her fashionable ladylike daughter. With a swift illogical anger that made her eyes go slanted and stormy, she wished him joy of his evening, but as for herself she could think of nothing so dull and tiresome.

"Goodbye," she said distantly.

He looked down at her face silently for a moment. Then, to her surprise, he put his hand under her chin and lifted it. "I am dining with the Governor," he said easily, "and it would be most impolitic to be tardy."

He pushed the wayward curl out of her face again, and for a brief moment his eyes rested on her mouth. Then he smiled faintly and turned away, and she watched, bemused, as he cantered down the drive in the drenching rain and turned out of sight beyond the gates.

The door opened behind her. "Oh, dear, I knew this would happen. Here you are dripping wet, and now you'll have a chill on the lungs."

Page turned. Mrs. Chudleigh stared at her and hastily drew her inside.

"My dear child, what on earth do you mean, standing outside in that condition? I don't wish to offend you, but even in my day it was considered quite fast for a girl to dampen her muslins."

Miss Eliza came into the hall and said in her quiet voice, "It was the rain, Charlotte."

"Of course," Mrs. Chudleigh said with relief. "But where is his lordship?"

"You look pale, love," said Miss Eliza. "Were you frightened by the storm?"

Page looked at them for a moment without speaking.

"I am going home to Annapolis," she said then, a little blankly, "and Lord Hazard is sailing for London."

In the face of their silence she walked slowly up the stairs, holding a sodden bonnet and a bedraggled parasol that dripped an uneven trail behind her.

9

It rained for three days, a gray smoking downpour that hovered like vapor above the sea, lashed Mrs. Chudleigh's flowers into tatters, and gurgled continually into the cisterns. On the morning of the fourth day the sun rose on a drenched island washed clean of dust and heat, its brilliant emerald and pink and white sparkling beside a blue-green sea.

Page stood in the drawing room, looking out at the garden. She wore a yellow pelisse over a high-waisted gown of cambric and the poke-bonnet framing her face was charmingly tied with yellow ribbons, but she felt no gratification at possessing such a fashionable costume. She felt quite ill, in fact, but other than smoothing the lace gloves over her fingers she held herself very still and straight.

Mrs. Chudleigh bustled into the room, followed by a servant who carried a huge straw hamper. "I've packed a basket of delicacies for you," she said. "The food aboard ship is quite miserable, I understand, and I couldn't bear to think of you eating wormy biscuits, or whatever it is sailors dine upon."

"Thank you," Page said. "You are very kind."

"Not at all, my dear child. Are you ready? Eliza has

put your trunks in the hall, and Lord Hazard just rode up. I think you had better use the barouche, since Eliza wishes to go with you to St. George's, and there will be plenty of room for everything." Mrs. Chudleigh's eyes filled with tears. "You will forgive me, I know, if I remain here. Partings are such sad affairs, and I'm not at all well. Oh, my dear, I do hate to see you leave us."

She wandered out, trailing her shawl behind her. Page heard Hazard's steps in the hall and his low voice as he spoke to Mrs. Chudleigh, and then he was in the drawing room, pulling off his gloves, striding toward her across the faded carpet.

"So you are finally going home," he said. "Did you think the day would never come?"

She considered a number of appropriate answers, but by the time she had thought of one sufficiently cheerful and noncommittal, the moment for speaking had passed.

"Never mind," he said. "I quite understand that you wish to spare my feelings. After all this time of telling me how badly I've treated you, at the last minute your conscience is paining you."

She kept her eyes on the reticule in her hands. "I'm sure this is a happy day for you, sir."

"Happy is not an easy word to define. Let us say, instead, unusual."

She looked up warily. "Why unusual?"

If his voice had been light and amused, his face was not. But it told her nothing, and she could not look at him long without fearing to betray herself. It was ever thus, she thought despairingly; she would never know what he thought or how he felt, or the secrets that lay behind the remote gray eyes.

"For the first time in my life," he said, "I am break-

ing my word. I promised to take you home myself, but
unfortunately my superiors, estimable as they may be,
are more concerned with their own problems than
mine."

"It was kind of you to promise, but unnecessary."

"Except, perhaps, for my self-esteem."

Page retorted, "You have entirely too much of that
as it is," and immediately felt better.

"I knew such unnatural civility couldn't last long,"
he said. "Do you feel more like yourself now? You
looked almost ill when I came in."

"I'm afraid I'm journey-proud," Page said ruefully.

His smile held a great deal of sympathy. "I suspect
you're only weary of ships and men and traveling
about."

"Not all of it has been unpleasant," she said. "You
will be surprised to hear it, I daresay, but I will miss
you." She paused, finding it necessary to draw another
breath before she could finish. "So much has happened
since that morning in Annapolis, it will seem strange to
know that I won't see you again."

He lifted a dark brow. "But I thought you would be
pleased beyond measure to see the last of me."

He was making it very difficult, a piece of perversity
entirely like him. "I'm pleased to be going home," she
said, "but it isn't the same thing."

"I'm gratified to hear it," he said, "because I have
every intention of returning to America." His smile
reached his eyes, warming the cold gray. "Surely you
can't expect me to go through life without learning
what Samuel Bradley would have said had one of his
daughters brought home two British spies and a copy of
Don Quixote as a peace offering. And you should also
remember that I left two valuable horses behind at
Bradley's House."

Page remembered the horses with a pang of guilt. "We shall take the best care of them."

"See that you do," he said, "because I shall be back to retrieve them."

"If you cannot," she said, striving to keep her poise intact, "I assure you that Papa will pay you their worth."

"But you have it all wrong," he said, quite gently. "It is I who will be indebted to Papa."

Before she could unravel the meaning in this cryptic remark, Miss Eliza said from the doorway, "I don't mean to hurry you, love, but shouldn't we be leaving for St. George's?"

Page took a last fleeting look at the rainwashed garden, the white walls and silk curtains and stiff English furniture, Hazard's impassive face, Miss Eliza waiting by the door with her bonnet in place. Then she walked slowly into the hall, where Mrs. Chudleigh was tearfully patting her face with a wispy handkerchief.

"I don't think I can bear it," she said chokingly, and embraced Page so fervently that the satin turban teetered dangerously. "Partings are so disagreeable, and just when we had become so fond of you. Take care of yourself, my dear, and do send word as soon as you are safely home."

Finally they were on their way in the old-fashioned barouche, baggage on the seat facing them and Hazard riding beside the carriage. Seeing the brass-bound trunks, Page said with dismay, "Surely there weren't enough clothes to fill two trunks."

"But the bonnets would have been crushed," Miss Eliza pointed out, "if I had put them in with the gowns. In any event, I'm sure you will have any number of handsome young seamen to carry them about for you."

"If only Lord Hazard had to carry them," Page remarked, "he would be well served."

"I fancy so," Miss Eliza said. She added sedately, "But one can't help admiring his excellent seat, and the symmetry of his profile. He may be a villain, love, but admit him to be a well-favored one."

Page laughed. "I'm sure he knows how well he looks on a horse, else he would have asked for a seat in the carriage."

"No man will ride in a carriage if he can possibly excuse himself. What if the horses bolted, my dear, or we were attacked by desperate brigands?"

The horses, however, jogged soberly toward St. George's Town, and apparently no desperate brigands were abroad on that gentle road winding past small whitewashed cottages, green fields, rambling Bermudian mansions with their formal gardens, and occasional stretches of dazzling blue sea. Hazard, whether or not he was conscious of his superb horsemanship and the symmetry of his dark profile, appeared to be engrossed in his own thoughts, riding the entire way beside the barouche without once glancing at it or even seeming aware of its occupants.

The rooftops and steeples of St. George's Town, blindingly white against their canopy of green trees, sloped up a hillside overlooking a calm blue bay. The public square drowsed in the sun as the carriage turned toward the waterfront, but the harbor was bustling with activity. There were few wharves to accommodate loading and unloading, but fully a dozen merchantmen swung to their moorings in the quiet bay and several British naval vessels were anchored below the town. Gigs and longboats skimmed the water, supplies were being taken aboard a stout black-and-white frigate, and at the foot of the square a longboat manned by neat seamen in queues and tarred hats waited the bidding of a young mate who peered impatiently toward the approaching barouche.

Noel Stuart, wearing a splendid new uniform, stood with Commander Jacobs. The American officers, along with Duncan MacDougall, were escorted by a dozen young midshipmen who stepped back courteously as Stuart and Hazard shook hands with each officer. When the Americans had climbed into the waiting boat the midshipmen did a sharp about-face and marched back across the square.

Noel Stuart, hat under his arm, made a little speech declaring that he had been delighted to make Miss Bradley's acquaintance and hoped she would have better luck with an American captain than she had with a British one. Bowing over her hand he said, "May your voyage be a pleasant one. We will miss you, you know."

Then he turned abruptly to Hazard and murmured, "I must see to those midshipmen," and went off immediately across the square.

Page looked at Hazard, but now that the moment had actually arrived, she could not manage even the simplest of good-byes. Her hands were icy cold and her heart thudded unevenly, and she felt dangerously close to weeping. Partings, as Mrs. Chudleigh had said, were sad disagreeable affairs.

His hands, warm and strong, closed over hers.

"You haven't seen the last of me," he said. "One day you can expect me to come knocking at the door, inquiring after Samuel Bradley's fourth daughter."

"We will be very glad to see you," Page said in a small voice.

"Will you?" he said quietly. Then, without waiting for an answer he added, "Keep yourself safe."

His face was hard, almost stern. He bowed, and for a single instant his mouth touched her fingers. Then he straightened, looked down at her with eyes that seemed to be more black than gray, and took her arm to help her into the waiting boat.

"Don't bid me farewell yet, love," Miss Eliza said at her shoulder. "Charlotte strictly charged me to see that your accommodations were adequate, so I asked permission to accompany you to the ship."

Hazard's hand fell away and he stepped back, but Page did not look at him again. She sat in the stern with Miss Eliza and resolutely fastened her attention on the reticule in her lap. The seamen at the oars watched her curiously and Duncan MacDougall scowled at her across the length of the boat, but Jacobs, after one glance at her face, tactfully drew his officers into a discussion of the Bermudian climate and the excellent hospitality of St. George's Town.

"A lovely ship," Miss Eliza said softly in her ear. "See how her masts seem to touch the sky."

Page raised her eyes indifferently, but they widened as she saw the *Caprice* swinging to her anchors just below a tiny walled islet. She was an ocean-going schooner, rigged fore-and-aft, and at first glance she appeared small and insignificant beside the British frigate, anchored no more than a cable's length away. But Page, seeing the clean graceful lines of the little ship, felt a catch of excitement in her throat.

"Do you remember the captain's name?" she asked Miss Eliza under her breath.

"Daniel Mason," Miss Eliza answered, "and I believe I hear it mentioned that the ship's home port is Salem, Massachusetts."

No, Page thought fiercely, no Salem ship ever built had that long low hull with its flaring bows, the tall raking masts, the eager look of a greyhound straining at a leash. From his name the captain might well be a dour New Englander, but Page would wager her life that the *Caprice* was built on the shores of the Chesapeake.

She caught a glimpse of MacDougall's face as he looked at the ship and knew she was right. The *Caprice* was a Baltimore schooner, and the unexpected sight of her, slim and lovely in the midst of fat English merchantmen and massive naval vessels stabbed Page sharply with homesickness.

She was sailing for home in that splendid ship, and home was Bradley's House, peaceful and quiet above the Bay, and Papa and Bessie MacDougall and a houseful of sisters, and a familiar countryside without an Englishman in sight. Once she was there again, she would surely look back with amazed disbelief at a Page who had wanted to weep on the quay in St. George's Town, who had known a bitter sense of loss all the more childish and unreasonable when one considered, in all honesty, that she had left nothing behind in Bermuda but a sprigged muslin gown too delicate to survive its brief taste of war.

She lifted her chin and held to the reassuring thought of home, and when she stood on the deck with Miss Eliza, waiting while the captain greeted Jacobs and his officers, she managed to look around her with interest.

The *Caprice* looked as neat and shipshape a vessel as any British ship-of-war, her flush deck holystoned to a spotless white, her brasswork gleaming in the sun, her crew going about their duties with a quiet air of competency.

"Even with a white glove," Miss Eliza said with satisfaction, "I daresay one couldn't discover a single speck of dust."

"There is no dust at sea," Page said in a queer little voice, and turned her back so that she could not see St. George's across the water.

Then Jacobs came toward them to present Captain Daniel Mason. He was younger than Page had expected, with a look of being too thin for his height, and he had a New Englander's lean sober face above a plain blue coat and neat neckcloth. Dull and conscientious, Page judged him immediately, a respectable and proper young sea captain from Salem who would doubtless think her a wanton for her misadventures, and perhaps hold services every Sunday at sea to pray for her salvation.

She eyed him uncertainly, thinking sadly that the *Caprice* deserved a different sort of master, and noticed that his oddly-colored hazel eyes widened slightly when he saw her.

But he bowed courteously at the introductions and ordered a seaman to take her trunks and show her below, and she reflected that, whatever one's opinion of New Englanders, one might surely assume that they were taught their manners, even in Massachusetts, and could be no more difficult to deal with than the English.

Miss Eliza agreed. "A pleasant gentleman," she said when they were alone in the tiny cubby assigned to Page. "Quiet and unassuming, I'm sure, and from the looks of his ship an excellent seaman."

Page sat on the edge of the narrow bunk. "I don't know how to say good-bye. We've become such good friends, and I hate to think that we will never meet again."

"Then don't think it," Miss Eliza said tranquilly.

"Bermuda is a long way from Annapolis."

"But then you are such a seasoned traveler, are you not, that a few hundred sea miles cannot matter so much." Miss Eliza unfastened one of the trunks and lifted out a gown. "In these modern times, love, one can dash back and forth across oceans with no great fuss at all."

Page glanced absently at the dark gown. "You packed one of your gowns by mistake," she pointed out. Over her head she heard feet thumping across the deck and the unmistakeable bellow of a bo's'n. "You had better hurry, or you might find yourself unexpectedly at sea." The thought, despite her dismal spirits, brought a smile to her face. "And that, I can tell you, will be only the beginning of your woes."

"Surely not," Miss Eliza said, quite cheerfully. "I must confess that I'm looking forward to it with the greatest enthusiasm. Do but consider, my dear, how dull my life went on before I met you."

Page stared at Miss Eliza, unhurriedly taking clothes from the trunk. "But you can't mean—"

"Yes, love?" Miss Eliza looked around the cubby with a measuring eye. "Do you know, ships would be much more comfortable places if men weren't such dim-witted creatures. I daresay it never occurs to a ship builder that a hook to hang one's clothes is quite as important as the placement of a gun."

"I hesitate to ask," Page said slowly, "for fear you may think me stupid, but do you intend to sail to America with us?"

The dark eyes lit with bright laughter. "How could I think you stupid," Miss Eliza said, "when I've been at such tiresome pains to keep you from guessing? I do hope you won't mind excessively, but Charlotte thought it most improper for you to travel alone with so many men, however gallant and charming, and I must admit I've been longing for a glimpse of America since I left London."

"I wish you had told me sooner," Page said unsteadily.

"Don't cry, my dear. This is a tiny space for two people, but we should do tolerably well. There is another bunk, you see, quite cunningly contrived to be lowered at need, and I promise not to be too much in your way."

"It's only that I'm so glad," Page said quietly, "and you never gave me the slightest hint." A sudden thought struck her. "But how will you get back?"

"Your father will surely be able to untangle that puzzle. I hope so, because I wouldn't care to run the risk of being hanged for a spy, love, in Lord Hazard's reckless fashion."

Page asked carefully, "Did he know?"

"Yes," Miss Eliza said. "Would you mind very much if I said he was entirely responsible? I was delighted, of course, but it was Lord Hazard who suggested it and then made all the arrangements at Government House "

Page, struggling with a number of conflicting emotions, said nothing. She stared bleakly before her, chin in her hands, hearing about her all the cheerful noise of a sailing ship getting under way, the lively chantey as the crew walked-up the anchor, the patter of bare feet on the deck, the chant of men high in the rigging as they unfurled the sails.

"Why don't you go on deck for a breath of air?" Miss Eliza asked gently.

Page shook her head. She could not explain, but to her great relief Miss Eliza said no more, going quietly about the business of unpacking the trunks.

It was not necessary, Page thought wearily, for her to go on deck to know how it was. The sails were unfurling aloft like white wings against the blue sky, throwing patterns of light and shadow across the bleached deck; now they were slowly filling with wind and sun, billowing out into great golden curves. The slim black ship was coming alive, gliding across the translucent emerald water, trailing astern a widening wake of white, reaching eagerly for the open stretches of sea beyond the harbor.

She took off her bonnet slowly, seeing in her mind's eye how the green islands and ships and busy wharves were dropping away behind, and the white roof tops and steeples of St. George's Town, and the drowsing public square, wide and empty in the sun.

The living quarters aboard the *Caprice* were strained beyond their capacity. Although the ship was primarily a merchantman, with roomy holds for her cargo and ample cabin space for passengers, her long narrow hull was designed for speed and her fore-and-aft rig for a minimum crew. At the beginning of the war fourteen carronades were mounted on her flush deck and her crew increased to nearly a hundred men. Now, with the men of the *Worthy* added to this number, the conditions below deck were so cramped and uncomfortable that many of the men slept on deck rather than face the sweltering heat and congestion of the forecastle.

"I wish I could do the same," Page said longingly after the first hot night in the tiny cabin. "It would be pleasant to sleep under the stars, with only the wind and sea for company."

"Not to mention fifty snoring sailors," Miss Eliza remarked, "and a deck which must grow quite hard by morning. Are you already so weary of my company?"

Page was not, but she had discovered that privacy was a luxury rapidly receding into the distance with the hazy outline of Bermuda. Aft there were eight small cubbies lining a narrow center salon where meals were served, and a wide stern cabin for the captain. The first day out, however, Captain Mason offered his cabin as a common room for the passengers; and with its cushioned stern transom, its sideboard with decanters and glasses, its hanging shelf of books and charts, they found it an agreeable place to gather when the cubbies began to shrink unbearably.

"But they spend hours and hours talking of the war," Page complained, "and having interminable arguments about sea battles already fought and forgotten by everyone else. I do believe they know the results of each shot fired, and the precise direction of the wind, and the tactics used by every captain who has won or lost a sea engagement since the beginning of time."

"But how can they know it bores you," Miss Eliza said reasonably, "when you listen with such eager interest?"

Page laughed, obliged to admit that she liked to curl up on the transom seat of an evening, while Miss Eliza worked at her embroidery and the American officers talked and laughed and argued amiably, and discussed in the sailor's casual ordinary words such splendid and heart-stirring sagas of the sea that Page listened with wide entranced eyes.

Their stiff and punctilious formality toward Miss Eliza had not long survived the close quarters and her cheerful good humor; and from the beginning they had all adopted an elderly-uncle attitude toward Page which she strongly suspected had been initiated by Hazard, at his most provoking, when they were all together on the British ship-of-the-line. By the third day out they were teasing her, ordering her about, supervising her diet and her manners, teaching her the rudiments of those card games they considered genteel enough for a young lady, and even, at Lieutenant Biddle's request, giving her a stern homily on being too much in the sun without a bonnet.

"I don't know what it is about me," Page said with some perplexity, "that makes everyone consider me a helpless fugitive from a nursery. I may be small for my age, but I am eighteen, after all, and in a family the size of mine one soon learns to shift for one's self. It seems odd that every man I meet thinks he must behave like a governess and tell me exactly how to go on."

Miss Eliza looked amused. "A helpless air can be very useful," she said. "You should cultivate it, love." Then, choosing a strand of embroidery thread with great care, she added, "Captain Mason, at any rate, doesn't behave in the least like a governess."

Page, sitting on her berth with her feet tucked under her, looked at Miss Eliza warily. "He is a most unusual man. He looked the soberest New Englander alive the day we sailed, and now it appears he was born in Baltimore and spent a good deal of his life sailing up and down the Bay." She laughed a little. "It's a trite platitude, saying how small the world has become, but do you know, he once carried a cargo from Annapolis that included Papa's tobacco and corn, and he even remembers meeting Papa at his agent's office."

"How nice for you," said Miss Eliza, biting off her thread. "Does that mean, in America, that one may consider him a family friend, as it were, with all the privileges of familiarity?"

Page said ruefully, "You know perfectly well it does not."

"Well, I admit I wondered when I came upon the two of you on deck last evening. From the look on your face I had a distinct impression that he had only finished saying something slightly improper."

"He had," Page admitted. Her eyes slanted with swift laughter. "Do you wish to know what it was? He asked if my gown came from Paris, and said every man should feel indebted to the French for decreeing that fashion should set off a lady's charms to such perfection."

"Dear me," said Miss Eliza. "No wonder you were so diverted."

"Are you shocked? That isn't all. He said he was quite surprised that the English had let me go so meekly, and it was his good fortune to profit from their mistakes."

"Not exactly shocked," Miss Eliza said calmly, "but perhaps it is just as well that I came on deck when I did. One cannot always trust a man's reaction, love, to a helpless air."

Page said gravely, "But I find I like a man who pays me improper compliments and can't be trusted without a chaperon at hand. I'm very weary of men who think me too plain for gallantries and too young to have any interesting conversation." But Miss Eliza said nothing, refusing to be baited, and Page finally relented with a ripple of laughter. "Do you know," she said, "he looks at me now and then as if he thought me a ripe peach ready for plucking."

After a moment Miss Eliza said, "You succeed in surprising me, love, at least a dozen times a day."

"Did you truly think me so young and innocent? Oh, well, I daresay he's been at sea a long while, and is only practicing his charm before he tries it on the Baltimore belles. One day in port and I'm sure he'd never look at me a second time."

"Then enjoy it while you may," Miss Eliza said amiably, "and I promise to stay within call at all times."

But as she readied herself for bed Miss Eliza thought

not for the first time, that it was remarkable how the child remained so unaware of her power. She sat on the bunk wearing nothing but a thin shift in the stifling hot night, her skin tanned a warm honey, the small vivid face, far more fascinating than pretty, dominated by those incredibly blue eyes so quick to laugh, to weep, to open wide with wonder, to gaze with candid directness at a complicated world. Miss Eliza could only sigh for an innocence that knew so little of vanity.

She had not been as surprised as Page at Captain Mason's about-face. Hazard had told her at the start that he doubted the man's credentials, but that any American captain who found himself in Bermuda in the summer of 1813 would be a fool not to affect Federalist politics and a New England home port. Daniel Mason did not have the look of a fool, and like his ship he had come to life only when the land was safely behind; but Miss Eliza was not entirely sure that she trusted anyone who could change so easily and deceptively before one's eyes.

Besides that, he was undeniably handsome; and Miss Eliza, like Page, had seen him looking at the girl with something alive and speculative and dangerous in his face. Page might think she could cope with it, but Miss Eliza considered the long miles to New York and cravenly wished the voyage already at an end.

She wondered, with a wry amusement, if Lord Hazard had suspected the formidable size of the favor he had asked of her. After a very short reflection, she decided that he knew very well. His lordship, after all, was less a fool than any man she had ever known.

10

The next morning Page and Miss Eliza ate breakfast alone in the salon, all the others apparently having eaten earlier, and when Page went on deck she saw them all aft, clustered around Captain Mason with serious faces that warned her immediately that something was afoot.

She stifled her curiosity and stood by the lee rail across the deck from them. Since they left Bermuda the sea had been a clear deep blue under a friendly sunlit sky, but this morning the sun seemed to glitter through a faint haze and large swells were rolling up astern, lifting the ship only to plunge her backwards as they passed under the keel and swept on.

Page stared suddenly at the sun. It was surely in the east, as all morning suns since the dawn of the world, but it was also definitely to port. The *Caprice*, she realized incredulously, was bearing southeast.

She turned abruptly, only to find Jacobs already at her elbow. "I see from your face," he said gravely, "that you are already aware of my news."

"Are we going back?"

"Not all the way," he said reassuringly.

"But why?"

He hesitated, and behind him Captain Mason said,

"Tell her. I'll wager she's not one to weep on your shoulder."

"I was only thinking of all she's suffered," Jacobs said with a kindly smile for Page, "and wishing I did not have to add to it."

Mason's voice had a pleasant drawl. "But you will have the consolation, sir, that it was I and not you who made the decision."

Page looked at Daniel Mason. Instead of the sober merchant's clothes he wore a striped seaman's jersey and canvas dungarees, and his brown hair, streaked like her own from the sun, was far too long on his neck. Standing feet apart on the slanting deck, with hands on his hips and a gleam of pure deviltry in his eyes, he could more easily pass for a corsair than a respectable captain.

"You may as well tell me," she said curiously.

He smiled at her. "A British convoy left Bermuda three days ago, Miss Bradley, with two sloops-of-war as escorts. I knew the sailing date, but with the British navy looking on I thought it best to hurry away like a good innocent lad with my shipload of passengers."

He laughed, and the young officers behind Jacobs looked at Page uncomfortably and tried without notable success to keep the eager anticipation out of their faces.

"But now we're going to have some nasty weather before the day is out, and no merchantman has ever been known to keep her station in a storm. They'll be scattered to the seven winds, and the *Caprice* will be on hand to gather up a straggler or two."

"And if there is a fight?" Jacobs asked slowly.

"I don't think it will come to that. If it does, I will certainly regret the presence of two ladies aboard." Mason's eyes were a light hazel, almost amber in the sun. "But my course of action, gentlemen, will remain the same."

He bowed briefly and left them with an abruptness which effectively ended the discussion. Duncan Mac-Dougall, who had come up beside Page during the conversation, stared after Mason with a gleam of admiring respect in his eyes. Like the young officers, his face betrayed an unmistakable eagerness, but it disappeared when he glanced down at Page, replaced by the familiar scowl of responsibility. Page, guessing at his chagrin smiled at him. Then she turned to Jacobs.

"But I thought Captain Mason traded with the British, and even had a license issued by Admiral Warren to protect him."

Jacobs shrugged. "He has a license to trade with Portugal, a British device to feed Wellington's army which deceives no one. But for every cargo he's delivered, I understand, he manages to exact a rather high payment."

"He carried a load of rotten grain to Lisbon last month," Mr. Biddle said with a grin, "but the Portuguese had nothing to trade and the British army agent was obliged to pay him in hard gold. Then he cruised the coast for less than a week and took one vessel loaded with British cavalry horses and shoes for the army, and another with an entire month's payroll aboard for a goodly number of Wellington's men."

"A reasonable price, I would say," Jacobs remarked, "for a bit of rotten grain."

Page watched their faces as they laughed. If it were not for her and Miss Eliza they would be delighted that Mason was turning back; they were spoiling for another fight, another bloody battle, another chance to pull the tail of the British lion.

She sighed. "He runs a great risk. Either the British

will hang him as a pirate, or the Americans as a traitor."

"There's a risk," Jacobs agreed, "but so far he's done a splendid job for his country."

"He carries a letter of marque from the President," Mr. Biddle explained. "It's all tight and legal, as much as if he wore an American uniform."

"Then what was he doing in Bermuda?" Page asked.

They grinned at each other in an infuriatingly masculine way. "Don't bother your pretty head with men's affairs," Mr. Biddle said. "Mason has the nerve of a rascal and the luck of a saint, and that's all you need to know."

It was all they intended her to know, at any rate, so she gave it up and went below to tell Miss Eliza the latest development.

Miss Eliza did not seem unduly perturbed. "We have a number of our own privateers in Bermuda," she said, "and I've learned to recognize the earmarks. A lean and hungry look, as it were, and a certain air of cleverness. We should have known it from the start, love." She added, with her usual calm, "He must have a great deal of experience in such matters, and I daresay will bring us off safely."

Page felt obliged to say apologetically, "But they are British ships."

"Don't distress yourself," Miss Eliza said. "You and I can do nothing about this provoking war, and all our anxiety would not change its course by one iota. It may be poor-spirited of me, but I for one refuse to waste my emotions so foolishly."

Page said nothing. It was all very well for Miss Eliza to look at the war with tranquil objectivity; what was a captured ship here and there, or a battle lost, to a country with the greatest navy in the world and an army powerful enough to push back Bonaparte's elite Imperial forces? When one was certain of eventual victory one could overlook the small defeats, as one might brush aside an irritating gnat; but Page, who had had a brief glimpse of British might and British confidence, thought of the pitifully few ships of the American navy and the paper armies so dear to the Washington generals, and wondered with a weary despair how it would all end.

Hazard had said he would come back, she thought soberly, and he was not a man to give his word lightly. Undoubtedly he was sure that the British would win; and what if they did? Might Bradley's House and Annapolis and all the Bay belong to England again, and the western lands beyond the mountains? Could a country be defeated and remain free, or would British ships and armies rule supreme as once they had done? Perhaps Hazard intended to return like a conquering hero, riding arrogantly up to Bradley's House, smug and complacent with a British victory.

Surely not, she told herself with an angry defiance. The end could not be defeat, there was too much to lose. No American, even a Federalist, would surrender a freedom so dearly bought. If pushed back from the sea they would fight in the mountains and forests, where the Redcoats had lost a battle or two before. Not all the king's men, nor all the king's wars, could wrest America away again.

"Pray don't glare at me so fiercely," Miss Eliza said. "You put me quite out of countenance." She smiled fondly. "You and I cannot be enemies, love, no matter how the war goes."

Page sat down on the bunk, all her defiant anger draining away. No, it was impossible to imagine Miss Eliza as anything but a dear friend, and the vision of an arrogant Hazard returning in triumph to Bradley's House did not hold true when she remembered his quiet voice saying, "A declaration of war cannot force men to hatred." It was exceedingly difficult, she reflected honestly, to keep a proper perspective in the midst of a war.

"In any case," Miss Eliza said, "I am more concerned with the news of approaching bad weather. Miserable sailor that I am, I think I shall fetch a basin and be prepared for any eventuality."

By nightfall the eventuality was upon them. The weather worsened steadily, the wind backing to the southwest and blowing so strongly that the *Caprice* lay over in a shower of spray, making it impossible for meals to be served in the salon and scrambling into chaos everything not securely lashed down.

Miss Eliza lay back on the bunk with an air of patient resignation, but Page begged a tarpaulin coat and sou'wester from the steward and went on deck, where she held to the companionway hatch for a few exultant moments, fascinated by the enormous seas racing by.

The *Caprice*, like all Baltimore schooners, was a wet ship, her deck awash with green fingers of water that swirled about Page's feet; but she ran before the storm like a gull, heeling gracefully to the gusty squalls that marched across the sea in the wake of white flaring lightning and rolling thunder, surging through the water with all the joyful abandon of a porpoise. From the crew, battling to take in more sail, came a tattered shred of laughter blown on the wind, and Daniel Mason's face as he walked toward Page was exhilarated rather than apprehensive.

"Go below," he ordered, "and stay there. I don't want to lose you overboard." Then he grinned, as if he understood her instinctive dislike of being shut up in a small prison below decks. "The *Caprice* and I have weathered worse blows than this. She's a stormy petrel with a taste for rough going."

As did her captain, Page suspected, but when she was once again in the tiny cubby, hearing the thundering pressure of water against the thin hull and conscious that the ship was but a tiny lonely island in that wild stormy sea, the brief sense of reassurance she had felt on deck faded away; and she remembered, with an unexpected stab of pain, another wild night when she had slept as peacefully as a babe and wakened in the gray dawn with Hazard's arms still holding her safe from all harm.

Soon there was no time to be afraid. Miss Eliza finally succumbed to seasickness, and Page tended her with a sympathetic care all through the night. "Do go away," Miss Eliza murmured once, still able to smile faintly. "It can be infectious, you know." But Page refused to leave her, and by morning she was almost as wan and exhausted as Miss Eliza.

The storm had abated with the dawn, however, and Jacobs, coming to offer his assistance and an invaluable flask of brandy, brought word that the convoy had been sighted to leeward at first light, scattered over a considerable expanse of sea. But the *Caprice* had continued on to the south and was now about to reap her reward; a large West Indiaman had apparently suffered damage aloft from the storm and was falling behind the convoy, its nearest protector now being hull down on the horizon and disappearing rapidly.

"It would be wiser," Jacobs said, "if you and Miss Wyndham went below the waterline until we see what might happen."

"But we cannot," Page protested. "You must see that it would be the worst cruelty to move her now."

She thought of the horrible time of waiting in the *Falcon*'s hold, with the rats and sour smell of bilge and the sickening sense of being shut in a coffin, and said definitely, "We will stay here and take our chances."

Jacobs frowned anxiously but he did not press her. Miss Eliza, indomitable still, whispered weakly, "You should go below, love. I will be quite safe here, with my basin as buckler and shield."

Page laughed. "So will I," she said, "unless British marksmanship has improved greatly."

The next hour, nonetheless, was a torment of suspense, laced by the rumble of the guns being run out and the disciplined noise and confusion of a ship preparing for battle. Then there was nothing but silence for an interminable time, finally broken by the roar of a carronade close overhead.

It was only a summoning gun, Page assured Miss Eliza, ordering the merchantman to heave to, but privately she wondered if the other ship was as heavily armed as the *Caprice* and if her crew was even now standing to her guns, matches waiting for the order to fire.

But there was no answering gunfire. Page, on her knees beside Miss Eliza, could distinguish no sound at all except the rush of water along the hull and the slight creaking of top hamper as the *Caprice* rolled in the ground swells following the storm, and the uneasy quiet was somehow more ominous than the anticipation of what might follow.

Then they heard a loud burst of cheering, followed by a patter of bare feet on the deck. Someone shouted, "Step lively, lads, or they may change their minds," and a sally of cheerful laughter answered him.

Page unloosed her fingers, one by one, from the edge

of the bunk. "They've struck," she whispered. "He's captured her without a battle."

"I knew he was clever," Miss Eliza said without opening her eyes. "Now if he could only devise a way to calm the ocean I would think him a delightful fellow indeed."

There was the unmistakable clatter of a boat being lowered over the side, but it seemed an exceedingly long time before it returned. No one came below to tell them what had happened, and when Page finally heard voices in the captain's cabin she was sorely tempted to go aft and brazenly find out for herself.

"Men's work," Miss Eliza said, "and they like to believe that women have no place in it."

"Perhaps it's just as well," Page said candidly. "I'm not nearly brave enough."

Miss Eliza smiled. "If I felt less ill, I'd tell you what I think of that notion."

But after another lengthy interval of waiting Page lifted her chin and said, "Well, I'm not so cowardly that I intend to sit here all day in ignorance. Something must have gone amiss, or they would have come to boast about their exploit before now." She combed her hair and washed her face, and put on a fresh gown, carefully choosing one Daniel Mason had openly admired. "A necessary precaution," she observed, "when one goes about intruding upon men's affairs."

"Very wise," said Miss Eliza. "If their business is at all grim, such as making Englishmen walk the plank to be eaten by sharks, I pray you will divert them." Then she added, quite casually, "Since I am so sadly indisposed, love, I hope you will hurry back with any astonishing news."

Page smiled. "I will be safe enough," she said.

Crossing the empty salon, she paused at the mahogany door to the captain's cabin. She waited there a moment, listening, then knocked and opened the door before she should lose her courage.

The conversation died away at once, and all eyes turned to the door. Page felt her face burning and wished fleetingly that she had not been so discourteous and presumptuous, but she forced a smile and said, "I only wondered what had—"

She stopped. MacDougall, turning to see her in the door, seemed to be suffering from a mixture of emotions, including exasperation, but surprisingly the most obvious one was a painful resignation. There was Jacobs, looking at her oddly, and the other American officers. There was Daniel Mason by the stern windows with a short portly man whose red face, scornful and enraged at once, indicated that he was the master of the merchantman. There, incredibly, was Farley, holding two portmanteaus.

And there was Hazard, leaning against the table with one boot crossed over the other, very big and dark in the white-panelled cabin.

Her first reaction was a surge of gladness so overpowering that her breath caught somewhere in her throat and came near to choking her. Swiftly on its heels came incredulity; fate, she reflected dizzily, was not usually so accommodating, nor chance so neatly dovetailed to please one's fancy.

He met her astonished glance with a rueful amusement in the depths of his gray eyes, but he did not speak.

"Miss Bradley," Daniel Mason said in his soft slurred drawl, "may I present Captain Carr of the *Fortune*?" The portly little man gave a brief angry bow.

"The other gentleman, as I presume you must know, is Lord Hazard."

Page did not dare look at him again. She managed an unsteady, "Yes."

"The *Fortune*," Mason went on, "was out of Havana for London, loaded with sugar and rum and ten thousand English pounds in specie." He added, still in that deceptively silken voice, "Not to mention Lord Hazard, a rather unexpected prize. Both Captain Carr and his lordship, I imagine, must wish they had not joined this particular convoy in St. George's Town."

Page said nothing. She felt such an irrepressible urge to laugh that she had to bite her lip sternly; she could not, after all, go into whoops of laughter over an affair that was obviously of the utmost gravity to everyone else concerned.

"It is piracy, sir," Captain Carr said, his voice cracking as it went higher with each word. "Barefaced piracy, if I may say so."

"You may say anything you like," Mason said politely.

"Then I will tell you, sir, that when you commit an outrage punishable by hanging in any civilized country in the world you are most certainly risking a determined retaliation by His Majesty's Navy."

"I'm sure of it," Mason said, and grinned. "But now, if you will excuse me, I have more important matters to consider." Ignoring Captain Carr's apoplectic anger, Mason put his hands in his pockets and looked around the cabin. After a pause he said, "The *Fortune* is too valuable a prize to be destroyed. Her damage is being repaired and I intend to send her into an American port."

The American officers waited impassively; only Jacobs, frowning slightly, seemed already to know, from his own experience at making such decisions, what Mason was going to say. Hazard, Page saw in a hasty glance, was watching Mason with that narrowed gaze of his that saw so much and revealed so little. How like him, she thought with an inner sigh, to appear so unconcerned by his predicament.

"The *Caprice* has been slightly crowded," Mason said, "with so many passengers aboard. The *Fortune*, on the other hand, is roomy and comfortable." He looked at Jacobs. "I propose to send you and your men to New York with her, along with the English prisoners. She has only a minimum of armament and won't outsail a skiff if you're unfortunate to be intercepted, but I'll put a small prize crew aboard and we can misname her a cartel ship." He added with a shrug, "The British find it convenient to have a polite system of exchanging prisoners, in any case, so I don't think they'll bother you."

"Your confidence is reassuring," Jacobs said drily.

Mason shrugged again. "If you're stopped you can always call upon his lordship to vouch for your good intentions."

Jacobs glanced at Hazard, who said nothing, and then asked quietly, "Is Lord Hazard to be considered among the prisoners?"

"The bigger the catch, the bigger the reward. A British viscount, I'd say offhand, will fetch a tidy ransom. Or at least a round dozen good American seamen in exchange."

Jacobs looked disapproving. "If it hadn't been for his good offices," he said, "the British might not have found it so convenient to manage an exchange for us."

Mason's face hardened. "I am engaged in fighting a war, sir," he said, "not in a tea party game to see who has the best manners."

Jacobs flushed. But he said mildly, "War or no war, we are still civilized men." Then he turned to Page with a smile. "It'll be a slow passage, but not too dangerous. Perhaps you'd better pack your things, and break the sad news to Miss Wyndham that she won't be on dry land as soon as she had hoped."

But Page, meeting Daniel Mason's eyes, hesitated. Something warned her that he was not finished, and that she had better stay to hear the rest.

"Miss Bradley is not going aboard the *Fortune,*" he said. "She stays here."

For a long stunned interval no one spoke. Then Jacobs recovered enough to say sternly, "I can't believe you serious."

Mr. Biddle, staring at Mason with a sudden hostility, took a step forward. "You are mistaken," he said. "If we go aboard the *Fortune,* so will Miss Bradley."

"Aye, so she will," Duncan MacDougall said, clenching a heavy fist.

Only Hazard seemed unaffected by the turn of events. His eyes, almost hidden behind the heavy lids, moved lazily from Jacobs to Mason, then back again. But not once did he glance toward Page.

Jacobs said, "What are your intentions? You may be in charge here, but I hold myself responsible for Miss Bradley and must reserve the right to judge what is best for her."

Mason laughed. "She must be gratified by your gallantry, gentlemen, but I assure you there is no need for such indignation." He looked at Page as if she should share his amusement. "I am taking the *Caprice* through the blockade to Baltimore, and my intentions should be clear enough. Miss Bradley's home is in Annapolis, is it not?" He added blandly, "Surely Miss Wyndham's

153

presence will safeguard Miss Bradley's honor, even without the protection of the United States Navy."

Young Biddle's hostility was not appeased. "Why can't both ships run into the Chesapeake? You'll stand less chance of losing your prize with the *Caprice* to defend her."

"The outcome of the war means more to me than any prize," Mason said. "You and Jacobs, and most of your crew, are from New York. The sooner you get back, the sooner you'll be at sea again to fight the British." He added, after a pause, "To be honest, gentlemen, I'll remind you that my ship's greatest defense is her speed, and I dislike the notion of her being slowed by the *Fortune*."

Page stood quietly by the door. The mention of Annapolis did not reassure her; she didn't trust Daniel Mason, or his easy drawl that explained everything so glibly, or the small amber flames in his eyes when he looked at her. But it would be futile to protest. Jacobs and Biddle would do with her what they would, smug in their masculine complacence that they knew better than she what was best for her. Even MacDougall, normally the most untrusting of men, looked positively feverish at the thought of getting home. Staring at the blue water beyond the stern windows, she wondered despairingly why Hazard said nothing and seemed to care so little what happened to her.

"There is one thing," Jacobs said thoughtfully. "Even if the *Fortune* should be retaken, we'll be allowed to proceed to New York. But Miss Bradley hasn't the same certainty, and there's no doubt she'd be safer on the *Caprice*."

"Slipping through the blockade, at any rate," Biddle agreed reluctantly. "The Chesapeake isn't as carefully watched as the Narrows, and there's not a British ship on the Atlantic station that could outsail the *Caprice*."

"This is all very interesting, but hardly to the point."

Hazard's low voice, clipped and decisive, held in the silence with the cold clarity of metal striking against metal.

He looked at Jacobs. "You have my thanks, sir, for acting in my behalf so conscientiously. But now that I am at hand, you need feel no further obligation in the matter."

Jacobs shook his head regretfully. "At the moment, my lord, you can hardly be of any assistance to Miss Bradley."

"On the contrary," Hazard said, almost indifferently.

He still leaned negligently against the table, relaxed and completely at his ease. But somehow he dominated the cabin; there was a violence inherent in the big shoulders and powerful size of him, in the hard face and edged voice, that was even more menacing for being so carefully controlled.

"I agree that Miss Bradley will be safer from the British aboard the *Caprice*," he said, "and since it is my pleasure and duty to see to her safety, we will both sail with Captain Mason to Baltimore."

After a moment Mason laughed. "For a prisoner of war, my lord, you take a great deal for granted." He put his hand, quite casually, on the big pistol at his belt. "Even if you were not my prisoner," he said softly, "you should know that the captain of a ship has absolute authority aboard her."

"You must allow me to offer you my sincere felicitations," Hazard said with a deadly politeness, "on reaching such an exalted position."

The silence in the cabin was absolute.

"I don't like Englishmen," Mason drawled, "and titles have never impressed me. Take care or I'll send you to New York in irons, and perhaps let my men teach you a few tricks they learned from your country-men in the bowels of a British ship-of-the-line."

Hazard said in a very quiet voice, "It wouldn't be your first mistake."

Mason's face was cold. "Don't try me too far, Limey."

"Why don't you use the pistol? Or call your men to bring on the irons? I am unarmed, Captain. It shouldn't be too difficult to carry out those brave threats."

Their eyes met and held; and Page, forgetting to breathe for the length of that moment, had the feeling that the other men in the room were on the verge of moving back involuntarily.

Then, to her surprise, Mason smiled. "Damn you," he said, "I've a mind to give you a pistol and call your bluff." The smile did not reach his eyes, but there was a grudging respect in his voice. "Stay aboard, then, and the devil take you. I've other things to worry about, and the Baltimore authorities will be glad to take you off my hands."

"It is most obliging of you," Hazard murmured, and bowed.

The air had cleared, swiftly and inexplicably. Mason had deliberately chosen to ignore Hazard's challenge, but Page was certain that he did not back away from cowardice.

"Transfer your gear," he said to Jacobs, as if nothing had happened. "The *Fortune* should be on her way before some ambitious sloop captain takes it in mind to search for her and we have it all to do over again."

They began to file out, their faces studiously blank, and even Jacobs was so thoughtful that he passed Page without a word.

But Mason paused at the door. "Don't forget that I

am captain of this ship," he said to Hazard, "and likely to remain so. I don't brook interference from any man concerning her crew, her destination or her purpose."

"I am only concerned with her passengers," Hazard said easily.

"That, too," Mason said, "I find disagreeable." When he turned, his eyes fell on Page. "We forgot to ask if you wanted to come to the party," he said, and winked impudently, "but I'll do my best to keep it from being a bore."

After he left them, MacDougall said, "I intended to go along with her," in a voice of such patent distrust that Page had to struggle against laughter. "There was no need for you to put yourself out."

Hazard regarded him impassively. Then he said gravely, "Every general should have reinforcements in the rear, my friend."

MacDougall, obviously wondering whether he had been promoted or relegated to the rear, gave Hazard a hard look. Then he went out, saying to Page, "If you've satisfied your curiosity, you'd best get back to your cabin."

When he had gone, the cabin was suddenly very quiet. Page, unexpectedly shy, took refuge in Farley.

"I see you're still guarding those bags as if they held the crown jewels," she said. "Do you think you'll ever get them safely back to London?"

He gave her one of his rare smiles, as if more pleased to see her than discretion would allow him to disclose.

"I trust so, ma'am," he said, "but if I may say so, the present prospect is somewhat dimmer than it was a few hours ago." He glanced at Hazard and added, "If you will excuse me, sir, I'll find Captain Mason's steward and arrange your accommodations."

"You're excused, but keep your wits about you.

We're among Yanks now and must tread carefully."

"Very good, my lord," Farley said. "I take it I am to follow your lordship's example?"

Hazard laughed. "I wouldn't advise it, my friend."

Then Farley, with a bow to Page, was gone. Her poise had deserted her entirely and she searched desperately for something to say.

"So we meet again," Hazard said, "and much sooner than we had expected."

She raised her eyes as far as his cravat. He had come much closer and was only a step away, towering over her.

"Yes," she said, oddly out of breath. "Are you very annoyed?"

"Are you?" he countered gravely. "You thought you had seen the last of me, and here I am again, taking charge of your affairs in my usual arrogant, high-handed way."

But his voice was not in the least arrogant; it was low and quiet and faintly amused, as she best remembered it, and suddenly the full impact of his presence there in the cabin of the *Caprice*, when she had thought she would never see him again, hit her with a stunning force.

She thought for a desperate moment that she was going to weep and turned away abruptly, knowing only that she must not let him see. But his hand closed over her arm, strong and warm against her cold flesh.

"Page," he said, "look at me."

There was no escape. She lifted her chin defiantly and thought, let him see the tears, let him think what he may, it's only that I'm tired and sleepy and hungry.

But she had forgotten that Hazard, whatever he saw or thought, was not a person to crowd one into a corner.

"We know each other too well to stand on ceremony," he said gently. "Has it been a difficult day for you?"

His arms went around her, pressing her hot face against his coat, and it was no longer necessary to struggle against betraying herself. She stood very still, refusing to think, while the tiredness ran out of her bones like rain dripping from an oilskin coat and the taut knots in her stomach began to loosen and let go at last.

He held her as he might a small child, offering her a silent matter-of-fact tenderness; and while a tiny corner of her mind protested that she was not a child and wanted no part of a child's meager portion, another lapped up the generous warmth and comfort within his arms like a starved and greedy orphan.

Then, gradually, the world came back. She heard Mason call an order on deck, and the muted voices of the men in the salon as they prepared to leave the *Caprice*. She raised her head and stepped back.

"I feel much better now," she said honestly.

He smiled. "I am at your service, ma'am," he said, "and available, I assure you, at a moment's notice."

She returned his smile. But she reflected, as she went back to the cubby, that it would never do to take any further advantage of his generosity; not, in any case, while it affected her so oddly, leaving her so shaken and limp that she almost felt ill.

Miss Eliza heard the latest news with obvious pleasure.

"So we are not rid of his lordship, after all," she said. "Well, I confess I prefer Annapolis to New York, and Lord Hazard to Daniel Mason."

Page did not confess anything. She went on deck to say good-bye to Jacobs and his officers and found them ready at the side. Since the crew had already been transferred and no one wished to delay the *Fortune*'s departure for safer waters, the farewells were somewhat hurried.

Jacobs and Mr. Biddle were the last to leave, and Page watched as they clambered down the side and were rowed across to the merchantman, thinking that she would miss them dreadfully.

"Don't look so distressed," Hazard said behind her. "They'll reach New York safely."

"I daresay," Page said, "but I always seem to be saying good-bye to people I've grown fond of, and will likely never see again."

As soon as she had spoken, she wished with some embarrassment that she had held her tongue. But Hazard only said, amused, "If your past luck holds, they'll turn up again when you least expect them."

They stood together by the rail, watching the *Fortune*'s sails unfurl and begin to draw. She moved with slow dignity to the northwest, but the *Caprice* soon slipped past and left her astern. With each minute she dropped further behind, until finally Page could see only her canvas, golden in the sun, dwindling to a small triangle. Then even that was gone, and the schooner was alone on a wide blue expanse of sea.

Mason came across the deck. "She'll ride like a gull now that we've unloaded our cargo."

He glanced up at the sails, at the raking masts so narrow and tall that they gave the illusion of bending and springing back with the wind to whip the *Caprice* forward like a live thing; and Page, watching his face, wondered if he would ever look at a woman with such proud affection.

"If my navigation is correct," Hazard said casually, "you'll soon be turning due east."

"I would," Mason agreed, "if I intended to run into the Chesapeake."

"And you have no such intention?"

Mason grinned. "No. Does it surprise you?"

"Not in the least," Hazard said calmly. "Why else do you think I insisted on staying aboard?"

For a brief instant Mason's tawny eyes glittered. Then he laughed. "You outguessed me, my lord. But don't be misled into thinking you can make a habit of it."

"I am seldom misled," Hazard said in his cool contemptuous voice.

Page found it difficult to feel either surprise or despair. Like a seaman perched at the mastcap while his ship swooped and dived endlessly from crest to trough of enormous swells, her emotions had been battered beyond the capacity to feel anything but an instinctive need to hold on.

"Am I to take it," she asked warily, "that the *Caprice* isn't going to Baltimore, after all?"

"But I have a convoy ahead," Mason said with an air of apology that did not deceive her, "guarded by only two sloops-of-war. Surely you can't expect me to turn tail and run home, Miss Bradley, with such tempting treasures dangling under my nose?"

Page sighed. "Surely not. I can't think of a single logical reason why I should expect you to go to Baltimore."

His grin was half malicious, half pure good humor, giving him a look both wicked and innocent at once.

"Now that you've visited Bermuda," he said, "you mustn't think you've seen the world. France is just over the horizon, you know, and sunny Portugal, and all the exotic lands along the Nile. Who can say where the convoy will lead us before we've done with it?"

Page's eyes widened. "Who, indeed?" she said faintly.

"Shall I tell you," Hazard said, his voice cutting levelly across hers, "or will it spoil the game for you?"

The two men regarded each other silently. But Mason, once again, did not accept the challenge; he merely shrugged and said, "Nothing you can do will spoil it," and sauntered off across the deck.

Hazard, looking after him, had an odd smile on his face. "Well, Miss Bradley," he said, "it would seem that you have made a conquest of our bold captain."

"How absurd," Page said without thinking. "He can't have been at sea that long."

Hazard threw back his head and laughed. Then he said, his eyes still warm with amusement, "I thought you would be feeling a great need to cry on my coat again."

"If anything," she said, "I feel an urge to tear my hair in a frenzy, but I doubt if it would relieve my emotions in the least."

Then she went below to tell Miss Eliza that they were not sailing to Annapolis with Lord Hazard, but stood a fair chance of seeing France with him, an abrupt change of plans one must apparently be prepared to accept as one of the strange peculiarities of sea travel.

11

Later, when she looked back at those bright sunlit days aboard the *Caprice*, she was to remember them as the happiest of her life.

At the time, however, she often wondered how it would be to live a quiet peaceful life again, her days marked by nothing more eventful than a county ball or visitors for tea, her world bounded by the slow march of the seasons and the lazy tidewater way of life, her heart stirred by nothing more dangerous than the stale news in a paper three weeks late in arriving. But that tranquil world lay far behind the misty haze that hovered along the horizon; and the past and the future were rudely pushed aside by a clamorous, unquiet present demanding all her attention and interest.

The *Caprice* was to take four prizes from the convoy before she was done with it, four fat wealthy West Indiamen loaded with sugar, rum, indigo, coffee, and enough British specie to make Mason a rich man many times over.

The two sloop captains, stamping their quarterdecks with enraged fury, could protect their charges only by bunching them together in close formation, a maneuver which necessarily slowed their passage and offered the *Caprice* even more time to scheme for another victim.

She would skim around the huddled convoy with the grace of a dragonfly, standing past it to draw one of the sloops after her, then suddenly coming about to slip down the leeward side of the convoy, her guns roaring at the frightened merchantmen as she passed. Before the clumsy sloop could round the convoy the *Caprice* would be alongside the other sloop, daring her to fight; and when both protectors and charges were confused and addled, the *Caprice* would dip her flags in a mocking salute and swing to the westward, not quite out of sight but always out of reach.

Then, just as the British captains thought it safe to draw a deep breath and sit down to an uninterrupted meal, the *Caprice* would be at her tricks again, seeming to be in a dozen places at once, harrying at their flanks, probing every weak spot, darting in to attack but never holding still long enough to taste their guns, an enemy as infuriating and illusive as a will-o'-the-wisp.

She accomplished her purpose with deadly ease. The naval captains and the merchant masters cursed Mason violently and grew bleary-eyed from tension and lack of sleep, and before two weeks had passed the *Caprice* had unhurriedly taken her toll, her only payment being a ripped sail and torn shroud lines, damaged when she fouled a merchant ship in the dark to facilitate boarding her.

Mason put prize crews aboard three of the merchantmen and sent them back to American ports, and the fourth he destroyed after transferring her cargo to the *Caprice* and setting her crew afloat in longboats to be picked up by one of the British sloops.

Page, to her surprise, did not find it at all frightening. Mason knew his ship intimately and handled her with a daring skill; and Page, who was not allowed on deck when the *Caprice* went into action, marvelled so at his seamanship that more than once she was plucked bodily from the stern windows, where she was discovered craning her neck to see what was happening and hugely enjoying the spectacle of the *Caprice* thumbing her impudent nose at the British.

"Whatever one thinks of his character," she said to Miss Eliza, "one cannot but admit him to be an excellent privateer captain."

To Hazard, one evening in the cabin, she remarked that Mason's success undoubtedly stemmed from an American trait engrained by long years of fighting against superior odds. No British captain, accustomed to victory and raised on the premise that His Majesty's Navy was invincible, could lower his unbending honor to the tactics of fighting only when the odds were even. Sailing blithely away from a superior adversary, whether in armament or numbers, smacked too much of cowardice, if not outright heresy, and British commanders were inclined to sneer that only an unethical Yankee would run away to fight again another day.

But Page, pointing out to Hazard the pitfalls of an honor so stiff that one must die to uphold it, remarked innocently that ethics would not fill the sugar pots of England emptied by Mason's exploits or pay the marine insurance rates that must surely rise sharply in London each time an American privateer put out to sea.

"They'll learn," Hazard said calmly. "Nothing is resisted so bitterly in England as change, but indignant citizens will write letters to the *Times* and retired naval gentlemen will argue loudly, and eventually some of it will pierce the foggy minds at the Admiralty."

"They'll never admit that a Yankee got ahead of them in anything," Page retorted, forgetting, as she so often did, that Hazard was also an Englishman.

"Never," Hazard agreed amiably, "but they might

begin to wonder why a Yankee would dare to try. They like to do things the sensible way, the way they've always done them, and they find it hard to understand how anything could be better."

"The sensible way isn't always the only way."

"Certainly not. Take the *Caprice*, for example. If the British captured her they'd immediately take ten feet off her masts and cut down her spars, and add some good sturdy planking to her hull. Then they'd man her with a crew used to a slow coaster or a ship-of-the-line, and wonder why she wouldn't log better than five knots for them. They've a great deal to learn from the Americans."

"If there were only more Baltimore schooners and more Daniel Masons," Page said, her eyes darkening, "we'd show them how to fight a war the modern way."

"You would need a great many more than you're likely to have," Hazard said quietly. "The odds are so uneven as to be ridiculous, even for the most courageous American captain."

Mason, coming into the cabin, heard Hazard's last words.

"The British are a complacent lot, Miss Bradley," he said. "They believe themselves ordained to rule the world, you know, a superior race with no equal on land or sea." He looked at Hazard and laughed. "How did they explain away the loss of the *Guerrière*, my lord, and the *Macedonian* and *Java*? Have the superior citizens of London ever heard of Hull and Decatur and Bainbridge?"

"They have," Hazard said coolly, "and know them to be excellent officers. They've also heard of the *Constitution* and the *United States*, as well as all the sizeable vessels in your fleet. Not a difficult task, you must agree, when there are so few. A handful of frigates, a few sloops, a number of gunboats—have I missed any?"

"You know a damned lot about it. Did you spend all your time in America spying?"

"The London newspapers carried the complete list months ago. They also printed a list of the British navy, at sea or refitting. Almost two hundred ships-of-the-line, two hundred fifty frigates, several hundred smaller vessels. Taken all together, over a thousand vessels."

Mason gave his characteristic shrug. "You have forgotten the *Caprice*, I think, and the hundreds like her."

"If you had many more hundreds," Hazard said slowly, "it would not signify. The British navy is occupied now with maintaining the lines of communications between England and Spain. Transporting men and supplies to relieve Wellington. Watching the French navy. But when Bonaparte has fallen, they'll have nothing to divert them from America."

"Bonaparte is a long way from defeat," Mason said carelessly. "We've plenty of time."

"But he will be defeated," Hazard said grimly, "sooner or later." The light from the lantern flickered uneasily in a draught, casting dark shadows across his face. "At the moment the Admiralty finds it difficult to send even a squadron to the western Atlantic. But how will it be, my friend, when they have all their ships and troops at hand?"

Page, for a fleeting moment, found herself close to hating him.

"I know how it will be," Mason said, his eyes cold and hard. "I once spent a few months in one of your seventy-four's, and another month or two in the hulks at Plymouth. I've the scars on my back and the memories in my soul to remind me of how it'll be." The cabin was silent. Mason added flatly, "The outcome isn't important, any more than the reasons it started. I do as I must, and so would you in my place."

"Yes," Hazard said briefly.

"Then why the gloomy pessimism? Do you think to warn me?"

"That, among other things."

"Thanks," Mason said, "but I've more wit than you credit me with. I don't need a Limey to open my eyes."

He left the cabin abruptly; and Page, her eyes on Hazard, whispered, "You cannot frighten us out of fighting, you know."

Hazard regarded her with inscrutable eyes. Then he went to the stern windows, resting his weight on his hands, and looked out at the foaming wake, silver in the moonlight.

"A few Englishmen might entertain that ludicrous notion," he said, almost absently, "but I am not among them."

Afterwards Page could not recall that there had been any of the usual dislike in their voices. Antagonism, yes, and even a cold wariness, but their opinion of each other in the context of war was apparently a thing apart, completely unrelated to their behavior where Page was concerned. She could not believe it possible that either of them considered her a more fit subject for enmity than a war, but she often had the disquieting sensation of being caught between a smoldering volcano and a deadly northern avalanche, either capable of setting off the most awesome devastation at any given moment.

It was Hazard, she well knew, who saw to it that she was never alone with Mason for more than a few minutes before Miss Eliza or MacDougall or Hazard himself appeared on the scene; just as it was Hazard's cool contemptuous voice that kept Mason at bay whenever he looked at Page with those dangerous amber lights in his eyes or began to tease her in a slightly improper way. Mason seemed to accept the situation with an outward amusement, but Page strongly suspected him to be merely biding his time until the moment suited him.

Miss Eliza, however, was unperturbed. "Depend upon it," she said, "his lordship knows precisely what he is about."

"I'm sure he does," Page said pointedly, "just as he knew when he stood on the quay in Annapolis and faced that murderous mob. But what would have been his fate if no one had come along to get him out of his predicament?"

"He would have managed," Miss Eliza said. "I daresay he's been in more than one bad squeeze, love, and is quite capable of looking after himself."

"I daresay," Page said thoughtfully.

The next afternoon as she stood beside him at the rail in the bright sun she had to admit that he did, indeed, have a definite air of being able to manage. She studied him from under her lashes, wondering what it was about him that set him so apart from other men. He was all clean sharp planes, from the high cheekbones to the inverted triangle formed as his shoulders tapered down to the cavalryman's narrow hips; he might have been carved from granite by a master sculptor with a sparing hand and a taste for strong elemental lines. But unlike a statue his hair was black as a crow's wing in the sunlight and his eyes, looking down at her, were the clear lucid gray of the sky on a cool morning just before dawn.

"You are very quiet," he said. "Tell me how I have offended you."

She grasped hastily at the first straw. "I was only wondering why Daniel Mason was allowed to sail openly into St. George's harbor. I would not have thought American ships welcome there."

"It's no secret," he said. "One of the important captains on the Bermuda station had been obliged to leave a lovely lady behind in Lisbon. So he arranged to buy passage for her on the *Caprice*." He smiled down at Page. "You can understand why Captain Mason was assured of a safe voyage and a hearty welcome at St. George's."

So that was why the American officers had been so close-mouthed about the whole affair. Page met Hazard's eyes and laughed.

"How like him," she said, and then did not quite have the courage to ask if the important captain had been acquainted with Mason before he entrusted his lovely lady to him.

"Precisely," Hazard said coolly. "That is why I made certain that Miss Eliza and MacDougall and Jacobs would accompany you to New York."

She was searching her mind for a suitably crushing retort when the cry of "Sail ho!" came from the bow and masthead.

Daniel Mason, standing across the deck with his first officer, swung up into the shrouds and leveled his telescope to the eastward, where the ships of the convoy, still herded together, set their slow stately courses across the blue sea. Then he shifted his scrutiny to the northwest, holding it there for some minutes.

Page, standing on tiptoe, saw the small white tip of a sail without difficulty. So did the ships of the convoy, beginning to flutter with signal flags that streamed in the wind from their main tops.

Mason jumped back to the deck and spoke quietly to

his first officer. Then he turned and tossed his glass to Hazard.

"Have a look," he called. "She must be one of those brave thousand ships you were telling me about."

Hazard looked through the glass, then without a word handed it to Page. She fastened it to her eye, seeing first the bold British ensign, then the black hull with its white band studded with gunports, then the towering white pyramid of sail bringing the ship down relentlessly on the *Caprice* and the convoy beyond.

Silently, with an emptiness at the pit of her stomach, she gave the glass back to Mason. But he only laughed and said, "A frigate, by God, and just in time to keep two sloop captains of my acquaintance from utter madness."

He raised his hand. The first officer, watching him, at once called the watch, and the men swarmed on deck. Within short minutes the *Caprice*, all sail unfurled and her bow wave flaring white, danced away to the southwest.

Page stifled a sigh of relief. But Hazard, glancing at her face, said provokingly, "Were you worried? Only last night you were boasting to me that a smart Yankee always knows when to fight and when to run away."

Beside her Mason leaned his elbows against the rail. "She might also have boasted," he drawled, "that this particular Yankee will take care that she'll never fall into British hands again."

Hazard said idly, "I'm afraid you're too late, Captain. She is already in British hands."

Page turned and looked back toward the frigate, rapidly falling astern, and the bunched white sails of the convoy that would soon be hull down on the horizon.

Behind her Mason's voice was quite soft. "So long as

she is aboard the *Caprice*, m'lord, I think I may safely say that the Redcoats, as so often before, have been put to rout by the Yanks."

"You may say it if you please," Hazard said, "but not, I must warn you, with any degree of safety."

Page turned abruptly to face Mason's mocking grin and a wicked gleam of devilment in the tawny eyes.

"Why don't we ask Miss Bradley which side of the war she favors?"

Hazard's eyes were like splintered ice. "Does the war enter into the question?"

To Page's great relief Miss Eliza advanced across the deck, calm and sensible in her gray gown and black shawl, making a matter-of-fact comment on the favorable weather.

"If it holds," Mason said, "we'll be off L'Orient in a fortnight."

"I presume you must have a good reason for wanting to go to France," said Miss Eliza, "but for the moment it has escaped me."

Mason looked surprised. "The best of reasons, ma'am. From L'Orient a fast handy ship may watch the approaches to the Channel and have her pick of prizes. She may cruise the Bay of Biscay and play havoc with the British communications." He glanced at Hazard with a slight smile. "Or, if she's bold enough, she can raid the coasts of England and Ireland with very little difficulty."

Hazard's face was guarded. "What of the British squadron blockading Brest? And L'Orient, surely, as well as Nantes?"

Mason shrugged. "They may be guarding the coast from Finistère to Gibraltar, but I think you'll find as many American ships making safe harbor as before."

"You've the ship for it," Hazard said noncommitally.

"And the nerve," Miss Eliza added. "But you may as well tell me, young man, what you intend for us. Surely you don't expect us to cruise the Biscay bay with you?"

He gave her a bland merry smile. "Not at all, Miss Wyndham. You'll have a comfortable room ashore in L'Orient with Miss Bradley, and I'll have two bright faces to greet me when I make port. The French inns are not the most luxurious in the world, but you'll be safe enough."

"I am an Englishwoman," Miss Eliza said calmly, "and my country has been at war with France for twenty years. You can hardly expect me to consider a French inn a safe refuge."

"But better than an American privateer," Mason said promptly. "You have your choice, ma'am."

Hazard leaned silently against the rail, eyes narrowed in the sunlight.

"And what of Lord Hazard?" Miss Eliza asked. "And Duncan MacDougall?"

"MacDougall also has a choice. He can stay aboard the *Caprice*, as one of my crew, or he can go ashore with you." After a brief pause, Mason laughed. "His lordship, of course, is a different matter. If you have any brilliant ideas on the subject, Miss Wyndham, I'll rely on you to share them with me."

"It might have been more brilliant on your part," Miss Eliza said mildly, "if you had allowed us to proceed to New York in the beginning."

"But not nearly so interesting. Never fear, ladies, I'll sail you back to Annapolis with dispatch, once I've finished my business on this side of the Atlantic."

But he did not disclose what plans he had for Hazard; and when Page questioned Hazard he only smiled and said, "Don't worry. We'll contrive something when the moment arrives."

The moment, Page feared, was swiftly approaching. Without the convoy to hold her back the *Caprice* raced along her way across a glittering sea, water and sky so clear and blue and the wind so steady that one memorable twenty-four hours she logged over three hundred miles. At night the stars hung low enough to dazzle the watch, and the wake creaming behind was a white fan touched with silver.

The ship might have been swallowed by the Atlantic. Page's life was no longer geared to land but concerned itself entirely with a routine so close to the sea that the rest of the world seemed distant and alien, dropped away below the horizon. The beautiful curving sails and the touch of wind on one's face, the desert of blue sunlit water streaked with white crested horses or lazy swirls of foam—these were the important things. Clocks were forgotten and the day was divided by the ship's bells, struck each half-hour, announcing mealtime or the change of the watch; the movement of the ship, soaring and swooping like a gull, became a more natural thing than the memory of an unmoving earth beneath one's feet.

It occurred to Page that she was not only becoming accustomed to a life of continual sea travel but was, indeed, in danger of liking it far too well. She spent as much time on deck as possible, sometimes lying in the shelter of a canvas rigged for her protection. But usually she stayed in the sun, liking the clean scrubbed feeling it gave her, letting her skin tan a deep burnished gold and growing hungrier, happier and more alive with each passing day.

She asked Hazard endless questions about France. It was astonishing but vastly exciting to think that she would soon see the ancient legendary land of Charlemagne and chivalry and brave knights, of brooding chateaus and fabled vineyards, of Versailles and Fontainebleau; the land where lovely princesses plaited their golden hair inside guarded turrets, and troubadours strummed their lutes outside the castle walls and carried love tokens next to their hearts; the land of Paris and the gray Seine, of Joan of Arc and Tristan and Lafayette.

And Bonaparte, Hazard would remind her gently, as if to warn her that the France of her imagination was not the same France dominated by the stout little man in a cockaded hat and olive green coat.

"Can he be so very bad?" Page asked pensively. "I daresay all Englishmen learn in their cradles to hate the French, but he is America's ally, after all, and surely no monster."

"By no means," Hazard said coolly. "Merely a cheat, a liar, a bully, and a ruthless bloodletter who plays with countries and armies as if they were cards, and boasts that the lives of a million men mean nothing to him."

Page regarded him gravely. "You more than hate him," she said. "Is that why you fight with Wellington's army when you could be safely at home in England, tending your estates?"

He withdrew behind his guard again, shutting her out. "No one is safe with Bonaparte at large," he said. "Don't look so distressed. You won't run the risk of meeting him in L'Orient. The Bretons are a proud lot and not overly fond of the Emperor."

She sighed and gave it up. He was a man who kept his own counsel and shared none of himself with anyone; the last day she saw him she would know little more of him than she had at the beginning.

She could not, in all honesty, complain. He was a charming and diverting companion, unfailingly patient with her questions, easily amused, solicitous of her comfort, always unobtrusively at hand whenever she needed him. No man could have accepted a tiresome responsibility with more graciousness than his lordship; she could not possibly expect more of him than he had already generously given.

But she stood on the deck one night, alone in the quiet moonlight, and examined her fancies with brutal honesty, and was obliged to sigh at herself for being so foolish.

"I don't blame you for sighing," Mason said softly beside her. "A pretty girl should never have to walk alone in the moonlight. Where's the British watchdog?"

Page did not answer. She would not tell him that Hazard was below with Miss Eliza, politely discussing the questionable merits of Lord Byron's poetry, and it was none of his business why she sighed, or why she was on deck alone, or what she was thinking.

"Like all Englishmen," he said, "Hazard's a damned cold fish." He laughed, and the moonlight glittered briefly in his eyes. "His intentions, however, are strictly honorable. Don't you occasionally find it dull?"

There was nothing to say that would not involve her, willy-nilly, in a most improper conversation. She turned her head to see if the helmsman was listening, but he was staring straight ahead, wooden-faced, absorbed in the wheel and his course and the set of the sails.

"Now, mine may not be at all honorable," Mason said, "but I'll wager you'd find them far more interesting."

She raised her chin. "I am not interested in your intentions, sir, honorable or otherwise."

"Have I insulted you?" he asked lazily, and grinned at her. "You might try striking me. Or look down your nose with utter contempt. Better still, faint dead away. In my arms, of course."

She had to laugh, but it caught in her throat when she felt his hands on her shoulders, pulling her against him. He bent his head swiftly and kissed her, and for the space of a startled moment she was conscious of nothing but a vast exasperation.

She tried to push him away but he was much too strong for her; and it seemed so undignified to struggle that she simply stood there, while his lips moved from her mouth to her eyes, to her cheeks, then back to her mouth. But her mind, not wholly stunned by the turn of events, noted calmly that it was quite dull and uninteresting, and might just as well have been strictly honorable.

"May I interrupt?" Hazard's cool voice cut through the moonlit silence.

Mason raised his head. Then he smiled and put Page away from him. "Certainly, m'lord."

Miss Eliza stood just behind Hazard, but she said nothing.

"I think we may dispense with the usual civilities," Hazard said. "We've put it off too long as it is."

"I agree," Mason said, and added, "Have you done any sparring, sir?"

"Now and then."

Mason smiled again. "Then you wouldn't be averse to a bit of exercise."

"Not at all," Hazard said. Without taking his eyes from Mason he added, "Miss Eliza, I believe you and Miss Bradley have a number of urgent matters demanding your attention below."

"Surely," Miss Eliza said serenely. "Come, love."

There was nothing to do but go with Miss Eliza, but

once in the captain's cabin Page asked with exasperation, "Why didn't you say something? How foolish for two grown men to behave like schoolboys, and you stand there meekly as a lamb, not doing a thing to stop them."

"But men frequently behave like schoolboys," Miss Eliza said, "and at the risk of losing your esteem for me, love, I confess that I am not one to change man's nature." She smiled reassuringly. "It is not so foolish as a duel with those lethal-looking pistols, and it might have come to that. A good mill will clear the air, and we will go on more comfortably after this."

"But it was only a kiss," Page said. "I daresay I should have known how to avoid it, but it was not so very terrible, after all."

"Well, it was not very wise, as you see, but I'm glad you enjoyed it."

"I didn't," Page said, "but if I'd known it would cause such a stir, I might as well have. A duel, indeed."

A polite cough from the door made her turn. Farley, holding a tray with two cups of steaming tea, was watching her with a small frown.

"A duel, ma'am?" he echoed.

"Only with their fists," she said, "which is a great piece of nonsense."

Farley's face cleared. "He has a punishing right, ma'am, and has always shown to advantage, if I may say so, with the best prize fighters of England." He put the tray on the table. "If you will excuse me, ma'am, I believe I will go on deck. His lordship, you may be assured, will have the situation well in hand, but it is always wise to have a sympathetic second at one's back."

"Like master, like man," Miss Eliza murmured. "I

suspect most of the crew will also find excellent reasons for going on deck in the next few minutes."

A heavy thud sounded directly over Page's head. She sat bolt upright on the transom seat, trying not to wince at the next jarring crash, but in a few minutes her shoulders ached from stiffness and her throat was painfully dry. She hoped that the cheers of the crew did not mean what she sadly imagined, and that the deck was not the scene of shambles and havoc indicated by the ominous sounds jolting the deck. The impeccable Viscount, she thought despairingly, should have kept to his pistols.

"I had no idea they would go at it so vehemently," Miss Eliza said. "They seem to have thrown themselves into the spirit of the thing with a good deal of abandon."

Page winced again as some object—she refused to think further—rolled across the deck and came to an abrupt halt against another solid object. Something overturned with a metallic clatter and a man's voice shouted a cheerful obscenity that resounded in the cabin with devastating clarity.

"Perhaps I should tell you to put your hands over your ears," Miss Eliza said, "but I've always held the opinion that closing one's eyes and ears to reality does not make the nasty thing go away."

Page smiled absently, waiting for the next violent thud. But it did not come, and except for a babble of voices and one loud burst of laughter, there was no more sound from the deck.

The silence was worse than anything that went before. It lasted even longer.

Page stood up abruptly. "Well, I won't wait here with bated breath for someone to bring us the glad tidings."

"I'll come with you," Miss Eliza said. "Whoever comes down the steps first will be vastly disappointed to find only me."

"I hope they've knocked each other senseless," Page said severely, "in which case neither of them will be coming below for anything but the surgeon's care."

"I don't believe the *Caprice* carries a surgeon," Miss Eliza said pensively. "Do you think perhaps I should—"

"Don't be so kindhearted. Neither of them deserves it."

Miss Eliza said, "You are very fierce," but she followed Page into the salon, dimly lit by one swinging oil lantern. They had been given separate cubbies when Jacobs and his men left the ship, and now Miss Eliza said good night and waited at her door for Page to go inside her cabin.

But the door leading to the companionway clicked open and Page, with a tiny gasp, whirled around.

Hazard stood there. His shirt was torn and clung to him damply. His short dark hair was wet, as if someone had poured a bucket of seawater over it, and a cut lip still bled slightly. His right knuckles were bound carelessly with a handkerchief. He looked disheveled and dirty and very pleased with himself.

For a long moment they stared at each other across the salon, and Page heard Miss Eliza's door close softly.

Then Hazard said, in his deep quiet voice, "It is settled."

"Are you hurt?" Page whispered.

His smile flashed white in the dim light. "I'll feel it tomorrow," he said. "So, I'll wager, will the captain."

"Is he—" she stopped, not sure she wanted to know.

"He's on his feet. Did you fear for him?"

She didn't answer. Looking at him there in the doorway, battered and tired but no longer remote, his face alive and unguarded, an indefinable air of triumph about him, she felt something inside her quicken with an exultancy so primitive and shameless that she was shaken beyond words.

He pushed the door shut behind him. He came toward her.

She found her voice, but it was husky and tremulous, not her voice at all. "What will he do to you?"

He paused beside the table. "Curse me, I should imagine," he said, amused, "until his muscles stop aching."

It was not what she meant, and he knew it. The lantern was behind him now, so that his face was dark and shadowed. He regarded her steadily, his eyes almost black, his shoulders blotting out the light.

Then he said absently, "It was a fair fight. I doubt if he'll hang me." He laughed. "At least he gave no indication of it a few minutes ago when we drank a mug of rum together."

Her eyes widened. It was hard to believe, but she didn't question him. He was very close. She could see the pulse beating evenly against the smooth brown of his throat.

"What are you thinking?" he asked, very quietly.

She shook her head. She could not see his eyes now, they were hidden behind the dark curve of lashes. His mouth was unsmiling but it was no longer hard. She fastened her eyes on it, realized the danger of doing so too late, and knew a strange terrifying sensation that her very bones were dissolving helplessly.

But when he finally moved it was to reach around her to open her door. He put his hands on her shoulders and turned her.

"Good night, little one," he said, and the sound was no more than a faint breath in the silence.

His hands fell away. The door closed with a tiny click, leaving her alone in a darkness more forlorn and empty than any she had ever known.

12

...—◆◎◆—...

Miss Eliza, who had declared that a good mill would clear the air, was proved right. The threat of violence had spent itself, like a summer thunderstorm left behind to rumble harmlessly on the horizon.

Mason came to breakfast the next morning with one eye closed shut and the other puffed uncomfortably, and a long ugly bruise purpling his chin. But if Page had expected the moment to be an awkward one she was greatly relieved when he grinned at her across the table without the least hint of anger or mortification.

"As you see," he said ruefully, "I came to grief. My crew was prevented from putting Lord Hazard in my place only by my forcible reminder that an Englishman commanding an American privateer might set back our cause a dozen years."

Page gave him a look of polite incredulity, but he went back to his breakfast with an appetite matching Hazard's. They appeared to think nothing more worthy of their attention than the huge amount of ale, beefsteak, eggs and bread before them. Hazard did not look battered or triumphant or dangerous, and there was nothing in his eyes when he smiled at Page to suggest that he remembered that strange moment in the salon;

he was once again clean and impeccable and remote, and obviously hungry.

Just before noon the *Caprice* spoke the American brig *Molly Ann*, Captain Joshua Miller, out of Nantes for New York, and learned that the British blockading squadron, aided by the long spell of good weather, was holding outside Brest and L'Orient so closely that only by the grace of good luck and an excellent pilot had the *Molly Ann* escaped its clutches. The harbors were full of privateers, Captain Miller reported, chafing impatiently at their moorings and waiting for a westerly gale to blow into the Biscay Bay and disperse some of the crowd.

"I haven't time to wait for a gale," Mason said, "and the British will see to it that no pilots sail out to offer their services." He whistled under his breath for a moment. "I see only one thing to do. I'll follow my own nose and we'll run in after dark."

Captain Miller was rowed back to his ship still frowning at so rash and dangerous a decision, and the *Caprice*, setting her course straight for France, soon left the *Molly Ann* astern.

Mason reassured Page. "It may not be L'Orient, but we'll find an anchorage somewhere along the coast. I've been chased in and out of every harbor in Finistère, and can remember more than a few handy ones."

Page did not doubt his ability to bring them off safely. But the uncertainty of her future, as well as Hazard's, once they were in France, was a worry that haunted her sleep and effectively took away her appetite.

Hazard noticed it, of course, and found an occasion to say, "I should think you would have learned to trust me by now. I still have your affairs in hand, you know, and there is very little reason to make yourself ill with worry."

"I don't know what you think you can do," she retorted, "locked fast and tight in a French prison."

"You have a remarkable imagination," he said, sounding amused. "I assure you that I am not in the least likely to be locked fast and tight anywhere, much less in a French prison."

His confidence was comforting, as was his presence beside her that night when the *Caprice* ran silently toward the Brittany coast and Page stood on deck with her heart in her throat and an ominous prickling up her spine.

They had made landfall just at dusk. France was a thin blue line floating on the horizon, and the tiny white feathers to leeward, barely visible in the hazy distance, were undoubtedly the sails of a portion of the blockading fleet. But darkness fell before either the land or the ships were appreciably nearer, and the schooner made her cautious way in toward the rocks and reefs that guarded the Breton harbors as stoutly as ten fleets.

"They'll be watching Brest and L'Orient," Mason said, "so we'll stay between them. They won't expect us to know the coast well enough to go in after dark."

The moon was hidden by scudding clouds that swept in from the Atlantic before the fresh wind, and the *Caprice* might have been a phantom ship, ghosting silently through the night. Only Mason and the helmsman stood erect by the wheel, their faces barely illuminated by the shadowed binnacle light; the rest of the crew was sprawled around the guns with their cutlasses and muskets at hand or waiting alertly for orders to handle the sails.

Page's memories of that endless night were somewhat unreliable, a jumble of unimportant details etched by the imprint of a few sharp moments of utter panic: the terrified thud of her heart when a large hulking mass, darker than the night, rose up suddenly on the starboard bow and the two ships passed each other by no more than a musket shot apart; the sudden shout of the British lookout as the *Caprice* melted away into the night and left the aroused frigate behind; the roar of breakers on a submerged reef somewhere on the port beam, a menacing sound that haunted the ship for miles.

A lookout peered into the blackness off the bows, a man in the forechains took soundings, and Mason, in a quiet calm voice, gave orders to the helmsman. The tension seemed unbearable at times. Page, standing still and anxious by the companionway amidships, was grateful for the warm strength of Hazard's hand holding hers through all the long dark hours of waiting.

Then a few scattered lights pricked the night and Mason, with a weary grin, spoke to the first mate. The watch swarmed aloft, the *Caprice* turned into the wind and lost way, and before the anchor had been let go the sails were neatly furled.

"The weather was on our side," Mason said. "We needed that breeze to offset the tide and keep us off the rocks." He looked at the lights ashore and laughed. "No Brittany village forgets its night lights. The good wives may all be sound asleep, but more than one will leave a candle in the window for fear some smuggler's ship may be counting on the lights of home to guide her in."

The night was very quiet and peaceful, and Page gave a long unsteady sigh.

"My thanks," Mason said to Hazard, "for not giving us away to that bloody frigate."

"Did you think I would?" Hazard asked drily.

"No," Mason said, and laughed again. "The crew deserves a tot of rum. Would you join us, m'lord?"

Page turned and went below. Her berth seemed oddly still, but she soon fell into an exhausted sleep that might have lasted around the clock if Miss Eliza had not waked her shortly before noon, bringing her breakfast and the news that Mason had lowered the jolly boat some time before and had gone off ashore, taking Hazard and a number of the crew.

Page did not feel hungry. "Do you suppose that the captain has gone to turn him over to the French?"

"I am too old for the folly of supposing, love. Come on deck and take your first look at France."

France was a wide bay ten miles long and at least as wide, sparkling an intense blue under the noon sun. From the water the hills swept upward in green moors crisscrossed by the darker green of hedges and thin thickets of trees. The *Caprice* was anchored below a small village whose bone-white houses climbed a hill above the harbor and gazed serenely down on a fleet of fishing boats.

The first mate handed Page his glass and she looked with eager curiosity at the stone quays weathered to a silvery gray, where old men in berets and sabots sat and drowsed in the sun, and women in black gowns and incredibly high white caps strolled back and forth like dignified black frigates under a press of canvas.

The first mate frowned and said, "Only women and old men left. The young ones have all been taken as conscripts for old Boney's armies. Half the fishing boats are rotting on shore, and the rest are kept close in the bay by the blockade. It looks to be a long hungry winter in Finistère this year."

But at the moment, sleeping in the bright September

sunlight and smelling delightfully of gorse and green turf and the heavenly land scents that came down off the windswept moors, the village seemed a sheltered happy place, far removed from Bonaparte and Imperial armies and the devastation of war.

Page saw the jolly boat returning and levelled the glass on it with unsteady fingers. But even without the glass there was no mistaking that dark head, bare in the hot sun, and the dazzling white cravat; he had been right, then, about the French prison, but surely he did not find everything in France so easy to order to his will.

She was mistaken. His lordship, it appeared, still had her affairs well in hand.

The *Caprice*, he explained briefly, could not linger long in the exposed and undefended bay and must slip back through the blockade southeast to L'Orient. Miss Eliza and Page were to go ashore immediately, where a carriage waited on the quay. Until Hazard had determined the wisest course of action they would stay in the home of Madame Gouret beyond the village.

It could not possibly be so simple. Page, regarding Hazard with a fascinated awe, said, "And you?"

"I'll tell you later," he said, and swung down the companion steps to find Farley.

Mason grinned. "I had the same feeling of futility," he said, "when I watched him storm France single-handedly."

"Didn't they know him for an Englishman?"

"He speaks French as well as any Frog. I do the thing in bits and pieces myself, and since most of the villagers speak Breton, it was a fair jumble for a while. But we stopped in the tavern and had a glass of cider, and inside thirty minutes he knew the names of all the English sympathizers in town, those suspected of being

Bonaparte's spies, and the ones most likely to offer shelter to two homeless American ladies."

After a moment Page asked, "Isn't there an inn?"

"Hazard didn't like that notion at all. After another glass of cider someone mentioned Madame Gouret, who lost three sons to Bonaparte and prays for his defeat at any cost."

Page gave him a direct curious glance. "I thought you intended to see him imprisoned."

"Did you?" he said lightly, and smiled at her.

"Why did you allow him to stay on board the *Caprice*?"

He shrugged. "I liked him," he said. "I would to God he had been born a Yankee."

Page stared at him disbelievingly.

"He's British and an enemy," he said, "'and I'll fight him to the end with any means at hand. But he's a man worth knowing, for all that."

She liked him very much at that moment, and straightway forgot all the unpleasant moments of the voyage.

"I suppose I should apologize for making life so difficult for you. I knew from the start how it would be, needing only one look at Hazard and another at you, but it goes against my nature to let anything slide away so easily." His slow easy drawl was teasing. "Don't be angry. You're such a pretty lass I couldn't withstand the temptation."

MacDougall came on deck then, his face a mixture of apology and defiance, to tell her that he intended to sign on the *Caprice* as a seaman for the length of time they were in France. Page thought it an excellent idea, but saying goodbye to him made the farewells even more melancholy.

"Don't congratulate yourself that you've seen the last

of me," Mason said cheerfully. "L'Orient isn't too many kilometers away, and when his lordship decides what to do with you, I'll be glad to be of service."

Page did not look back at the schooner. The *Caprice* had become an old friend and her crew spoke in familiar American voices; ahead lay Bonaparte's France, and a strange house belonging to a resentful Breton lady, and an uncertain tomorrow. It was enough to make a stone weep, and she stared resolutely ahead to the village and its stone quay.

The carriage was old and worn, drawn by two horses as ancient as the old man holding the reins. But they went at a plodding pace through the white houses and eventually reached a wide plateau of moors sweeping over and around the hills.

Finally Miss Eliza asked the question Page could not bring herself to pose. "Will you stay with us here, my lord? I cannot think it wise for you to go about so openly. The Bretons may not be fond of Bonaparte, but his agents are surely in every corner of France."

He gave her a faint smile. "I've no doubt of it, ma'am." Then, in the same level voice, "I am returning to Spain to join Lord Wellington."

Miss Eliza, for the first time since Page had known her, looked somewhat taken aback.

"Then we are to remain here—" she hesitated, then finished quietly, "—indefinitely?"

"I'm afraid you have no choice. The *Caprice* will not be returning to America for some time, and Mason agrees with me that it would be unwise to obtain passage for you on another privateer at this time." His mouth had a grim look, as if he was not entirely reconciled to leaving them alone in France. But he said, "My orders were to report to his lordship as soon as possible, and I intend to go directly to Spain. How long it will be before I can return depends, of course, on the extent of his winter campaign."

Page was silent. The carriage creaked slowly along, and somewhere outside in the blinding sunlight a gull cried sharply.

"How will you go directly there?" Miss Eliza asked.

"I'll look for a smuggler who's had a lean year, and pay him to take me out to one of the British ships."

Miss Eliza said thoughtfully, "Will it be so easy to return?"

"It doesn't signify," he said briefly.

They continued on their way without speaking again. Page stared out at the passing landscape, but she was never afterwards to remember any of it, nor any of the introductions at Madame Gouret's beyond noting numbly that Madame was small and withered and leaned on a cane, and wore a towering white lace bonnet.

She said good-bye to Hazard on the steps, where the old-fashioned carriage waited to take him and Farley back to the village.

He bowed over Miss Eliza's hand and said, "I shall rely on you and Madame Gouret," straightening to give her a warm smile.

But when he turned to Page the smile faded.

"Keep yourself safe, sir," she managed unsteadily.

He took her hands in his, looking down at her with his eyes hidden and narrowed, and for a long moment he said nothing at all.

"Promise me," he said at last, "that you will wait for me here."

It was so ridiculous that she smiled. "You know very well that I have no choice in the matter."

The hard lines in his face broke up, and his gray eyes

laughed down at her. "But like your father," he said, "I have never learned to trust the French."

He swung into the carriage, which squeaked alarmingly, and Page stood on the steps and watched as it descended the hill on the narrow road, plainly in sight on the treeless moors until it had diminished into a small black beetle pursued by a cloud of dust.

Then it dropped down into the village and disappeared between two rows of white-washed houses, and the dust it had stirred up drifted lazily across the silent upland slopes and settled at last on the bracken and yellow gorse.

San Sebastian, a stout fortress perched on a great rock jutting four hundred feet out of the sea, had only recently fallen to Wellington's lengthy siege. Hazard, landing soon after the surrender, found the town occupied by the Fifth Division and immediately appropriated a decent mount from one of General Leith's staff officers.

Riding up through the mountains in a drizzling rain, he headed for the village of Vera on the upper Bidassoa, held by the Light Division against the French positions on heights across the river. Wellington was reputedly in the vicinity, although he was known to move his headquarters overnight and might presently be anywhere along the front from the coast to Roncesvalles in the east.

The army, as was its wont, had established itself snugly in the hills; Wellington's men, accustomed to snatching their comforts as they found them, always made the most of any bivouac, however brief. The French Marshal Soult's last big thrust through the passes had ended in defeat, with his center smashed, his flanks routed, and most of his supplies left hurriedly behind in the retreat. The river Bidassoa, rushing down to the sea between rocky gorges, was so full of dead Frenchmen that the stench was overpowering, mixed as it was with the pungent odor of the goat herds, avidly collected and cherished by every British regiment in that land long since ravaged clean by the French.

Hazard glanced at Farley, huddled on his saddle inside an ugly frieze coat that did not keep out the rain, and said, "Perhaps you would have done better to stay in France, my friend. It will get worse, I warn you, before it improves."

Farley immediately stiffened and sat straighter. "I trust I shall be able to survive any hardships that your lordship must endure."

"But I've been at it for some time," Hazard said, "while you were sleeping in your comfortable bed in London."

Farley said, with the first glimmer of amusement since they landed in Spain, "As to that, my lord, the time I've spent in various ship forecastles has done much to dim the memory of a comfortable bed."

Hazard laughed. "We fare well enough at head-quarters to have roofs over our heads most of the time, but I can't guarantee a bed or any degree of comfort. The fleas are legion in Spain, you know, and even Lord Wellington frequently tries to outwit them by sleeping on a table."

Farley was no longer as skeptical as he might once have been. The soldiers of the Peninsular army were so different from those in peacetime barracks in England that Farley had at first sight mistaken them for foreign troops. Their uniforms could hardly be called by that dignified name; with jackets so ragged and faded that no insignia of rank or regiment could be distinguished, breeches patched with any means at hand, and shakos bleached by weather and long wear, the general impression of Wellington's troops was one of a motley crew of undisciplined cutthroats.

But Farley, no fool, could see the unmistakable signs of a discipline so engrained that it needed no outward show to maintain it. Wellington's men might not be dandies in bright uniforms or march with a brisk military step, but despite their ragged clothes and slouching stride there was something in their hard sunburned faces and impudent wary eyes that spoke well for England's chances in the war.

"When Bonaparte is defeated, my lord," he asked, "will these same men be sent to fight the Americans?"

Hazard said soberly, "I should think so."

"Then I might venture to say that it will be over in short order, sir. If the French armies cannot withstand them, surely the Americans will be easily routed."

"But the Americans, as you should know by now, are not the same as Bonaparte's conscripts. And British armies, my friend, have already lost one war in America."

Hazard was as unsure as Wellington that an extensive land campaign in America would bring the war to a swift close. There were no concentrated objectives, no cities of any size to lay under siege, no Spanish guerrilleros to strike the enemy's rear, no constant stream of supplies from an England just over the Biscay Bay. Just as Bonaparte had been vanquished by the vast impenetrable steppes and cruel snows of Russia, so might England's armies overrun the entire American seaboard and still find victory an illusive will-o'-the-wisp.

"But Lord Wellington has never yet suffered a serious defeat, sir," Farley persisted.

"The men fight like tigers for him," Hazard said,

"but he has already said that he wants no part of an American campaign. And you seem to have forgotten that we have not yet defeated old Boney."

Not that he had any doubts that the thing would be done. Wellington had been hampered every step of the way by lack of money, incompetent officers, jealous politics at home, the unpredictable Portuguese and Spanish. But behind him now were the victories of Ciudad Rodrigo, Badajoz, Salamanca, Vittoria; and today his army looked down from the Pyrenees upon the broad plains of France.

Hazard had heard aboard the British seventy-four bringing him to Spain that a grateful Prince Regent had made Wellington a Field-Marshall; he grinned ruefully, certain that his lordship would pay no more heed to being a marquis than a mere baron. But he deserved the honors, just as his men deserved more praise than they would ever be likely to get from their country. They were tough, obscene, hardbitten troops who had endured four years of discomfort and dangerous campaigns in bitter-cold rains and blazing sun, in dirty vermin-ridden Portuguese villages and the hungry devastated plains of Spain, cheerfully unconcerned that their pay was usually in arrears, their clothes in tatters, and their stomachs not always full. Yet they had, as he told Farley, fought like tigers, not so much for their country as for their fierce pride in their corps and their serene faith in Old Crooked-Nose, as they affectionately termed their Commander-in-Chief. If Bonaparte's empire, wrought out of violence and pillage and the blood of millions, was beginning to totter, they deserved no small part of the credit.

The rain had stopped by the time they rode into Vera, crowded with the green-jacketed Rifles and scar-

let coats of the fifty-second Division. A laconic Rifle-
man told them that headquarters was, as late as the
night before, at Lesaca, four miles to the rear.

When Hazard finally dismounted in a muddy street
in Lesaca, a small town nestled in wooded hills, he
shrugged his shoulders to relieve the stiffness and said,
"If he's not here, we'll wait. I've no mind to chase him
all over the Pyrenees."

He ran up the steps of an old delapidated house
while Farley, sore and wet, patiently held the horses.
He did not feel entirely at ease. Although accustomed
to the clamor and incredible racket of London, he
found the noise of a foreign town, crowded with troopers and chattering natives and the inevitable hodge-
podge of camp followers, somewhat unnerving.

But he stood as straight as possible in the hampering
frieze coat, never moving when a squadron of jingling
dragoons went by him at the trot and spattered him
with mud, ignoring the vigorous cursing of a wagon
driver as his heavily-loaded vehicle foundered in the
slimy ruts, staring with cold dignity at a street vendor
shrilling some foreign babble under his nose.

The horses were army mounts and not disturbed by
the uproar, but Farley breathed a sigh of relief when
Hazard came back down the steps. He was surrounded
by several officers who pelted him with questions and
pounded him on the back at intervals, impeding his
progress with so much laughter and raillery that it was
some time before he reached the horses.

"My dear fellow, where the devil have you been?"

"Lazing about at home, I daresay, while we've been
marching and countermarching all over Spain, wearing
ourselves to the bone to whip the French for you."

Farley was obliged to admit that the officers did indeed look worn, their uniforms neat but faded, buttons

slightly tarnished, faces all thinned down to a lean brown leather.

But Hazard only grinned and retorted, "You look in better shape than the last time I saw you. What's the matter, has his lordship eased up on you at last?"

They all laughed, one of them remarking ruefully, "To be sure. We all get at least four hours sleep, one meal a day if we eat as fast as his lordship, and we seldom wear out more than two horses before night."

"How was America, Joss?"

"He doesn't have to answer that. Damn his eyes, have you ever seen anyone so well-fed and well-groomed?"

"Not since the Blues and Life Guards arrived, all pink and shining. Fitzroy took dispatches to them outside Vitorria, Joss, and was told politely that from the looks of Lord Wellington's A.D.C.'s it was past time the Household Cavalry came out to show us how to fight a proper war."

After the laughter died away Lord Fitzroy Somerset grinned. "It didn't take long," he said. "A few wet bivouacs and long marches, and a rearguard action or two."

"Rearguard?" Hazard said, raising a brow. "Are you still playing that old game of advancing and retreating? I had hoped matters might have improved, now that Soult is running for cover."

"Devil a bit," Lord March said cheerfully. "We've spent the last half month taking mountains and giving them back again."

Hazard laughed. "What about winter quarters? Are you staying here?"

"Who knows?" Somerset said. "The entire army is going to the devil, when all they ask is to go to France, and his lordship sits and scratches his nose and thinks."

"And curses his staff," Lord March added. "Thank God you're back, Hazard. He can look down his crooked nose at you for a change, and perhaps the rest of us will get a leave from his bad temper." He added thoughtfully, "I trust you brought him good news. If not, we shall immediately toss you into the Bidassoa and forget we ever saw your black face."

"Good and bad," Hazard said. "Where is he, by the way?"

"Out with de Burgh, galloping around to see if pickets are posted properly and all the Frogs on their side of the river."

Somerset said, with a look of cunning, "I'll wager a bottle of good claret I'll know if we're moving soon from the way Wellington greets you, Joss. If he's pleased to see you, it'll mean another campaign is on and he wants every man at hand. If he curses at the sight of you, it's winter quarters here and the devil take you for coming around to drink his lordship's wine and steal all the pretty girls from under his crooked nose."

They all shouted with laughter. "Speaking of wine," March said, "I suggest we throw a grand dinner to welcome the wanderer back to the fold. You furnish the wine, Fitzroy, and the best brandy you can find. I'll have my batman bring in enough mutton for the whole lot."

"Wine?" Hazard said, amused. "Brandy? Roast mutton? Lord, it's not the same army I left."

"We're only ten miles from France, old boy, and the Basques and the French peasants see no reason to make life more uncomfortable than necessary. But if you're above dining on smuggled sheep, you've only to say the word."

Someone made a rude sound. "If I remember correctly, it was Hazard who stole two scrawny hens from

Pakenham's cook just before Salamanca, which put him in such a rage that he carried the day for us."

"Joss, have you a uniform?" Somerset asked. "I saw Cotton this morning, and if there's to be a banquet you can depend upon it that he'll turn up."

"I had hoped him at the other end of Spain," Hazard said ruefully. Stapleton Cotton, the elegant cavalry commander, was always a vision of splendor, and despite Hazard's service with Wellington, who cared nothing for uniforms, could not be persuaded that a cavalry officer had any higher duty than swanking about in a smart pelisse, his accoutrements always shining and his helmet at precisely the most dashing angle. "I left my uniforms in London."

"Cotton's a damned fine officer," Somerset said, "but I pity his batman. One engagement and the whole lot has to be scrubbed and polished again. He brought a wagon-load of new uniforms from London in the summer, however, and if you like I'll do a bit of pilfering for you." Then, while the others went toward their horses, Somerset stepped closer to Hazard and said quietly, "Did it go well, Joss? Any trouble with the Yankees?"

"None to speak of."

"I hope your report will help matters. Wellington has had a devil of a time with Lord Bathurst, you know. The eminent Secretary of State for War and the Colonies seems to think Wellington the only military adviser available to the government, and pesters him with the most tiresome details."

"I didn't think Bathurst capable of so much perception."

"I daresay it's an honor," Somerset said dubiously, "but his lordship considers it a damned nuisance. They're at him about Canada now, and with no maps or reliable information he's expected to draw up a magnificent plan of defense and attack. Damn it all, you'd think they'd allow him to finish one war before starting on another."

"Unfortunately," Hazard said, "the Americans won't wait."

"Well, I trust you spied out enough information to help him with his correspondence with old Bathurst."

Hazard said idly, "Don't throw that word around so lightly, Fitzroy."

Somerset smiled. "That's right, I had forgotten. You were only visiting dear Louisa. How is she, by the way?"

"Quite well, thank you, but determined to remain in Virginia."

Farley, thinking with pleasure of seeing the master in a dashing hussar uniform again, saw two riders approaching and wondered if he should warn the master that it might be the great Field-Marshall himself. But one of the men was obviously too young, and the other could not be anyone of consequence. He was a cheerful-looking red-faced gentleman in a cocked hat, dressed plainly in a neat blue coat and pale pantaloons. As he rode up he spoke affably to a group of Riflemen passing by, laughed heartily at something his companion said, and dismounted to tie his big brute of a bay to a post with all the air of one accustomed to doing things for himself.

But then Farley noticed the splendid high-boned nose, and saw the tall gentleman coming toward the master with outstretched hand.

"I wonder," Fitzroy Somerset murmured softly, "if I have won myself a bottle of claret."

"By God, I'm damned glad to see you, Hazard," said Lord Wellington in a loud blunt voice.

13

···—◆◉◆—···

The first month in France passed slowly for Page. The second dragged unbearably. The third, with Christmas fast approaching, was so dark and dreary that Page, struggling to hide from Miss Eliza the depth of her hopelessness, found herself beyond even the comfort of tears and lay awake at night staring with wide dry eyes into the lonely darkness.

At first it had been pleasant to sit beneath an ancient apple tree in Madame Gouret's walled garden, enveloped in the utter quiet of a world seemingly forgotten by time.

The bright September sunlight dazzled on the old white-washed granite walls of the house and lay on the grass in pools as yellow as Breton butter, and the *mouettes* flew up from the bay to perch on the steeply-pitched slate roof like white sentinels watching for ships far out on the horizon. The smell of herbs from the kitchen garden spiced the air and mingled with the delectable smell of fresh bread, drifting out of the house in early morning when Marie-Thérèse did her daily baking.

Marie-Thérèse was a girl from the village with bright dark eyes like currents in a pudding and a clean round face beneath her tall white lace *coiffe*. She was Madame

Gouret's only servant, other than the ancient old man who drove the carriage and took care of the garden, and at first she regarded Miss Eliza and Page with silent suspicion. But after they made a valiant effort with their schoolbook French, at its best no match for the Breton tongue, Marie-Thérèse laughed at their struggles and unbent enough to teach them several Breton words. The lesson was adequate for no more than the briefest of exchanges, and for some time they communicated in a sort of pidgin language that served, with much Gallic gesturing, to make clear the most essential matters of daily living.

Page was not allowed to go into the village, and few people passed by Madame Gouret's gate. The house, like most Breton homes, sat square and uncompromising in its plot of land, but it was larger than most country houses and screened from the road by a gloomy stand of dark pines.

Isolated as it was, there was a sense of timeless security and peace about the house and garden, as if Bonapartes and kings and wars could come and go and never disturb the sun-drenched tranquility; and Madame Gouret herself, always gracious, endlessly courteous, offered a generous hospitality that never faltered. She was quite frail and spent many days in her bed-chamber; but on her good days, when she came downstairs to sit with them in the stiff parlor with its heavy dark furniture, she never gave a sign that her heart was heavy with grief and bitter resentment, nor spoke of the three sons who had died for the Emperor.

Marie-Thérèse was not so reserved. "She says one died at Trafalgar," Page told Miss Eliza. "He was an officer aboard the French seventy-four *Intrepide*, which burned after it was taken." After a moment she went on quietly, "Madame's second son died in a cavalry charge

202

at Austerlitz. The third, her youngest, was conscripted for Bonaparte's march to Russia, and died in the retreat."

Miss Eliza, head bent over her embroidery, sighed. But there were no conventional words to fit a tragedy of such magnitude, doubtless repeated in homes the length of France, and neither of them spoke of it again.

September blew out in a wild gale that swept up from the bay with a foretaste of winter to rattle the shutters and stream in wet gray torrents down the narrow window panes.

Marie-Thérèse built fires in all the fireplaces against the cold draughts, and the firelight gleamed on polished wood and pewter and flickered uneasily over the three small portraits framed in silver on the wall. One, a young man dressed in a green uniform with a crimson sash, looked down over Page's shoulder as she sat by the fire, and some trick of the candles and firelight caught in the painter's brushstrokes and brought them to life, putting a smile in the dark eyes and a twist to the mouth so that it sometimes seemed on the very edge of speaking. With the wind howling about the chimneys and the shutters banging as if a rude hand outside in the stormy night demanded admittance, Page was not entirely sure that the young man in the portrait did not actually speak, once or twice. It gave her an uncanny sensation that prickled along her spine, and she was very glad when the gale blew itself out in the hills and the sun reappeared, pale and watery but dispensing, in that thrifty Breton household, with the need for fires.

The road before the house was always empty except on the Sabbath. Then the country people walked down to the village church, the women wearing their best dark gowns trimmed in velvet and covered with gay aprons, and elaborate starched *coiffes* of the most intricately fashioned white lace, while the old men walked proudly in yellow waistcoats and flat black hats dangling with ribbons.

But in October the road was filled from morning until night with creaking carts piled high with apples, wine-dark and crimson and tawny and butter-yellow. The whole countryside smelled of apples and cider, so sweet and tangy under the crush of the presses that one could feel intoxicated merely from breathing; and in the garden Page sat on the grass and ate her fill of apples and yellow cheese and crusty bread with such happy gusto that Marie-Thérèse, who loved an appreciative appetite, baked her a panful of delicate meringues, laced with heavy cream, flavored with apple, and dusted lightly with spice.

"You'll be fat as a pig in no time at all," Miss Eliza said, "and his lordship will never recognize you."

Page looked at her with her eyes slanted and thoughtful. "Do you really think he'll come back?" she asked curiously. "At times I have an odd presentment that he has disappeared entirely, as if he had never existed, and we shall be left here forever."

"Nonsense," Miss Eliza said briskly. "He will come when he can, depend upon it, and when he does he will see us off to America."

Page wished she could share Miss Eliza's confidence. At times she missed him so dreadfully that the serenity of Madame Gouret's garden closed about her like a prison. Hazard's return meant no more to the quiet Breton country folk than his departure. If he never came back they would go on fishing, tending sheep, pressing their cider, donning their best clothes on the Sabbath and the Saints' days, hiding their sorrows behind quiet resigned faces. The stormy tears soaking a pillow, the warm surging blood, the fierce despair and fears and hopes, the desperate protest that one was still alive and young and waiting—what did these foolish things matter, in the end, against the slow march of time? The sun would blaze on the white-washed houses, as it had always done, and the gales continue to blow in from the sea, the winter rain would still stream endlessly down the wavy window panes, and in the neat parlors the portraits of young men in uniform would flicker in the firelight long after all the wars and emperors and wayward passions had been forgotten.

Before October was gone the weather turned cold and wet. The wind blew unceasingly, the clouds rolled over the moors in great shaggy herds, almost touching the chimney tops, and the slow rain dripped from eaves and trees, chilling the soul and aching in old bones.

"If it is this damp in Spain," Miss Eliza remarked, "the army will surely be bogged down for the winter."

Page gave her a startled glance. "All winter?" she asked.

"If Wellington cannot advance, love, he might be willing to spare one of his staff. I do not wish for his campaign to be halted, of course, but if nature stops his army it cannot be unpatriotic to rejoice a little in strictest privacy."

After that, Page, who was not obliged to be patriotic for English armies, regarded the miserable weather with a more favorable eye. But they heard no news from the south, and in November the sun came out unexpectedly and they had a fine bright spell. The roads hardened again and the air was crisp and brilliant, and on the moors the bracken was silvery with autumn and the gorse still tipped with yellow.

One morning two wounded veterans hobbled slowly down the road, feet wrapped in rags and dirty bandages covering their unhealed sores, and were grateful to stop at the gate while Marie-Thérèse and Page brought them cider and bread and cheese. In blank flat voices they spoke of a great battle at Leipzig in Germany, where Bonaparte had retreated before the Russians and Austrians and Prussians in an utter rout that left eighty thousand of his Imperial Army dead on the field. Those who escaped across the river Elater were ridden with typhus and rotting wounds, and in the mud and rain more thousands had dropped by the wayside.

The soldiers seemed dazed and confused, and Page silently refilled their cups with cider, not having a heart to plague them with more questions.

But as they started down the road again Marie-Thérèse glanced at Page's face and called after them, "What have you heard of the armies in the south?"

One man shook his head. The other said, "There's a rumor that the British have crossed over into France. But the mountains are high, I've heard, and new conscripts were marching south all along the road from Paris."

He did not seem to care about the war in the south, and went on his way without saying more.

"I am sorry," Marie-Thérèse said. "Spain is a long way distant, and even if he were as close as Rennes it would be hard to get news of him in Finistère." When Page said nothing Marie-Thérèse said slyly, "I saw him, you know, when he first came to talk to Madame. You are lucky to have a man like that to wait for." She looked after the veterans and sighed. "The only two men below fifty I've seen in a year, and neither of them in one piece. I begin to think I will never marry."

Page smiled. "It would be a pity if such a good cook were to be wasted." She added softly, "The war will end one day, Marie-Thérèse."

But Marie-Thérèse, with a sober Breton practicality, said flatly, "There will be no young men left. They'll be dead, like those eighty thousand at Leipzig, and all over France there will be as many women who will lie alone the rest of their lives."

They walked back to the house in silence, the dark pines around them dripping mournfully as the rain began again.

With winter finally upon them the house settled into the monotonous routine of indoor living. The dreary days dragged into December, the fires sizzled beneath wet chimneys, bed linen and clothes felt damp to the touch, and from the windows one saw only a desolate black-and-gray landscape. Meals were sparse, despite Marie-Thérèse's struggles to vary the standard diet of fish, and fresh milk and butter became a thing of the past when Madame Gouret's only cow sickened and died.

When he heard the news, the old gardener shook his head sadly. Not long before someone had left the gate open and the cow had wandered across the moors; the gardener explained to Page, in an uneasy voice, that the black stones on the moors were possessed of evil spirits that walked at night, holding wild revels in the dark with creatures that never saw the light of day, and no Breton dared touch them on peril of being eternally haunted. Madame Gouret's cow, the old man whispered, had surely fallen into evil hands and died of an evil curse.

Page was amused at the thought of a haunted cow, but she doubted if anyone could live in the dark granite land of Finistère, washed by wild seas and gray mists, littered by strange pagan stones leaning up against the rain, and not be conscious of ghosts and werewolves and frightening creatures that walked the night. The Breton coast of sunshine and blue water had long since disappeared, and like Lord Hazard, seemed never to have existed except in a fantasy of her mind.

Miss Eliza, however, appeared unaffected by the gloomy atmosphere. She did not chafe at the dreary rain, the endless days of waiting, or the uncertainty of her future; and if she questioned the wisdom of her decision to leave her sister and the colorful warmth of Bermuda, she never once betrayed anything but a tranquil acceptance of her circumstances.

"I feel quite guilty," Page said, "when I consider that you left your family and friends because of me, and now must endure so much unpleasantness half-way across the world from home."

Miss Eliza smiled. "But it would not be very pleasant for me in St. George's Town," she said, "if I knew you were here in France alone and friendless." After a moment she added, "As for a family and home, I'm not sure how one measures such commodities. I have a number of relatives in England, all of whom were greatly delighted to see me off to Bermuda. And Charlotte, it is true, kindly offered me a home for life. But when one is a maiden lady with a negligible fortune, it is sometimes difficult to know precisely where one belongs."

"Would you have come with me," Page asked slowly, "even if Lord Hazard had not engaged your services?"

"Yes," Miss Eliza said gently. "He knew that, but he did not care to take advantage of my weakness. So I left Bermuda with my pride intact and my purse filled, and I have not yet had reason to regret the bargain I made with his lordship."

No, Page reflected honestly, Hazard was not a man to take an unfair advantage of one's weaknesses. But the advantage was his, fair or not, when a weakness had its inception in the very fact of his existence.

By the end of January Page's life was ruled by boredom and the increasing discomfort of living in a chilly wet climate with no warmer clothing than that designed for the hot sun of Bermuda. Miss Eliza fared better, her gowns being less fashionable but far more comfortable; her trunks also yielded a number of warm shawls more cherished than pieces of gold and generously shared by Miss Eliza with all the women in the household.

Page, shivering and blue with cold in her thin muslins, was finally persuaded to try one of Marie-Thérèse's warm black gowns, and she was wearing it one February day when Marie-Thérèse called her downstairs and she walked unsuspectingly into the parlor to find Daniel Mason and Duncan MacDougall waiting for her there.

For a long moment she could not speak at all. Quick tears burned her eyes, and she stood silently in the door, a small woebegone figure in black, wiping her eyes childishly with the back of her hand.

Mason's laughter was the most marvelous and cheerful sound she had heard in long dreary months.

"Lord, are you in mourning?" He caught her hands and held them tightly. "I've never seen such a forlorn sight. Dry your eyes, Miss Bradley, I've brought you a nasty-tempered Scotsman to keep you company. He's somewhat the worse for wear at the moment, but I'm sure you'll make a better nurse than the *Caprice's* carpenter."

She whirled to MacDougall with a gasp of dismay. He looked pale and disheveled, and beneath his heavy seaman's coat she could see the bulk of bandages.

"I'm not bad enough to be nursed," he said with a

wide reassuring smile. "I'm no good to the ship, but it's a clean cut and a week or two will see it healed."

"Oh, Mac," Page said on a long sigh, "I'm so glad to see you." She added anxiously, "Hadn't you better sit down?"

"Leave him be for a minute," Mason said. "I haven't long to visit. The *Caprice* is anchored below the town, and it'll be the devil to pay if some long-nosed English captain decides to take a look in the bay. Tell me how you've fared, and what your plans are. Where the devil is Hazard? Have you heard from him?"

She shook her head. "Not since the day he left us here."

Mason's strange tawny eyes were alert on her face. "The British army has had a busy time of it this winter," he said slowly. "We hear in L'Orient that Wellington has pushed the French back to Bayonne. It's not so far in terms of kilometers, but a major victory for the British to be fighting on French soil."

Page tried to place Bayonne, but the name meant nothing to her. "At this rate," she said bleakly, "they may take years to reach Paris."

He smiled. "That doesn't sound like a good Yankee. Do you want the British to keep winning battles?"

She was silent. Then, with a quiet desperation, she said, "I cannot stay here forever. Do you know of any ships in L'Orient that will soon be sailing for America?"

Mason put his arms across the back of one of Madame Gouret's high-backed chairs and studied Page thoughtfully. "He is probably safe and well, you know. It can't be easy for him to send word, communications being what they are, and if Wellington has kept him busy he couldn't possibly arrange a leave before now."

Page held his eyes steadily. But her voice was no

more than a whisper. "If anything happened to him, I would never know."

"Nothing has happened to him," Mason said shortly, "and if I know his lordship, nothing will." Then he added, "A few ships will be sailing for home shortly, but I'd not trust you to any of them. The British have increased their warships on the Atlantic stations, and they're thick as flies in Biscay Bay and the Channel."

"Do you plan to stay here indefinitely?"

"So long as the prizes hold out. Look, if you've had no word before I'm ready to take the *Caprice* back to America, I promise I'll take you with me. But give him a good margin of time, Miss Bradley. He won't think better of me for snatching you away while he's off fighting his war."

"Do you care what he thinks of you?" she asked, low.

"Yes," he said levelly. "Don't you?"

But he gave her no time to answer. He had to get back to his ship, he said, and before she knew what he was about he had kissed her soundly, told MacDougall to send him word at L'Orient when he was well enough to rejoin the crew, and was gone, the door slamming behind him as if a boisterous wind had passed by.

Madame Gouret's household settled back into its quiet winter solitude. But with MacDougall there the atmosphere was less oppressively feminine, and even the old gardener came into the kitchen at night to hear MacDougall tell, in his blunt Scots voice, the exciting saga of the *Caprice* and her master, Daniel Mason.

Page, her eyes sparkling, listened with a fierce hot pride. The little schooner, beating down the sea lanes, had taken ten prizes and sold them in L'Orient for more than half a million dollars. She had ranged the Channel, the Bay of Biscay, the coasts of Ireland and

England, and although it was rumored that an entire squadron of British ships were sent out to hunt her down, Mason had thus far brought her off safely from every danger.

"But I don't mind admitting it was a close thing once or twice," MacDougall said. "With another captain we'd never have made it, and like as not I'd be in Dartmoor prison now, or rotting in the Plymouth hulks."

Marie-Thérèse gave an exclamation of horror and immediately prepared him a posset of hot cider and spice. She nursed him tenderly and cosseted him outrageously, and her kitchen soon became the center of the house, with MacDougall enthroned in comfort beside the fire and Marie-Thérèse's laughter as bright as the copper pots she so zealously scrubbed every day.

March was wet and cold, with spring seeming a million dismal years away. There were more veterans returning to Finistère, telling of hordes of deserters from the Imperial armies streaming toward a stunned Paris, and Cossack patrols seen at Fontainebleau. The Allied armies, it was rumored, had close to a million men within the borders of France. They were closing in for the kill while Bonaparte, it was said by some who had been near his headquarters, ordered his regiments about as if they were at full strength, planned great campaigns with troops and officers long since dead, and screamed in a fury of winning back every inch of his vanished empire.

But of Wellington's forces in the south there was no news at all.

Page was very quiet and subdued those first days of April. She had grown quite thin, and the golden tan acquired in the long weeks aboard the *Caprice* faded to a pale translucent ivory. On mild days she often wrapped herself in a warm shawl and walked in the garden, gazing down silently at the wide empty bay.

The sun finally came out, weak and timid. The moors began to turn green, showered with wildflowers like small yellow stars, and in a sheltered corner of the garden a tiny mimosa tree threw a delicate lacy shadow against the house. But Easter turned wet and foggy again, and one chilly night when Page blew out her candle and climbed into bed with a warming pan, she felt a great admiration for the Breton strength of character that could endure such a wretched climate.

The rain had stopped before dark and was now only a thin wispy fog, and through the window Page could see the garden below, bathed in a pale light when the moon broke through, the trees half hidden in mist that floated eerily over the garden walls from the dark moors. It was surely a night for goblins and ghosts, and spirits that wandered the dark earth like the tattered uneasy mists; and Page, shivering a little, pulled the bedclothes about her ears and closed her eyes.

She was almost asleep when she heard the knock on the door, loud and imperative in the silent night. It was immediately repeated, echoing harshly through the house, and Page threw the covers back and lit her candle. Poor Marie-Thérèse, she thought, would think the devil himself on the step, for no respectable Breton dared to venture out at night or knock so arrogantly at lonely houses on the moor.

The noise ceased abruptly; someone, then, had found the courage to go to the door. She heard a faint squeaking on the stairs and steps outside her door, and could not resist the curious impulse to see what was happening.

Opening her door, she came face to face with

Madame Gouret, one hand on her cane and the other holding a wavering candle.

"Don't fear, child, all is well," she said in her frail voice as light and dry as the rustle of autumn leaves. She gave Page a hauntingly sweet smile. "My house and I know too well the sound of sorrow knocking at the door. But tonight the news is good, and we are both happy for you."

She patted Page gently on the cheek and went into her bedchamber. Page, her eyes wide and disbelieving, went slowly down the narrow stairs as they curved against the wall. She paused, half way down, and looked below into a blaze of candles.

The small hall was crowded with people, but she saw only Hazard.

Big, dark, assured, he filled the hall to overflowing. His caped greatcoat and his boots were heavily mud-splattered, and his hair and face glistened wetly with pearled drops of mist. He looked tanned and grim and hard as nails, and his eyes were frowning and tired.

She took another step, and he glanced up to see her standing on the stairs, one hand on the wall as if she needed the support.

His face changed swiftly. With one long stride he reached the bottom of the steps and looked up at her; and for a brief instant she met the gray eyes and saw the hard mouth curve into a smile so brilliant it took her breath away.

Then she was running down the steps and his arms reached up for her. He lifted her in the air and swung her around above his head, and when her feet touched the floor again he was holding her tightly and her face was buried in one of the capes of his coat.

"You'll be drenched," he said, his voice warm with laughter. "I brought most of the fog inside with me."

She didn't care a fig that she was wet, or that they were not alone, or that she was dressed in nothing but a flannel night shift.

Over her head his deep quiet voice said, "We don't have much time. I've a British frigate waiting out beyond the bay, and her captain advised me to be back aboard by dawn."

She lifted her head then, staring at him with a despair that shook her with its hopelessness. But he looked very pleased with himself, with the world, with Page Bradley in his arms.

"Paris has fallen," he said, and his smile blazed into little dancing lights in his gray eyes. "Napoleon has abdicated."

The hall was silent. No one spoke, or even seemed to breathe, until Marie-Thérèse gave a long unsteady sigh.

"We're sailing for England," Hazard said, "and you needn't say you won't go. My orders were given me by the Marquis of Wellington, and I stand the risk of court-martial if they aren't obeyed."

They all stared at him: Miss Eliza in her wrapper and night cap looking as pleased as if she had known all along it would be this way; the ancient gardener muttering, "England," as if it were a dark place haunted by more evil goblins than those that stalked the lonely Finistère moors; Marie-Thérèse, button-black eyes shining with excitement; and MacDougall, frowning, his eyes going from Hazard to Marie-Thérèse.

They all began to speak at once, their words running together in a little babble of confusion.

But Page, struck dumb by the familiar dizzying sensation of his nearness and his presumptuous way of sweeping everything before him with the force of a tidal wave, looked at him with slanted blue eyes and said nothing at all.

14

They landed in Portsmouth after a foggy Channel crossing that delayed them an extra day, and went immediately to the George Inn on the quayside, where Hazard left Page and Miss Eliza in Farley's care while he went off to hire a post-chaise-and-four to take them up to London.

MacDougall, at the last minute, had refused to come with them. "I've lost nothing in England," he said brusquely. "It suits me better to stay here and go off with the *Caprice* when I can. My arm's healed now, and when Mason comes back into L'Orient I'll join him there." Then he regarded Hazard with a searching scrutiny. "Can I trust you to do your best by her? In the fix she's in there's no denying you can do more for her than any of us."

"You may rest assured that I will take the best care of her," Hazard said in his cool amused way.

Page was not displeased. The *Caprice* was a happier choice for MacDougall than London, and he was very proud of his service on the privateer. But she could not understand the awkward apologetic smile he gave her until she took a second thoughtful look at Marie-Thérèse's round happy face.

Delighted, she said to Miss Eliza, "I hope I may be there to see Papa's face if Mac brings home a French demoiselle." After a moment's reflection she added, "I dare say a single one of her meals would change Papa's whole attitude toward the French. Only think what a regiment of Marie-Thérèses would have done for Bonaparte."

"I sadly regret," Miss Eliza said, "that I cannot do as much for England."

Page's first sight of England, however, was not in the least terrifying. The inn was crowded with naval officers with cocked hats and boisterous voices, but there was nothing menacing in the inn parlor with its cheerful coal fire, its red curtains, and its placid air of substantial comfort.

Everyone in Portsmouth seemed overjoyed, if not actually stunned, that victory was at hand after twenty long years of fighting the French; and the very sight of Hazard's uniform, worn and faded under his greatcoat, was enough to set off the most amazing demonstrations of cheerful affection. The landlord showed them an enormous deference, referring constantly to "my lord," and while Page privately considered Hazard's arrogance the inevitable result of such toad-eating, she had to admit that he never appeared to show such arrogance to grooms or servants or landlords.

She had not seen him alone for a single moment, and was not entirely sure that she wanted to. It was craven, she knew, to stay so close by Miss Eliza, but self-preservation demanded it, as well as pride.

Miss Eliza was not deceived. "Don't you think you're overdoing it, love? You can't expect his lordship to think you so eager for my company after such a long tiresome winter of it."

Page, standing by the fire in the George's parlor,

wished with some desperation that Miss Eliza, for once, would be both unimaginative and blind.

"I don't expect anything of him," she said carefully. "He likes to order people about, you know, and he thinks himself responsible for me." She added pensively, "He can also be very kind when he wishes to be."

"All those things are certainly true," said Miss Eliza, "but I would like very much to hear his lordship's reaction to such raving compliments."

Page said in a bleak little voice, "You must know how difficult it is for me."

"But he has done everything he could," Miss Eliza pointed out gently, "to keep matters from being difficult for you."

Page was silent. How could she explain the inexplicable, or put into words the cowardly but instinctive desire to retreat before certain and irrevocable disaster?

But Miss Eliza relented. "In any case," she said lightly, "I hope you will enjoy your visit to London. There is nothing more distressingly English than England, I'm afraid, but the city is something quite out of the ordinary way. We are fortunate to be staying with the Trevors. Their town house is in Grosvenor Square, and I assure you, love, that the beds will be quite comfortable."

Page smiled, as she was expected to do, but she was not cheered by the mention of Hazard's family. Miss Eliza, the respectable daughter of a Devonshire clergyman, could expect an amiable welcome; but no one with the least knowledge of English self-consequence would expect the Trevors to feel anything but a haughty disdain for a plain miss from America who had suffered such amazing misadventures.

But there was no delaying the event. Hazard, having

dispatches to deliver, was in a hurry to be off, and they set out for London in the bright sunlight. The chaise was well-sprung and the horses fresh, but Page was not entirely comfortable. Hazard, sitting opposite her, was his usual remote self, but whenever she raised her eyes his were there to meet them, a lurking smile in their clear depths; and while he was as affable and attentive to Miss Eliza as always, he seemed content to watch Page with a silent amusement that came close to unnerving her.

But the passing scenery soon caught her interest and she forgot him, sitting on the edge of her seat to look at England outside the chaise window.

It was a beautiful England, as sleek and prosperous and flawlessly fashioned as an enameled miniature. There were no beggars, no tattered veterans with festering wounds, no faces thin and pale with hunger; even the people in the fields looked well-fed and well-dressed. The chaise rolled past pastures with fat sheep and cattle, well-stocked farms and lush green fields, villages with geese and rosy-cheeked children and gardens in equal abundance; past buttercup meadows, wooded hills, thatched cottages smothered in spring flowers, and elegant country houses set among trees and wide lawns.

At a turnpike toll house they passed a top-heavy London coach blowing up for the gate, its fat redfaced coachman dressed in a bright green coat, a red waistcoat, and a yellow hat. In a small village with whitewashed brick houses and an ancient gray church, a girl in a smart Polish riding habit and her escort in high beaver and spotless boots waited impatiently for the chaise to pass; beyond, in the rolling countryside, a yellow curricle flashed past them, driven by a young gentleman with a supercilious nose and a groom in yellow livery to match the carriage.

Page leaned out to get a better look at such elegance, sneezed hugely in the cloud of dust, and was pulled back by Miss Eliza.

"Never mind," Hazard said. "When we get to London I'll take you driving in the Park in my perch-phaeton."

Page remembered too late that she had resolved not to gape at everything like some ignorant hayseed. But Hazard was smiling at her, and when he asked her, "What do you think of England?" she could not pretend a languid indifference.

"I think it charming," she said honestly. "It would be narrow and intolerant of me, after all, to dislike it simply because it is English."

His smile deepened. "I knew I could depend on you," he said gently, "to be neither of those disagreeable things."

Page bit her lip and turned back to the window. They stopped only once, to dine in a neat inn beside the road, but it was well after dark before they reached the outskirts of the city and Page saw very little of London that first night save wide streets with row after row of neat brick houses, and a confusion of carriages and people and oil lamps and noise that indicated no one ever went to bed in the city.

The carriage drew up at last before an imposing mansion; inside all was a blur of glittering lights and marble, and a great staircase rising above a hall full of doorways. Page, somewhat overwhelmed by the number of liveried footmen appearing out of nowhere, watched the butler's stiff dignified face break into a smile as he murmured, "May I say, my lord, that we are exceedingly glad to have you back?"

"Thank you, Sutton. How is her ladyship?"

The butler waved aside a footman and took Hazard's coat himself. "Quite well, sir."

Then a shriek echoed in the hall and a girl's voice cried, "Mama, it's Joss!"

There was a sudden babble of voices, and more shrieks, and a great rush of skirts on the staircase and Hazard was completely enveloped in a froth of ruffles and curls and laughter. The prodigal son, Page thought, feeling very alone in the center of the vast marble hall with Miss Eliza somewhere behind her and Farley disappeared out of sight.

A calm voice broke through the storm of greetings. "Anna, Sophie, do come away and give him a chance to catch his breath."

A tall dark-haired lady in a lace cap and flowing gown came across the hall, smiling happily as Hazard kissed her on the cheek.

"Jocelyn, is it really true? We heard the news about Bonaparte, of course, and then I had your letter, but it seems too marvelous to believe." She held his shoulders a moment longer, as if hating to let go of him. "You look tired," she said, searching his face, "but smug as a cat with feathers on his face."

Hazard laughed and kissed her again. "I've reason enough," he said lightly.

"Bonaparte's downfall, I daresay," Lady Hazard said with amusement, and turned to greet Miss Eliza. Then Page, trying not to dread her turn, felt Lady Hazard's cool lips against her cheek for a brief moment, and an affectionate arm around her shoulders.

"My dear, we are delighted to have you with us. If Jocelyn made the journey to town in one stage, a piece of nonsense very like him, I'm sure you must be wretchedly tired, and in no mood for introductions.

These are Jocelyn's sisters, Anna and Sophie, but they will have to wait until morning to talk to you." She took Page's hand and led her gently to the stairs. "Come along and I'll show you to your room, and the housekeeper will bring you and Miss Wyndham a tray of food and some hot tea."

The quiet soft voice flowed on with no apparent purpose, yet footmen began to move with alacrity, the butler sailed majestically off toward the back of the house, and Hazard, with a sister on each arm, grinned at Page and disappeared into a booklined room off the hall.

"They won't forgive me for snatching you away, but they've been so impatient for your arrival that I fancy they'd exhaust you in five minutes. They think you a most exciting heroine, you know, and were quite exasperated with their brother for keeping you in France all this long while."

So much, Page reflected with a dazed disbelief, for the stiff and haughty Trevors who would greet her with arrogant disdain.

"I'm convinced that Jocelyn has not taken as good care of you as he should," said Lady Hazard. "But we have you safely with us now, and intend to keep you as long as we can."

Page opened her eyes the next morning to a majestic canopy of silken hangings suspended from the claws of a large gilt eagle. The bedroom was a splendid apartment in crimson and blue, with satinwood furniture and delicate French paper reminding Page of Aunt Hester Carroll's drawing room in Washington. A few minutes earlier a cheerful maid had brought a brass hot water can, lighted a fire in the black marble grate, left a cup of steaming chocolate on the table, and ventured the information that breakfast was being served in the morning room.

Propped against the pillows, Page sipped the chocolate with a shameless pleasure in such indolent luxury. When she finished she rolled over on her stomach and rested her chin in her hands, contemplating the situation with an odd little smile, but she gave it up at last, if only because she knew the folly of trying to outguess her host.

She dressed quickly and started downstairs, meeting Miss Eliza in the hall, and they were obliged to ask directions of a footman before they finally found their way to the morning room, a sunny parlor at the back of the house overlooking a formal garden.

Lady Hazard greeted them cordially and said, "I do hope you rested well." She had clear gray eyes, Page noticed, and a way of smiling with so much friendly warmth that one could not long stand in awe of her. "Jocelyn has gone off to deliver his dispatches to Lord Bathurst, but he will be back presently. In any case, Anna and Sophie have planned to drive you about the city, and he would be very much in the way."

Anna was a young lady of nearly seventeen years who wore a plain round-necked dress hinting of governesses and schoolrooms and was still in the awkward stage of being all legs and feet. But she had the Trevor gray eyes, clear and candid, and her face lit up like a candle whenever she flashed her brilliant smile. Sophie, the eldest by two years, was very fashionable and smart, with elegantly-coiffed black curls and a gown of embroidered cambric. She had an enchanting gurgle of laughter and an impetuous way of speaking that endeared her to Page at once. Henry, the youngest Trevor son, was a young man who affected a lavender waistcoat and monstrously padded coat, and obviously thought of himself as a dandy of the first order; but he put out his hand with a boyish eagerness and said, "I'm not much for sight-seeing, you understand, but let me know when you can't endure the girls another minute and I'll come rescue you."

"I don't know what you'd do to entertain her," Anna said.

"Take her for a drive in my phaeton," Henry said, "and show her off in the park." He grinned at Page. "I'll be a regular social lion with an American up beside me."

"Everyone will stare at you in any event," Sophie said pointedly, "in that atrocious waistcoat."

"It's the latest fashion," Henry protested. "You know nothing about style, Sophie, or you'd cut more of a dash yourself."

Sophie took exception to this insult instantly, but the argument was amiable and ended with victory on both sides when Henry remarked loftily that, waistcoat or not, he intended to do his share as a host to entertain Miss Bradley, and Sophie retorted that he had better not drive her as far as the corner until Joss had given his approval of the new phaeton, purchased while he was safely away in Spain and could not object.

Page, seeing the phaeton later when Henry left the house, was relieved that she was not sitting up beside him. It seemed as high as a second-floor window, perched at an absurd angle that might be quite sporting but looked exceedingly dangerous.

"He would like to be as dashing as Joss," Anna remarked fondly, "but I don't think he has the remotest chance."

"I suggested he should imitate Richard," Sophie said, and laughed, "but he only said that if he was ever foolish enough to marry another Frances Milbourne he didn't doubt he would be as long-faced as Richard in no time at all." She explained to Page, "Richard is another brother, who lives in the Dower House at Hazard and helps to administer the estates for Joss. He is a dear, but the soberest Trevor alive, and Frances is an earl's daughter and has such an air of consequence that there's no enduring her."

"We're so glad you're not like her," Anna confided happily. "We knew we must try to love anyone Joss brought home, but I don't mind saying we thought it would be dreadfully hard. He is such a special person, but of course you know that."

Sophie, with great tact, interrupted to say, "Run and find your gloves, Anna. Mama's carriage is at the door."

There were undoubtedly other ways of seeing London, but Page and Miss Eliza agreed that it was vastly pleasant to see it from Lady Hazard's elegant carriage with its splendid pair of chestnuts and its driver and groom liveried in green and gold.

Page was completely dazzled. London was dirty, crowded, noisy, enormously large, and glittering with color and people and excitement; with so much to see and hear she gaped like any green provincial and swiveled her head until it ached.

In Bond Street she saw luxurious shops and fashionable ladies in low-cut and high-waisted gowns and young gentlemen of such incredible elegance that she felt terribly dowdy; she saw fashionable Piccadilly, and so many phaetons and curricles and barouches that they seemed to skim the street like brilliant dragonflies; she gasped at a gorgeously uniformed troop of Household Cavalry clattering by, marveled at the splendid portico of Carlton House where the Prince Regent was presently in residence, and was greatly impressed by the plum-red and white brick mansions lining the wide London streets.

"This is only a part of the city," Miss Eliza said. "You must see Westminster Abbey, and the crown jewels at the Tower, and the palace at St. James's."

"And the Parthenon marbles at the British Museum," Anna said, "and the opera."

Sophie laughed. "It won't all be so dull. Mama will have a small ball to introduce you to our friends, first of all, and then you'll be invited everywhere. And Joss will surely take you to the theater, and to the pleasure gardens at Vauxhall."

Anna clapped her hands. "We must persuade him to have a river party, Sophie," she said eagerly, explaining to Page that such parties were quite the rage, with boats bedecked with gay awnings and flags, and bands playing, and suppers prepared by Gunter's. "I'm not allowed at balls yet, you see, but I'm sure Mama would permit me to join a party on the river."

The sisters chattered on happily about routs and masqued balls and dinner parties, while Miss Eliza smiled at their enthusiasm and Page was silent with a growing apprehension that matters were progressing much too rapidly for her to cope with.

When they returned to Grosvenor Square the butler informed Page that his lordship wished to see her in the library.

Sophie smiled and said at once, "We'll go on up to see Mama," and drew a protesting Anna away toward the stairs.

Then Sutton said, with a face so expressionless that it conveyed his disapproval quite plainly, "A young gentleman left a note for you, ma'am, and desired that I should see that you received it immediately upon your return."

Page stared at the letter extended in his hand, then shook her head. "He must have made a mistake. I know no one in London."

"He mentioned you by name, ma'am," Sutton said, "and added that you were the young lady from America. He also specified that I was not to mention the matter to anyone but you."

Page, a little bewildered, took the letter and glanced at Miss Eliza, who said with a firm dignity intended for Sutton, "I daresay all will be explained when you read it, my dear, and if a mistake has been made we will inform his lordship."

Sutton's face did not change, but he quite plainly felt that it would be best to allow his lordship to handle the affair. Bowing stiffly, he went off across the hall, and Page, too curious to wait until she was in her room, tore open the letter.

The message was scrawled hurriedly across the paper, with a careless blot of ink almost eradicating the signature.

"I saw you in Portsmouth, and wasn't at all surprised that Hazard contrived it at last. If you think you can escape his eagle eye for an hour or so, I'll be in Hyde Park today, not far from the gates, between five and six. Since I'll be promenading under false colors, I'd rather you didn't ask his lordship to join us. He might not feel obliged to turn me in, but I'm in no shape to face that right of his again."

She knew, even without the signature, that Daniel Mason had written it, and the smear of ink was probably deliberate.

She wondered if her face had gone as bloodless as it

felt. Meeting Miss Eliza's concerned eyes, she whispered, "Daniel Mason is in London."

"Then he is in trouble," Miss Eliza said quietly.

"Yes," Page said, "I'm quite sure of it. He wants me to meet him in Hyde Park this afternoon."

Miss Eliza said thoughtfully, "We can surely arrange it, but do you think it wise?"

Page put the letter in her reticule and walked toward the stairs with Miss Eliza. "I don't care if it's wise or not."

It was incredible to think of him being in London. Wondering what dire event had forced him to leave the *Caprice* and venture into a country whose authorities had placed an enormous price on his head, Page's imagination immediately furnished any number of calamities, all of the most disastrous nature.

"I've been waiting for you," Hazard said at her elbow, startling her so badly that she jumped. He raised a dark brow. "Did Sutton forget to tell you that I wanted to see you for a moment?"

Caught unawares, she could think of no excuse. "He told me," she said awkwardly, "but I forgot."

His eyes rested thoughtfully on her face, measuring, she knew, the short few minutes since she had spoken to Sutton.

"Miss Eliza and I have been viewing the sights of London," she said hastily. "It is quite impressive." She smiled at him, instinctively hoping to divert him. "We have nothing in America to compare with it. I imagine there are more people here than we can boast in the whole of Maryland."

"I am glad you found it interesting," he said politely, not in the least diverted.

He stood aside, waiting for her to precede him into the library. Miss Eliza went away up the stairs, and there was nothing to do but go meekly with him; she felt Mason's letter burning her reticule like a hot coal, and wished she had waited until later to read it.

"Please be seated, Miss Bradley."

He was quite as elegant, Page thought, as any of the Bond Street dandies she had seen. His gray coat was beautifully tailored to fit his big shoulders and had a high standing collar of velvet, and the pale yellow breeches fitted him as impeccably as a second skin. He looked the perfect gentleman in his proper setting of splendid mansion and liveried servants and fashionable London, and he had never seemed so unapproachable.

"I have two pieces of news for you," he said. "First, I understand from Lord Bathurst that your father has stirred Washington into protesting your abduction by a frigate captain. Kincaid, you will be pleased to know, has received a severe reprimand from the First Sea Lord."

Page smiled at the vision of Papa storming at Mr. Madison and the other distinguished Washington gentlemen as if they had nothing else to occupy their minds in the midst of a war. But it was staggering to think of lords and admirals concerning themselves with her misfortunes.

"I hope they did not blame Captain Stuart."

"I assured Lord Bathurst that I was responsible for Stuart's actions. He was absolved of blame at his court-martial, by the way, and has a new command." Hazard smiled faintly. "His ship has been stationed for some time with the patrolling squadron off Brest."

She said nothing, waiting for the other piece of news.

Hazard picked up a letter from the desk. "When I joined the army in Spain I took the liberty of writing to your father to assure him of your safety. My letter was obliged to go through official channels, along with the usual dispatches, and Mr. Bradley did not receive it until early spring."

"But he knew what had happened," Page said. "You sent a boy from Hampton."

"The message reached your father, unfortunately, in a slightly garbled form. He was told only that his daughter had been carried off forcibly by the British, and that a high-nosed lord had paid hard gold for her."

Page's eyes widened. "And he has thought that," she said, awed, "all this time?"

"I believe so," Hazard said. "Apparently my letter did not convince him of my good intentions."

For a moment she felt a great sympathy for poor Papa, who thought his daughter disgraced and ruined; but it was so ridiculous, when Hazard and Miss Eliza had guarded her honor with such zeal for all those long months, that she had to laugh.

Hazard smiled. "Yes, it is amusing. But not, I fear, to your father. Here is a note from him, sent from Washington through the American minister at St. Petersburg. Two American commissioners have been there to discuss a possible peace, with the Czar as an intermediary, and when they arrived in London they asked Bathurst's cooperation in locating you."

Page took the letter warily. It took some time to decipher Papa's elaborate penmanship, but no time at all to realize that Samuel Bradley had been torn between an explosive rage and a valiant effort to comfort his daughter in her adversity.

He did not like the situation at all, despite Lord Hazard's reassurances that Page was undisgraced and well, and she was to come home as soon as safe transportation might be arranged. The British were arrogant devils with a great deal to answer for, and Madison a bungling fool for allowing enemy ships to violate the

Chesapeake. Page had no business going to town with MacDougall, and her misfortunes served her properly; nonetheless he would personally take his whip to any man, British or otherwise, who dared to insult her. Hazard's horse was a beauty and he would like to buy it, but he had missed most of the autumn hunting by rushing back and forth to Washington; Bessie had been a trial, weeping and wailing, and for days after the sad event no meals had been cooked, the girls went around with long faces, and so many chattering fools came to call that one would think a funeral was in the offing. For Samuel Bradley's part, he hoped Page would remember that she was his dearly beloved daughter and he would leave no stone unturned to affect her return; and while Lord Hazard might think himself too high and mighty to be censured, Samuel Bradley would see to it that he answered for his behavior if he had to seek his lordship out in London.

Page looked up to find Hazard watching her with inscrutable eyes. "It sounds very like he means to call you out," she said, her eyes bright with laughter. "I'm afraid your letter failed to conciliate him."

"His anger is understandable," Hazard said. Then, still watching her, he went on, "Bayard and Gallatin are now in London, as I told you, and I feel certain they would be delighted to take you and Miss Eliza under their protection. They travel under diplomatic immunity, and would be safe, at any rate, from British ships."

The laughter drained away, leaving only a cold empty sobriety. After a moment she asked, "Will they be leaving for America soon?"

"They are waiting for some word from Lord Castlereagh at the Foreign Office, and I doubt if it will be forthcoming in the immediate future. But there are quite a few Americans in London, despite the war, and if you wish it I will ask the commissioners to arrange for you to spend the remainder of your time in London with some respectable American family."

She knew what she must say. There was no alternative, it was the only possible thing to say. But something inside her protested so fiercely and vehemently that she could only look at Hazard in a dismayed silence, unable to force herself to say it.

Then he went on evenly, "On the other hand, you may depend upon my promise to see you safely home. It might take me a few weeks to arrange it, but it should not be too difficult. If your father knew the circumstances, I don't think he would have any valid objections to your staying here with my family."

Surely, she thought desperately, he didn't mean for her to decide. He could not be so ungentlemanly as to force her to such an awkward and impossible choice.

"Before you decide," he said, "there is a matter or two we must settle between us."

He came closer by a few steps, moving lazily and without apparent motive; he was very big, very tall above her, his face dark and unsmiling. Involuntarily, she took a step backward.

"You have been avoiding me," he said.

She shook her head.

"When I came to Madame Gouret's," he said, "I flattered myself that you seemed glad to see me, and not displeased to come with me to London. Have you changed your mind since then?"

She shook her head again, retreating.

"Are you afraid to face the truth? It isn't like you to be a coward."

She found her voice at last. "You don't know anything about me."

A smile flickered in his eyes. "On the contrary," he said, "I know a great deal about you. But I am not yet certain which of my faults you find most disagreeable."

She was against the bookcase now; she could smell the faint scent of oil from the leather bindings. "This is ridiculous," she said with a desperate attempt at dignity, appalled at the thought of Sutton's face were he to enter the library and find her backed into a corner by his lordship. "You aren't behaving in the least like yourself."

His face changed, was no longer grave. "I've grown slightly weary of that game," he said. "You must think me a bloodless wonder."

Her eyes widened. But she did not tell him that, to her misfortune, she had never once thought him anything of the kind.

"For almost a year I've behaved like the dullest and most honorable of elderly uncles. While you were dependent upon me for your safety, I could do no less and live with my conscience. But now, thank God, the American commissioners have arrived on the scene. From now on, Miss Bradley, if you want to be safe you'll have to apply to Mr. Bayard or Mr. Gallatin."

"Don't blame it on your sense of honor," Page retorted. "From the beginning you treated me as if I had run away from a schoolroom and a governess."

His gray eyes were warm with laughter, and something else that effectively took her breath away. "It may come as a surprise to you," he said, "but I have loved you since the first moment I saw you."

"You cannot mean it," she whispered.

"I never say anything I don't mean." The fire crackled loudly in the silence; after a moment he added, very quietly, "Is it so difficult to forget that I am English?"

At that moment she could have forgotten the war, Bradley's House, her family, her country; she didn't care if he was English, or French, or a Hottentot. All that mattered were his gray eyes, looking down at her with their laughter changing slowly to tenderness, and his mouth that was no longer hard, and the blessed sense of having come home after a long weary tormenting journey.

"Do you know," he said idly, "that I have never even kissed you?"

"Yes," she said, "I know."

He laughed. Then his arms went around her and tightened possessively, his face against her hair and his voice, low and not entirely steady, speaking gently in her ear. She remembered fleetingly the time he had held her in the cabin of the *Caprice*, but this time he was not carefully withholding himself as if she were an innocent child to be comforted. This time she knew, at last, how his mouth felt on hers, and the feel of his hard lean body, and the strength of his hands.

And now, she thought for a confused instant, I will need the comforting more than before, and there will be no comfort in all the wide world.

He raised his head and smiled down at her lazily. "Don't look so stricken. It isn't such a calamity, after all." He put his hand on her face, pushing back a wayward curl, his eyes never leaving hers. "Americans have been known to marry Englishmen before now. The war will be over one day, you know, and then no one can accuse you of giving aid and comfort to the enemy."

Her eyes were wide and disbelieving. "You wish to marry me?" she asked carefully.

"You sweet idiot, what did you think I wanted?" He looked very amused. "And to think I've considered you as innocent as a babe, all these months. Did you fear I'd make you an improper proposition?"

Still incredulous, she thought of his title, his position in London society, the wide impossible gulf between his life and hers, his consequence and hers.

"But your family—" she began.

His voice cut gently across hers. "I do not marry to please my family. But I can assure you that they would be delighted."

She tried to move away, but his arms held her tightly. "You can't know that."

"I know them very well, my sweet." He kissed her cheek, then rested his face against it. "They can see that I love you, and that is enough for them."

She was not convinced, but she had no time to speak. Behind them the library door rattled with an unnecessary loudness, and a determined cough preceded Sutton's dignified voice.

"I regret to disturb you, my lord, but Commander Stuart insisted upon—"

Then a brisk cheerful voice interrupted. "Don't bother to announce me, Sutton, I'll do it myself. Joss, you old dog, now that you've won the war and come home the conquering hero, with laurels on your noble brow and all the ladies of London at your feet, I warrant there'll be no living with you. How the devil are you?"

It was Noel Stuart, uniform as magnificent as always, bright blue eyes and hooked nose the same, chattering away with amiable tactlessness. He had not yet seen Page, backed against the bookcase to his left. As Hazard went to meet him, Page remembered with amusement the day on the British frigate when Noel Stuart had overlooked her presence in the same heedless way.

"Noel, it's good to see you again," said Hazard.

"But you don't look overjoyed. Have I come at a bad time? I couldn't wait, however, I'm on my way down to the old ancestral home to see the family. Then it's off to America again, with a shipload of troopers to fight the Yankees."

"Noel," Hazard said, "here is—"

But Noel, his back now to Page, could not be interrupted. "I daresay the whole affair will soon come to a shrieking close, now that Bonaparte is out of the way and Wellington can direct his attention to America, and I understand we'll have you to thank, my dear fellow, if we beat the Yankees in short order. I saw Fitzroy Somerset in Bordeaux, and he told me all about the tremendous job you did for Wellington in America." Stuart laughed. "You remember I accused you of something of the sort when I last saw you, and you tried to turn me off, sly as the devil."

"Noel," Hazard said curtly, "do you remember Miss Bradley?"

Stuart whirled around. "Lord, I should say so," he said with a wide smile. "My dear Miss Bradley, what on earth are you doing here? The last time I saw you, you were sailing off to Maryland."

She could not manage any words. She did not even look at Stuart. She simply stood and stared at Hazard, still hearing Stuart's heedless words like an echo reverberating in an endless chain of relentless sound.

Stuart glanced from Page's face to Hazard's, and his own flushed ruefully.

"I'm an awkward fool," he said swiftly, "And I should have learned by now that I only open my mouth to put my foot in it. I wouldn't offend you for the world, Miss Bradley, and I hope you'll believe me when

I say that I have every respect for your country, as well as yourself."

She gave him a faint automatic smile; it was not his fault, and she could not embarrass him further.

"Sit down, Noel," Hazard said coolly. "The more you say the worse you'll make it."

"I know, one can never undo a harm already done. Forgive me, Miss Bradley." He gave Hazard a half smile and shook his head. "You'll be wishing me at the devil, and I can't blame you. I'll be off now, and perhaps I'll see you at White's before I leave."

"No," Page said quickly, "don't go. Miss Eliza is waiting for me."

"Give her my regards," Stuart said. "I hope she has been well since I last saw her."

Page nodded and walked to the door, thankful that Hazard did not speak again. She closed the door behind her and ran up the marble stairs, so short of breath that an agonizing pain caught somewhere in her chest and brought quick tears to her eyes.

15

...—◆—...

It was not difficult, in the end, to arrange to drive to Hyde Park in the late afternoon. Sophie had a previous invitation to tea she could not beg off and Anna was engaged to take her music lesson, and Lady Hazard was assured by Miss Eliza that she knew her way about London quite well and would be delighted to show Miss Bradley the charms of Hyde Park.

The question settled, Page lay across her bed, staring blindly at the crimson hangings, and when Miss Eliza came to say that Lord Hazard wished to see her, she pleaded a headache in a small cold voice.

"You do look pale," Miss Eliza said. "Lie quietly, love, and I'll tell his lordship that you need to rest."

She came back later, her face more concerned than ever, and said in her calm way, "Lord Hazard has been called to Carlton House to see the Prince Regent, but he asked me to give you a message."

Page lay still, her eyes closed against Miss Eliza's perceptive gaze.

"You are to remember that he is not an elderly uncle," Miss Eliza said with no expression at all in her voice, "and if you have not recovered from your headache when he returns, he will come up to your bedroom to finish the conversation interrupted by Commander Stuart."

Page's eyes flew open. Miss Eliza regarded her with a dark tranquil gaze, but she said no more.

After a moment Page said, "He wouldn't dare."

"I don't think I would be too sure of that, love."

Page rolled over and hid her face in the pillow. For a long while she lay quietly, trying to think; but it was difficult to think clearly when her heart still lurched oddly and her breath came and went with painful irregularity. Still the truth must be faced; he was right, it wasn't like her to be such a coward, and she knew with a shameful self-reproach that she had refused to think clearly any number of times in the past year, and now her cowardice had brought her to this. *I knew*, she thought miserably, *I knew even when he kissed me.*

Her conscience might argue that she had done a terrible thing, but her heart as swiftly denied it. Love was not dictated by the color of a man's coat, and war, as Hazard had once said, could not force people to hatred. It was not such a calamity; unwise, perhaps, and certainly dangerous, but not an act of treason. All this she could tell herself, rationalizing away such impersonal matters as loyalty and patriotism and the cold distant politics of war, remembering only his dark face and his laughter and the feel of his mouth against hers.

But the other matter was something else again. She turned Noel Stuart's words over and over in her mind, growing so cold and numbed and frightened that her head actually began to ache.

"Do you intend to drive in the Park?" Miss Eliza asked quietly. "If you don't feel equal to it today, perhaps we could send Farley with a message?"

"No," Page said fiercely. She sat up. "He would only tell Hazard, and we can't put Mason in such danger."

239

Miss Eliza looked mildly surprised. "I don't think his lordship would be so underhanded as to report him."

Page said bleakly, "You can't know what he would do."

Miss Eliza seemed about to protest, but in the end she only said sensibly, "Then we had better hurry, I think, not to miss Captain Mason."

So they drove out again in the elegant chaise. Page, however, saw very little of London this time. They were bowling along a drive in the Park before she lifted her eyes and looked around her. The Park was a gay glittering place in the sunlight, all green foliage and brilliant uniforms and beautifully dressed ladies, and blooded horses groomed to a polished gloss prancing before curricles and barouches and chaises of the most gorgeous hues and luxurious upholstering.

"Everyone promenades in the Park of an afternoon," Miss Eliza said. "It is quite the fashion, you know." She added, after a pause, "I make no doubt that the groom's livery will be recognized, if not Lady Hazard's carriage. It isn't the most promising spot for a secret assignation, my dear."

"No one will recognize either Mason or myself, and I don't care about the rest."

"I was thinking of Lord Hazard, love. What will you tell him when he finds out, as he surely will?"

"I don't know that he will," Page said. "I must deal with that when the time arrives."

If she felt a brief qualm she banished it quickly. She had seen him angry before, and the memory was not reassuring; but she lifted her chin and reminded herself that she had never been frightened of him before and did not intend to begin now.

Miss Eliza put her hand on Page's for a moment.

"Don't worry, love," she said quietly. "Whatever happens, you know that I will always stand beside you."

Page, who had not been entirely certain of Miss Eliza's understanding or support, tried to find words to thank her, but they would not come.

"I grew quite fond of Daniel Mason before we left him," Miss Eliza went on, with a little smile. "Give him my very best regards, and assure him that I wish him only the best."

"Thank you," Page said gratefully. "I've been feeling rather lonely the past few hours."

She saw Mason then, strolling along by himself, clad in a sober but well-cut blue coat and a glossy beaver, wearing an indolent air of careless boredom as if Hyde Park at the fashionable hour of the promenade was not a thing to impress him greatly.

"Put me down," Page said to Miss Eliza. "I'll walk with him, and you can go around the Park and come back to get me."

Daniel Mason came up to the carriage, his smile as reckless and assured as it had been on the deck of the *Caprice*.

"I'm glad you came," he said in a low voice. "It's good to see two friendly faces."

He held out his hand and assisted Page to the ground.

"I'll be a model of propriety," he said to Miss Eliza. "But don't be long. It won't do for her to be with me any length of time. Someone might remember seeing us together."

Miss Eliza smiled sympathetically and the chaise drove away.

"How are you, my pet?" Mason said in his soft drawling voice. "I don't have to ask about Hazard. When I caught a glimpse of him in Portsmouth he seemed a bit tired and worn, but the same old Hazard for all that."

Page studied him for a long moment. He had lost much of his tan, and his face was thin and sharp, etched with tiny wrinkles under the eyes; and despite his well-cut clothes, he had the appearance of not having enjoyed a full meal for some time.

"What were you doing in Portsmouth?"

He smiled. "Come along, we'll attract less attention if we're walking."

"And what are you doing here in London? Where is the *Caprice*, and where is MacDougall?"

They walked along slowly, moving through the leisurely Park strollers until the walk was less crowded.

"I'm in London because I wanted to see you. I was in Portsmouth only accidentally, having arrived by coach the same morning, apparently, that you came ashore." After a moment Mason went on, "I find myself less conspicuous in a town, you see, so for some time now I have been traveling by coach from one English town to another."

"But why?"

She met a passing glance, openly admiring, from a young man in a cherry waistcoat, and Mason noticed it in time to rout him with a hard quelling stare.

His voice hardened. "The *Caprice* was taken in early March. It took two frigates to do it, but we had suffered some damage in a storm and couldn't get away. Before we could all get off she began to burn, and several of my crew perished. The *Caprice* burned to the waterline and sank."

Page felt the shock like a hard physical blow. After a long while she said with care, "And MacDougall?"

"Still safe and well at Madame Gouret's, so far as I know. I was to pick him up when I returned to L'Orient the next time." Mason laughed, and it was not a pleasant sound. "But we were caught as neatly as a mouse in a trap, coming out of La Rochelle one dawn. We had put in during the gale, and they were waiting for us when we came out."

Page stared at him remorsefully. There was nothing to say, or any words to ease his bitterness. Then he said, "I was taken to Dartmoor, along with the remainder of my crew. Two of them died within a week for lack of attention to their wounds. But the rest, like myself, are accustomed to hard knocks, and the last I saw them they were well enough."

Page thought numbly of the things she had heard of Dartmoor, that dreadful pesthole in Devonshire where the cold bitter winds blew eternally and dank fogs settled in the bones, and the ill-fed, poorly clothed prisoners died from typhus and pneumonia and smallpox, or else wasted away for years, forgotten by the world.

"But how did you escape?"

He told her the rest of it then, in plain matter-of-fact words that took no notice of the dangers of being an escaped prisoner, or of walking boldly in Hyde Park, or of planning to go back to fighting the British as soon as possible. When Bonaparte abdicated and the French prisoners were released from Dartmoor, he said, a great number of Americans went with them; few French deaths were ever reported by the prisoners, and on the day of the release the names of the deceased were used by any Americans who could speak passable French.

"You wouldn't think I'd qualify," Mason said with a faint grin, "but our Devonshire guards couldn't tell the difference between French and cockney."

He had left Dartmoor with the first group of French to be released, and when they were marched to Plymouth he had managed to escape. He could not go back to France without his crew and officers, and they were planning to try the same ruse with the next list of departing French; those succeeding were to meet on the Cornish coast, where smugglers could be hired to take them to France.

"So I'm biding my time," Mason said, "traveling about on abominable British coaches and learning a lot about the British character."

"I don't understand how anyone could mistake you for anything but a foreigner," Page said. "Aren't you afraid they'll pick you up again?"

"But I make no bones about being an American," he said. "I simply mention that I don't approve of the war, and prefer England to America, and since they think any reasonable fellow would feel the same, they aren't at all surprised or suspicious."

Page walked in silence for a few minutes, and around her the laughter and bright heedless conversation of fashionable London seemed as shallow and insubstantial as the pale English sun. There was nothing menacing about the people who paraded in the Park, unless it was their arrogant self-satisfaction, their assurance, their obvious belief that as English they were superior to anyone else in the world. They lived in a smug privileged world bounded by Grosvenor Square and Bond Street and St. James's Park, by the great country estates scattered over a lush green countryside; and not the least of them would be even fleetingly interested in two unfashionable strangers of little consequence and no English blood.

"If I'm lucky," Mason said then, "I'll get back to France and find myself another ship." He paused, and when he went on his voice was hard and blank, as if the thought of sailing another ship after being master of the *Caprice* was not a thing to dwell upon. "I promised I'd take you back to America when I went, and so I'm here to repeat the offer. It'll take a bit of maneuvering, but I think I can get you out of England. Do you still want to go with me, or have matters changed since I last saw you?"

"I don't know," she said slowly. "Everything has become so confusing."

"I had an idea," he said, "that you and Hazard had come to an agreement of sorts."

She could not answer for fear that she would weep.

"No need to give me an answer now," he said easily. "Look, I'll be in London for a day or two yet. Here is an address; memorize it and destroy the paper. Don't dare to come yourself, but a message will reach me there."

The chaise stopped beside them. Mason took Page's hand and held it for a moment.

"Take care," he said, "and don't worry about us. If an American can't outwit an Englishman any day, we've no business fighting a war."

Regardless of the attention she might attract, she stood on tiptoes and kissed his cheek. Then she allowed him to help her into the carriage, and smiled unsteadily at him as he tipped his beaver with an elaborate politeness, his amber eyes laughing at her as the carriage drove on and left him standing there alone on the walk.

"Is everything well with him?" Miss Eliza asked softly.

"The *Caprice* was taken and burned," Page said. "Mason lost some of his men in the action, and more when they were taken to Dartmoor Prison. He has been there himself, since March."

"I see," Miss Eliza said, and her voice betrayed that she did indeed see.

So the lovely Baltimore schooner was at the bottom

of the Biscay Bay, Page reflected, and her captain a
hunted man; her crew, or what was left of it, was imprisoned in a filthy pesthole where men died like flies
from wounds or disease. But the *Caprice* was not an
exception; it had happened before to other ships and
other men, and would again.

I must be resolved, she told herself rigidly, to do
what I must, and not allow any foolish weakness to
blind my judgment.

In Grosvenor Square she went into the house with
Miss Eliza and asked a footman if Lord Hazard had
returned.

"He is in the library, ma'am."

She met Miss Eliza's calm thoughtful eyes. "I have
something to say to him," she said, "but I don't think it
will take long."

She raised her chin before she knocked on the library
door; then she opened it and walked in, despising herself for her lagging reluctant feet.

He was standing with one arm resting on the mantel,
looking down into the fire. When he saw her he
straightened and looked across the room at her with the
hooded gaze and inscrutable face he affected so well.

"Did you have a pleasant drive?" he asked levelly. "I
trust you have recovered from your indisposition."

"What did Noel Stuart mean?" she asked carefully.
"What kind of a job did you do for Wellington in
America?"

"Nothing very important. Noel has a trick of exag-
gerating trifles."

She stood quite still, watching him come toward her,
but when he reached out for her she could not bear it.
"No," she whispered, and moved away from his hands,
putting a chair between them.

He did not move. He looked at her silently for a

moment. "Page," he said, his voice gone very gentle, "I love you."

She shook her head helplessly. "You said you were only visiting your sister. You didn't tell me Wellington had sent you to America."

"I did visit my sister," he said. "For the rest, I didn't think you needed to know."

She stared at him. "Were you spying?"

He didn't answer at once. Then he said evenly, "That's an ugly word, sweet."

"It's an ugly thing," she said, her eyes wide and unfriendly.

They were only a few feet apart, but it might as well have been a million cold separate miles. Page felt waves of chill sweep through her, as if she had left a warm room for a dark draughty corridor.

"Did you tell Lord Wellington the best way to attack Washington, and how to sack it when it finally surrendered? Did you spy out all our defenses, so it would be easier for his soldiers to finish off the Yankees the way they did Napoleon?"

"I could tell Wellington nothing about America's defenses, or lack of them, that his lordship did not already know."

"Then you did spy for him," Page whispered. "You were a British agent."

There was a dreadful, unnatural silence.

Hazard walked across the room and leaned his back against the desk, resting on the palms of his hands.

"Wellington is a victorious general," he said, "and for some time the Government has asked his advice in military matters. But he does not care to advise when he knows little of a situation, and my job was to bring him the necessary information."

It did not help matters, Page thought numbly, to

explain. There was a subtle difference about him, an unconscious assumption of authority, decisive and competent, that a man acquired from years of command. He might as well be wearing a scarlet uniform; it was in his voice, his face, even the way he looked at her, with impersonal appraising eyes.

"He wanted to know the popular temper, the actual feelings of the American people toward England and France, the probable course of public opinion in the country. He wasn't as interested in gun placements and military movements as in the assessment of America's will and ability to fight."

"It amounts to the same thing," Page said dully. "If we are defeated, you will be partly to blame."

"Whatever I did or did not do, the United States stands a fair chance of being defeated." Then he said, with a hint of compassion in his voice, "I did my duty as I saw it, Page, and were the questions to arise today I'd do the same again. Did you expect it to be otherwise?"

She hadn't expected anything, and so she had been fool enough to think she might avoid disaster; but now she had fallen into a trap of her own making, and there was no escaping the pain, no softening of the blow.

"Even for you, my sweet," Hazard said quietly, "I cannot change the color of my coat."

"Nor can I," she said bleakly.

She felt drained of every feeling. They might have been struggling in a nightmare neither could control. Hazard, standing motionless by the desk, studied her with narrowed frowning eyes, his face pale under its tan.

"I wish you would trust me," he said, low. "You have done so before and come to no harm."

She shook her head, beyond words. Going to the

door, she thought desperately that if he spoke to her again in that quiet tender voice, or asked her to reconsider, she might well be lost; but he did not speak, and she closed the door and went slowly up the stairs, passing both Farley and the groom who had been on the carriage, without seeing them.

In her bedroom she sat on the bed with a tiredness that ached inside her and said to Miss Eliza, "Do you have a pen and paper? I must write a message to Daniel Mason."

16

Page left London, as she had once left Annapolis, on a warm gray day with a drizzle of summer rain wetting the cobbles and dripping aimlessly from green leaves and brass lampposts and red brick porticoes.

It had been surprisingly easy to arrange. Miss Eliza, with her usual perception, seemed to understand Page's need to get away; and while she looked exceedingly grave when Page confided her plan to sail to America with Daniel Mason, she said only, "Perhaps we should leave London. Once he has left England it will be difficult for him to contact you here."

And so, at breakfast on the second morning after their arrival in London, Miss Eliza professed a great desire to visit her aunts and cousins and assorted kin in Devonshire, and suggested to his lordship that Page might also enjoy the trip.

Hazard, without an instant's hesitation, said coolly, "An excellent idea." He would be busy with his agent most of the week, he said, discussing matters pertaining to his estates, but he was sure that his mother would give them every assistance in preparing for the journey.

There was a veritable storm of astonished protests from Anna and Sophie and young Henry, but Lady Hazard, after one swift glance at her eldest son, cleared the atmosphere by saying calmly, "Do be more considerate of our guests, children. They will be in England for some time, you know, and we can't keep them selfishly to ourselves the entire time. Run along now, and allow us to finish our breakfast in peace."

But Page noticed a tiny frown between the lovely gray eyes, and felt a sudden stab of regret that Lady Hazard should think her ungrateful and churlish. Her ladyship, however, continued to be as friendly and warm as before, and even Anna and Sophie, having been reminded of their manners, appeared to accept Page's departure with compliance if not approval.

They were to travel to the west of England in his lordship's own crested traveling chaise, equipped with a driver, grooms, and two brawny outriders; and if Page, tearless and silent, felt a cold creeping misery that Hazard had accepted her refusal so swiftly and dispassionately, sending her off across England without a protest or even seeming to care, she was obliged to admit that his indifference made the parting more bearable.

Henry told her good-bye brusquely and went off with a long face to order his phaeton, and Anna and Sophie said their tearful farewells in the morning room beside their mother.

"Thank you for being so kind to me," Page said, with some difficulty. She imagined that Lady Hazard gave her a rather searching look, but in the end she simply kissed Page gently and said, "Hurry back, my dear."

Hazard went out to the steps with her, and behind him the butler and footmen faded away and disappeared.

"By the time you return to London," he said, "the American commissioners will probably be ready to sail for home. Do you want me to make the arrangements while you are gone?"

Because she did not want him to suspect anything she said, "Yes, please."

He looked down at her silently for a moment. Then he said easily, "I wish you joy of Devonshire and all the Wyndham relatives."

"Thank you," she said stiffly, and turned to go down the steps to Miss Eliza and the waiting carriage.

"You're an absurd child," his voice came from behind her, low and amused and caressing. "Do you think you've stopped loving me?"

She did not dare look at him again. "I never said I did," she said in a small voice.

"But I did," he said gently. "Don't forget it."

He handed her into the carriage, but she did not speak again. After he had said good-bye to Miss Eliza he spoke to the driver and stepped back, yet even at the last minute Page could not trust herself enough to look at him again. Farewells, she thought numbly, were a form of torture no one should be obliged to endure.

For a long while, as the well-sprung carriage moved through the streets of the city and out into the English countryside, she pondered the echo of laughter in his voice and the casual amiability with which he had said good-bye. It was not at all like him to give in so easily; but then, she reminded herself dismally, he had no way of knowing that she did not intend to return to London.

"Perhaps it would be wiser," Miss Eliza suggested thoughtfully, "to sail with the commissioners. They would take the best care of you, I daresay, and it would surely please your father to have you returned to America so properly."

"Properly or not," Page said, "I want to go home as

soon as possible. The commissioners may be in London the rest of the summer."

The very thought frightened her. When one had neither the opportunity to fight for one's country nor the strength of character to hate those who fought against it, the prospect of having to cope daily with such a contemptible weakness was not pleasant.

"Even so," Miss Eliza persisted in her quiet way, "the waiting would not be so tiresome. London will be an exciting place this summer, with all the ruling princes and statesmen of Europe there to celebrate the end of the war. Lady Hazard intended to introduce you to society, you know, and see that you received invitations to all the balls and dinners." She added, with a hint of amusement, "Confess, love, that it would be delightful to have his lordship's escort to all the gala events."

Page said nothing, despising herself for the small painful ache of regret she could not resist.

"The ladies would dislike you bitterly," Miss Eliza said, "but the men would all want to know what it was about you that could interest one of the most eligible men in town. Within a fortnight you'd have a dozen offers, I dare swear, all of which you could refuse with the utmost contempt. Do but consider the satisfaction of knowing you had taken the enemy by storm and defeated them handily."

Page was obliged to smile. But she could not prevent a wistful thought of London as it would be that gay festive summer. Anna and Sophie had talked of nothing else, and Page had found it impossible to escape the infectious excitement.

She could imagine the glittering balls, where exquisitely-gowned ladies in satin and diamonds waltzed with the Cossacks, the royal Prussians, the hussars, the German princes, all in uniforms of a dazzling splendor . . . The afternoon parades in Hyde Park with the magnificent horses and dashing equipages and escorts of cavalry in their plumes and scarlet cloaks . . . The crowds in the streets watching the Prince Regent as he rode by with his clattering troop of Household Cavalry, cheering the Emperor of Russia and his scarlet-and-gold guard of honor, straining eagerly to see the bestarred generals and bemedalled kings who had fought by England's side to defeat the Corsican . . . The rockets showering golden clusters of fire above the London chimney pots, the stirring band music, the radiant transparencies flickering in every window, the pageantry, the merrymaking, the gaiety, the exhilaration because the war was over and done with at last.

But the war with America was not done with, she thought sadly, and she had no place in a rejoicing and festive England.

"Daniel Mason and MacDougall will take good care of me," she said steadily, "and see me home properly. The plans are already made, in any case, and I would not like to think of them waiting off the coast for me, in the greatest danger, only to learn that I had changed my mind."

After a moment Miss Eliza asked gently, "And if they find it impossible to manage? I am sure Captain Mason has only the best of intentions, but he has any number of obstacles to surmount. A suitable vessel to be found and purchased, for one thing, and the business of outfitting her and signing on a crew. Not to mention the risk of holding off the coast until a message can reach you. In the end, my dear, you may be in England longer than the American commissioners."

But not in London, Page thought, and perhaps a long

peaceful time of waiting in remote Devonshire would erase the turmoil inside her. Daniel Mason, she was certain, would not consider any obstacle insurmountable. Sooner or later, in the dark of night, someone would tap lightly on the door in Plymouth where Miss Eliza's trusted friend lived alone with her cats and dogs, and she would send the word on to Page and Miss Eliza.

"They must manage," Page said stubbornly. "I will not go back to London."

"Nor shall you," Miss Eliza said promptly, "if you don't wish it. Do look, love, at the elegant mansion to your left."

Page looked obediently, seeing but another of the imposing country mansions with rolling lawns and spreading elms, and tall iron gates boasting a massive coat of arms.

"One might be vastly more impressed," said Miss Eliza, "if one were not aware that the owner barely escaped being imprisoned in the Fleet when he could not pay a gambling debt for some forty thousand pounds."

Having deftly changed the subject, Miss Eliza talked cheerfully of Devonshire, and there was no further chance to ask her the delicate question Page had been turning over in her mind since they left London. She had considered a dozen different ways to phrase it, but there was really no polite way, after all, to ask if the gold guineas in Miss Eliza's purse had been furnished her by Lord Hazard.

They paused for luncheon in a small bustling market town where substantial old houses crowded along the cobbled streets and looked down with satisfaction upon the red-faced farmers and their country wives, the laughing milkmaids and servant girls, the well-fed and well-mounted squires, the blacksmiths and saddlers and masons, the tattered bright-eyed gypsies in red coats, the abundance of the countryside heaped up in the market stalls.

Directed to the town's only inn, Miss Eliza and Page dined contentedly on trout and roast lamb, a yellow omelet, a salad sprinkled with oil and vinegar, and a plate of sugared cherries. When they came out again into the pale sunlight, they found their carriage surrounded by curious townspeople who smiled at them broadly and looked with respect at the crest on the carriage. Page, feeling rather conspicuous, returned the smiles shyly and wondered if the good-natured curiosity might turn to anger were she to announce that she was both enemy and an American.

But Miss Eliza laughed at such a notion. "They would only shake their heads at such foolishness," she said, "and then sympathize with you for being a foreigner, poor lamb, and not fortunate enough to be English. They're a long way from wars here, you know, and news is slow in coming. I'll wager only a few of them know that England is at war with America, and those have probably forgotten it."

"But I cannot," Page said quietly, and felt an astonishing urge to weep when she met Miss Eliza's compassionate eyes.

She turned to look out at the passing landscape, seeing it for the first time with a rising resentment. Beyond the town the placid countryside began again, incredibly green and lush, its lanes leading through sun-filtered woods and curving past thatched cottages almost hidden by flowers and vines, past velvet fields and chestnut coppices and hedges all pink-and-gold with shepherd's rose and wild honeysuckle.

A lovely England, she thought, secure and complacent and tranquil; not unlike the Chesapeake country before the Englishmen from these very cottages and hamlets had come to pillage it. She wondered how the prosperous countrymen of Surrey and Dorset would feel to have their houses and barns burned, their crops ruined and livestock stolen; but then they were a long way from wars, she reminded herself bitterly, and that sort of news would never reach them.

"It is just as well that nothing came of it," she said drearily. "No one who is born an American can think with an English mind."

Miss Eliza did not pretend to misunderstand. "I imagine he has always known that, love," she said calmly. "He has a vast deal of intelligence you have never credited him with." Then she added, with a faint smile, "I have an idea he prefers your mind as it is, every whit American."

Page shook her head. "He thinks I should ignore my conscience and see matters as he sees them," she said hopelessly.

She longed to say more, but she knew it would be useless. Even if Miss Eliza knew the truth, which was very likely, she would think him only a brave and gallant patriot; the coin of truth had two faces, equally fair, and no one could see them both at once.

Miss Eliza remarked casually, "I seem to recall something you said to me once about men and the foolish things they will do to uphold their honor. You told me, if I remember correctly, that you thought it all a great piece of nonsense."

Page sighed. "I still think it," she said. "You see what confusion I've made for myself by getting involved in men's affairs. But once one has a lion by the tail, it is difficult to leave go of it." She stared through the window for a while before adding, "It is not so much honor, or even conscience. It is remembering all the others who have suffered so much more than I, and those who will yet suffer before it is finished."

"But not because of him," Miss Eliza said quietly. "Remember that, now and again."

But no one could be sure of that, Page reflected miserably, arguing the thorny question over and over in her mind until she was almost ill with it. By the time they stopped for the night she was thoroughly exhausted, and the sight of the neat inn with its gleaming oak furniture and sanded floors, and its copper and pewter shining in the firelight, was so comforting that she went up to bed without dinner and fell immediately asleep in a goosefeather bed with astonishing depth and softness.

The next day was equally tiring, although Miss Eliza deftly kept the conversation on a cheerful impersonal level and refused to allow Page's mind to dwell on anything more unsettling than a game of chess, played on a pocket-sized board with tiny Chinese chessmen fashioned of creamy ivory.

But that evening, prodded by the thought of Devonshire coming nearer with each hill and gentle valley, Page determined to get the matter straight between them. The inn was small and they were obliged to share a bedchamber, and Page looked at Miss Eliza in the candle light with searching eyes.

"What will you do," she asked slowly, "when I am gone? Will you stay in Devonshire, or return to London?"

Miss Eliza buttoned up her flannel night shift, finishing the task neatly before she spoke. "I thought you understood, love, that I have no home in England. Oh, I daresay I could make a place for myself with a cousin who has six children and a delicate constitution. She would be pleased, I'm sure, being a thrifty soul who dislikes to hire housekeepers and nursemaids. Then there is the elderly aunt we are going to visit. She is a lifelong invalid who has a wretched temper and an enormous draughty house, and I know she would be delighted to have me on hand to give her hot milk and sympathy."

Appalled, Page said, "But couldn't you live in London, in a small place of your own?"

"Not on my meager fortune," Miss Eliza said, somewhat apologetically. "I have been faced with this dilemma before, you know, and that is why I accepted Charlotte's offer to live with her in Bermuda."

Page, subdued by an awful sense of guilt and self-reproach, went to the window, looking down through the dark green foliage of a great elm into the walled kitchen garden of the next house. A lark sang once, spiraling down the sky, and then was silent; the twilight was blue and quiet, so still that even the echoing footsteps of a passerby seemed serene and unhurried. It was a small charming village of old weathered walls and crooked streets, of sheltering trees and bright gardens tucked into unexpected corners. Here, in this remote and forgotten backwater, London was a world away and France a legendary distant place of men with tails like monkeys, and only the schoolmaster might recognize such foreign names as Maryland or Bermuda.

She felt very lonely, of a sudden, and unbearably homesick.

"Can you afford to take passage back to Bermuda?"

"Thanks to his lordship's generosity," Miss Eliza said, "I can. But it seems rather foolish for us to sail to the westward in separate ships. I had hoped you would want me to go on to America with you, love, and visit Bradley's House until I could arrange passage to Bermuda. I have a conscience, too, you know, and it would never be easy if I allowed you to go off alone with Daniel Mason."

"Are you still in Lord Hazard's employ?" Page asked, very quietly. "Is he paying you, even now, to stay with me?"

Miss Eliza laughed and blew out the candle, and in the blue shadows of dusk it was impossible to read her face or guess at the reason for her amusement.

"While you are visiting my relatives in Devonshire," she said, "his lordship can reasonably expect me to watch over you. But he has nothing to do with my determination to stay by you until the bitter end."

Waiting for Page to climb into bed, Miss Eliza efficiently tucked in the bedclothes against the evening chill, and for a brief moment her hand rested softly against Page's cheek.

"My affection for you, love, cannot be bought by any amount of gold."

Reassured, Page closed her eyes. It was a blessed relief to know that Miss Eliza intended to sail with her; they had been much together for a lengthy time, and the thought of losing her, along with everything else, had been a bleak heavy burden to bear.

"I hope you won't regret it," she said sleepily. "Please don't think me obstinate for wanting to sail with Daniel Mason."

"Well, never mind," Miss Eliza said lightly. "I suspect it was only a bit of feminine nonsense on my part to disagree. Doubtless I would find that both of your American commissioners are younger than I and married in the bargain, and a long sea voyage with them would serve no good purpose."

Page laughed into her pillow and was asleep almost at once, and so never knew that Miss Eliza soon lit the candle again and stood by the bed for a moment, looking down at Page with a small fond smile curving her mouth.

Then she took paper and quill from her luggage and settled herself quietly at the table to write a long and precise letter to his lordship, Viscount Hazard.

In Devonshire Page sipped tea and ate clotted cream and strawberries, and made polite conversation with the elderly aunt whose temper was as atrocious and house as draughty as her niece had described them. But out of courtesy, and gratitude to Miss Eliza for not deserting her, she endured the slow quiet days of waiting with as much grace as she could muster.

The Wyndhams were kind to her, even the invalid aunt, and the Devonshire woods and coppices and chocolate-brown fields were a delight to see; and it was no one's fault but her own, after all, that nothing in that beautiful peaceful summer could ease the sense of dull depression that settled in her bones like an ache from an old hurting illness.

Sometimes she despaired of ever leaving England, and Miss Eliza comforted her, in the most sensible of ways, by diverting her mind from the message that never came. One morning, as a last resort, she took Page to view the magnificence of a country house in the neighborhood. It belonged to an earl of immense wealth, she explained, who resided in London most of the year and allowed his housekeeper to open the mansion on certain days for the delectation of the curious and envious.

"It is not quite so elegant as Hazard," Miss Eliza said, "but since you had no chance to see his lordship's seat in Leicestershire, this will give you a vague idea of it. His mother told me that he has always spent more time at Hazard than in London, and indeed the entire family prefers the country."

Page, who had not admitted to herself for an instant that she had the faintest curiosity about Hazard's country estates, gave Miss Eliza a wary glance and said nothing.

The carriage drove past a lodgekeeper's house and through the big gates, but a cable across the avenue soon forced them to leave the groom with the carriage and walk the rest of the way through the deer park, a distance of almost a mile.

"How arrogant," Page said. "Does the earl think his prestige would be lowered if he allowed the peasants to drive up to his door?"

"I daresay," Miss Eliza said. "Now I am not necessarily arrogant, but I find I don't care to have my small prestige lowered by being classified as a peasant. Lift your chin and look down your nose, love, and the other visitors will surely mistake us for members of the family."

Page laughed, her momentary irritation gone, and admired the acres of green lawn tailored to the last blade of velvet turf, the profusion of flower beds, the willow weeping over a quiet lake.

"There are dairies and hothouses and stables," Miss Eliza said with a sweeping gesture, "and an entire village of workshops. The earl hires more than three hundred men, they say, merely to work in the grounds." She added casually, "Hazard, of course, is much more impressive. The house itself, I understand, is five miles from the gates, and the park is nearly twenty miles around."

The journey through the house consumed most of the morning, and Page, warned not to linger behind Miss Eliza and the housekeeper, was astonished to discover that a visitor had once been lost in the labyrinth of corridors and rooms for an entire day.

Once when the housekeeper stepped aside to speak to an upstairs chambermaid, Miss Eliza whispered, "I fear I'm beginning to feel the strain of so much splendor. Do act impressed, love, and perhaps she will condescend to ask us to tea in the third parlor. Or the second, indeed, if you remark on the earl's excellent taste."

Page, a bit overwhelmed by the wealth of damask and velvet, the Italian and French paintings in gilded frames, the fine mahogany and rosewood furniture, the Sèvres china and oriental carpets, could only feel a surge of thankfulness that she would never be obliged to be mistress of any such monumental splendor as this. Granted, her chances had been remote from the outset, but now she could truly see the insanity of any notion that a Page Bradley could rule over half a thousand workers, or a deer park twenty miles around, or a mansion with too many rooms to count.

The very thought made her smile wryly, and the housekeeper, who had just proudly remarked that the earl spent more than five thousand pounds a year to dress his lady, immediately stiffened and added, "But them that hasn't, miss, don't know how to respect them that has, and I always say it's a poor kind of folk who don't know their betters."

"But I'm an American," Page could not resist saying, and the housekeeper's eyes bulged with as much horror as if she had been guilty of entertaining a red savage in the master's hallowed halls.

They were ushered out in icy silence, without an offer of any refreshment at all; and despite their aching feet and parched throats, they laughed impenitently all the way home.

There they found a letter from Miss Eliza's friend in Plymouth, asking them to come at once for a visit.

Page, with a long sigh, went to pack her things, and Miss Eliza wrote a number of letters which she sent off at once to be sure, she said ruefully, that all her relatives could breathe freely again to be rid of her.

"I was beginning to doubt him," Page said, "but I should have known he would come, no matter what."

"Always trust a Yankee to do the impossible," Miss Eliza said. "Any number of English gentlemen, to their sorrow, must have been forced to learn that hard lesson."

She and Page said their farewells to all the Wyndham cousins and aunts and went south to Plymouth to visit the little house on a crooked street where Miss Eliza's friend of independent means and mind was beside herself with excitement to be included in such a wildly romantic plot. Then, on a dark still night, they put to sea in a small fishing vessel manned by men whose faces were only blurs in the darkness, and after a stealthy exchange of signal lights they at last climbed aboard the *Esperance* and were greeted by Daniel Mason's flashing grin and familiar soft drawl.

"I want to be out of the Channel as soon as possible," he said cheerfully. "Take your things below, and the next time you see the dawn we'll be sailing for home."

Page's spirits lifted perceptibly, and when she went below and found Duncan MacDougall and Marie-Thérèse, wearing absurdly blissful expressions, she amazed herself by laughing and weeping at the same time, her self-control suddenly in shreds.

"You see I found a husband," Marie-Thérèse said proudly, "despite Bonaparte. We had our wedding in the village church, and even Madame Gouret came to the ceremony." She smiled slyly at Page. "And I myself cooked the food for the feast."

"When it came to the point," MacDougall said gruffly, "I couldn't leave her behind."

Page smiled at them, pushing away the treacherous thought that they had been far more courageous than she. To her relief, they did not ask about Hazard. Indeed, there were no questions asked at all; he was forgotten, erased from their lives, left behind to vanish like the long hazy line of land on the horizon that was England.

"It seems strange," Page said once to Miss Eliza, "that I heard no word from him while we were in Devonshire."

"Why do you think it strange, love? He is a gentleman, after all, and he could not wish to distress you after you made it so very plain what you thought of him."

"I didn't mean that," Page said quietly. "I only thought he might wonder when we were returning to London."

"Oh, I had a short note from him some time ago," Miss Eliza said casually, "asking me how we fared and if we found Devonshire peaceful enough for us. I would have mentioned it, but I didn't wish to upset you." She added, matter-of-factly, "In any case, I fancy he has been much too preoccupied to be concerned about our return. He has a great deal of business to attend to, and London is so gay this season that he is probably deluged with invitations."

Page said no more about it. And since no one aboard the *Esperance* mentioned England or France or the war, it should have been very easy for her to forget everything but the delight, felt by every American aboard, to be sailing for the United States again.

The *Esperance* was a French brig, purchased by Mason in Nantes and refitted to his specifications, and if she did not have the speed and grace of the *Caprice* she was roomy and comfortable. Swinging south to find the trades and make their westing, they sailed along steadily with a northerly wind behind them. The sea was a friendly warm blue, the wind constant, and in the emptiness of the Atlantic they sighted only one sail, a tiny triangle which dropped below the horizon almost at once.

Life aboard was quiet and monotonous. The food was excellent, due to Marie-Thérèse's continual visits to inspect the galley, and the atmosphere cheerful. Since no one spoke with any interest of anything but the number of days it might take to raise a landfall, the most exciting topic of conversation for days was the wager among the crew as to which day the ship would first turn her bows west with the trades and begin the long slow curve to America.

Page found the voyage interminable. It was a safe peaceful trip with no tension, no alarms, no fights on the deck, no arguments or hostility. Miss Eliza was her usual calm self, MacDougall and Marie-Thérèse had eyes only for each other, and Mason, while he talked to Page by the hour and teased her in his usual way, never once overstepped the bounds of propriety. The *Esperance* sailed sedately along for week after week after week, and even when they raised the South Carolina coast, and the whole crew cheered lustily, Page could not rouse herself out of the strange lethargy enveloping her.

They spoke an American ship off Charleston and were warned that the British were swarming in the Chesapeake. Mason, with a grim set to his mouth, put into Charleston at once, avoiding the blockade by his usual habit of slipping through it in the dark. There, quietly anchored in an American harbor, the *Esperance* lingered for more than two weeks.

Even the crew chafed impatiently, wanting to be off to the Chesapeake at once. But Mason refused to take any such risk with women aboard; until he could be reasonably sure of finding a port still free of the enemy, he would keep the *Esperance* in Charleston harbor. Nor would he listen to any suggestion that the women might be sent north by carriage. It would be a miserable hot trip, he said firmly, and they could easily be a month arriving in Washington; by that time there was no guessing what turn the war might have taken.

Puzzled, Page remarked, "It's most unlike him. Do you recall how he went off to take on an entire British convoy, and never once talked of any risk to us?"

Miss Eliza smiled. "Perhaps he is thinking that he owes your father the courtesy of looking after you. Mr. Bradley's temper seems to make a great impact on all who know him."

"Daniel Mason doesn't know Papa that well," Page said, "and he isn't one to fear any man's temper."

Finally even Mason tired of trying to make any sense of the bits and pieces of rumor drifting south. They could not stay in Charleston all summer, after all, and the most reliable intelligence indicated that the British were not hovering in Lynhaven Bay but were further north in the Chesapeake. In the end, Mason decided that the *Esperance* might, with care and vigilance, fetch Norfolk safely.

They set sail on a bright August morning, with not a single British ship in sight. Page, watching the roof tops of Charleston fade astern, was as eager as the crew to be off again. Charleston might be an American port, but home was up the familiar blue reaches of the

Chesapeake; and home, the British notwithstanding, was where she longed to be.

Mason, who knew the shoals and channels of the Bay as well as the lines of his hands, took the *Esperance* into Norfolk in the moonless dark of midnight, and so it was not until dawn, when a harbor official came over the side to welcome them, that they learned the truth about the British activity in the Bay.

A mighty armada of four ships-of-the-line, at least twenty frigates, and an untold number of military transports loaded with British soldiers was anchored at the mouth of the Potomac. Rumor had it that they were soon to attack Washington, but the Secretary of War himself had reassured the worried citizens of the capital that the British effort would be directed against Baltimore.

Mason went off ashore to learn what he could of the situation. When he returned he announced that he had sent a messenger to Samuel Bradley, telling him their whereabouts and expressing the hope that they would be able to reach Washington without running afoul of the British.

"But I'm not convinced I should allow you to go near Washington or Annapolis so long as the British might attack at any moment," he said thoughtfully. "I can't escort you. I'll have to stay with the ship, ready to take her out to sea again if the British turn south. You might be safer here in Norfolk than on the road north, with nobody knowing where to expect the British next."

Page admitted the logic of his argument. But she said, "I would like to go home. Even if they land their troops in Virginia, we could stop in Gloucester County with my sister and be as safe as in Norfolk."

Mason smiled at her rather absently. "We'll see. You're a heavy responsibility, my pet, and I can't risk letting you out of my sight until I'm reasonably sure you'll come to no harm."

"You're not responsible for me," Page objected, "and surely it is my own business if I choose to risk the journey."

It took a great deal of argument, however, before he finally arranged for a carriage to drive them to Washington. MacDougall, surprisingly enough, agreed with Page that if matters worsened she would be better off at her sister Julia's or even at Hester Carroll's Washington house. But he would not think of staying with the *Esperance* while Page and Miss Eliza and Marie-Thérèse went home by land, and it was his decision to escort them, Page suspected, that persuaded Mason to let them go.

"They're saying that Washington is of too little consequence to attack," Mason said, "and that Commodore Joshua Barney has a flotilla of gunboats to protect it. Well, I've plenty of trust in Barney but none whatsoever in gunboats. Still, even if the British go up the Potomac I imagine the news will reach you in time for you to turn inland."

Page looked away from the tawny eyes, not wanting him to see the despair plaguing her since he brought back the news that the British soldiers were veterans who had fought with Wellington, and their commander, Major General Robert Ross, one of Wellington's most brilliant brigadiers. Cockburn, the hated and odious scourge of the Chesapeake, was present, as well as Admiral Cochrane, who had replaced Warren; both men, it was well known, were harsh, rough, overbearing officers with old bitter grudges against the Americans. Washington, it was whispered in Norfolk, was almost defenseless, having no regular troops at all and only a handful of untrained militia to face the British regulars of a force some thousands strong. The enemy had been expected for over a year, yet President Madison and his generals were now scurrying around in a chaotic daze of confusion, searching frantically for battalions and supplies and ammunition that did not exist except on paper.

It was a frightening, humiliating situation. It was even worse, to Page, to remember Hazard's certainty that this was how it would be when Bonaparte was defeated and the British turned all their attention to America. He had undoubtedly foreseen all the foolish hurry and confusion and panic and Page wondered, with dismal bitterness, if his report to Wellington had been a deciding factor in the arrival of the British troops and ships-of-war in the Bay.

"Don't look so concerned," Mason said. "Even with ten thousand regulars they can't hold all of Virginia and Maryland. And it might be, with Redcoats marching about the country, that we'll get together and muster a few troops of our own. We've needed something like this to stop all the bickering and back-stabbing."

He took two tough seamen from the *Esperance* to ride escort along with MacDougall, and hired a Negro driver and a groom for the carriage.

"Don't try to hurry," he warned. "You'll have to rest the horses, and in any case it's too hot for you to make fast time." He had a final jest for Marie-Thérèse, a courteous bow for Miss Eliza, and for Page a cheerful grin that did not deceive her. "Don't worry," he said, "we'll defeat them yet. As soon as I can get the *Esperance* up the Bay I'll come to Annapolis and pay my respects to your father." Then he added, his face going grave, "You and I know that they're not all rascals and villains. Remember that, whatever happens."

Page pondered his words as the carriage lurched and rattled over the ill-kept rutted highroad to Washington. Whatever happened, there was much to remember and much to regret; but none of it mattered now. The British were in the Chesapeake in force, and she was going home under circumstances as uncertain as they had been at any moment in the past year. She must learn to cope with the present and forget the past, and not weep and sigh over the painful prospects of the future.

17

The road to Washington was a long dusty red ribbon under the August sun.

The carriage, pulled by tired sweating horses, moved with interminable slowness through the stifling heat of the Virginia summer, past parched woods and baked red fields and pine barrens stretching in sullen silence on either side of the road.

Inside, the heat was even more suffocating, for the windows had to be kept shut against the clouds of sifting red dust, and the uncomfortable jolting over the rough road was so constant and without relief that it had long since become a torture to be endured in an agonized silence.

Page sat with her head against the upholstery and looked with passive indifference at the sun-parched countryside. She and Miss Eliza did not often speak, nor did a miserable Marie-Thérèse; they needed all their energies to fight the heat and insects and plaguing dust.

"Do you remember telling me once," Miss Eliza said, "that there was no dust at sea? Did I dream it, or was it really true?"

To smile was an effort, but Page managed it. "We seem to travel from one extreme to the other," she said.

"Only think of the miles of sea we've crossed, and the days at Madame Gouret's when we were tired of the very thought of rain. And now I'd give all I own for one small wet creek or a single shower."

"Well I daresay the Chesapeake hasn't yet dried up," Miss Eliza said comfortingly. "It can't be much longer, love, before we're there."

But Page was beginning to doubt if she would ever reach Bradley's House again. It was always just over the horizon, hovering out of reach, and sometimes she had a strange fear that when she was finally there and put out her hand to open the door it would fade away into nothing, as in a dream, and she would find herself as far away as before.

Nor could she bring herself to care very much any more. One could cope with pain and wretchedness only so long before it became a dull fixed habit, hardly noticed except as an agony one had grown used to, and finally it became impossible to remember a time when life had been anything but a tedious grind of hours stretching from one dull day to the next.

Now that they neared Washington the rumors were wilder and more ominous than they had been in Norfolk. It was said that General Winder, who had never commanded more than a brigade, had been riding desperately over the countryside searching for men to defend Washington; Maryland and Virginia had not yet produced any militia to help; the British were unloading thousands of hardened soldiers along the banks of the Patuxent River; a fleet was advancing up the Potomac; Washington was being evacuated and civilians were fleeing in all directions.

The last they knew to be true. The road, empty and deserted for all the miles from Norfolk, began to be crowded with loaded wagons and carriages, the drivers whipping on their horses as if the British were only just behind them.

"Perhaps we had better change our destination," Miss Eliza suggested, "and turn back for your sister Julia's."

"No," Page said firmly. "If the British reach Washington before us, we don't have to cross the Potomac." Then she said, trying not to betray her apprehension, "If they are landing from the Patuxent they won't be far from Bradley's House. I can't hide in Virginia while everyone at home is in danger."

"But do you think it wise, love, to try to reach Bradley's House when the enemy is so close?"

Page met Miss Eliza's eyes directly. "They are not enemies to you," she said steadily. "Will you help us?"

She hadn't needed to ask. "You know I will," Miss Eliza said, "if I can. But I am not at all sure that I would know how to deal with an army, if we happen to meet with one."

"Perhaps we won't," Page said, seeing Marie-Thérèse's wide startled eyes. "If we do," she said lightly to Miss Eliza, "we must all pretend to be British ladies frightened to death of the Americans, and no doubt they'll be gallant enough to protect us."

Miss Eliza's answering glint of humor was mixed with affection. "An excellent notion," she said. "You had better allow me to do the talking, however. I am obviously English, and not so obviously a poor liar."

Reassured, Marie-Thérèse began to relax again, but Page and Miss Eliza looked at each other briefly with sober eyes.

The road was becoming so crowded that progress was growing more difficult by the moment, but theirs was the only carriage going toward Washington. In a steady stream the fleeing citizens of Washington poured into Virginia, stirring up choking clouds of dust as they urged on their horses. The coaches and carriages were packed with pale terrified passengers and the wagons, piled high with hastily packed household possessions, teetered unsteadily in the press of haste.

At the Potomac bridge their carriage was held up for over an hour; even when an occasional lull in the traffic might have permitted them to pass, so many people tried to dissuade them from going into Washington that MacDougall and the two sailors were obliged to ride before the carriage, clearing the way and scowling so fiercely at anyone thinking to stop them that they were finally allowed to go forward.

MacDougall agreed with Page that they should go straight to Hester Carroll's. "Her husband is one of the President's officials," Page explained to Miss Eliza, "and perhaps he will know enough of the situation to advise us."

Washington, a small straggling village of eight thousand inhabitants, was usually a drowsy unhurried place in the steaming heat of late summer. As a capital only half-finished, the streets were unpaved and all but a few houses were scattered among fields and unkempt patches of wood where rabbits and quail abounded. The federal buildings on the hill and the warehouses on the river at the Navy Yards were the only landmarks distinguishing Washington from any other sleepy Virginia village. But on that August Wednesday it was full of turmoil and bustle, seething with rumors, confused by constant alarms that the British were coming, echoing to the distant sound of cannon, and in such a grip of panic that Page hardly recognized it.

When the carriage finally drew up before the Carroll's large house with its iron gate and wide pillared portico, the peaceful quiet pervading the street was such a contrast to the rest of town that Page was seized with foreboding.

"I warrant they have already left," she said, exasperated. "It would be very like Aunt Hester to run away at the first alarm."

The house was plainly closed and locked, but after repeated knockings one of the Negro servants opened the door a small crack, and MacDougall immediately pushed it the rest of the way.

Aunt Hester Carroll, it seemed, had left that morning for Georgetown, and Mr. Carroll's whereabouts at the moment were unknown. The servant, badly frightened, knew only that the British were definitely marching on Washington and that the hastily mustered American force had already left the city to meet them. In the panic of the moment no one had given the servants any instructions, and now they were huddled in the cellar, terrified that they would soon be victims of the British monsters.

"Maybe we'd best go out by Georgetown ourselves," MacDougall said. "We can't go towards Annapolis if there's a battle at hand, and this is no place for women."

Page lifted her chin. "Nonsense," she said. "I will not run away with all the other faint-hearted cowards. We'll stay here until we know something more definite."

"While we are deciding our next move," Miss Eliza said, "I think it would be the better part of valor to go inside."

The street was no longer empty. Small groups of militia came by, moving with no sense of urgency but seeming tired and dispirited, and somewhat dazed; a number of them were carrying no weapons of any kind, and only a few wore uniforms.

Mason's men stopped one of the men who wore the uniform of the Baltimore militia.

"There's been fighting at Bladensburg," the man said dully. "Ten thousand British regulars, they're saying, but it looked twice that to me."

"If there was a fight," one of the seamen said harshly, "why ain't you there? Running away, the whole lot of you?"

The soldier glared at him with angry eyes. "We were ordered to retreat. General Winder himself was the first to leave. Go fight the Redcoats yourself, if you're so anxious. I've had enough of it, marching and counter-marching all night with a bunch of old nannies quarreling over which way to go, and nobody knowing where the British were. The commissary wagons got lost and nobody's drawn a ration since Tuesday morning, and half of us were never issued ammunition."

The seamen, appalled by the inefficiency and confusion of a land war, stared at the soldier with astonishment. MacDougall was silent, but there was a bitter shamed twist to his mouth.

"The devil take the generals, and the British, too," the soldier said furiously, and stalked off down the street.

There were more retreating troops now, filling the street, and two riders on sweating horses galloped by and disappeared in a swirl of dust.

"We'd better go inside," MacDougall said. "I don't like the looks of it, and it's likely to get worse."

They all went into the Carroll house, sending the carriage to the stables. MacDougall put Mason's men to work closing the shutters, while he locked the doors as if preparing for a siege. The rest sat in the drawing room, an elegant chamber furnished in crimson velvet and silk-upholstered furniture, and looked at each other with bleak silent faces.

The drawing room shutter in the window facing the street was left cracked, and for some time they watched the American troops retreating through Washington, hungry, tired, dispirited men whose flight was obviously spurred on by the thought of the British regulars on their heels.

Then there was a lengthy silence, uneasy and ominous, and the street outside was empty again. Washington might have been utterly deserted except for those there together in the drawing room; but Page, seeing a curtain flutter briefly in a window of the house across the street, knew that they were not the only ones hiding in a locked house. The men had fled, running from the British, but more than one woman had been left behind.

She stared down at the empty street, feeling a sense of defeat so bitter and helpless that she was torn between anger and tears.

Then MacDougall said, in a harsh unbelieving voice, "Here they come."

A troop of British soldiers marched down the street, moving in a steady cadenced step, their scarlet uniforms brilliant in the hot sun. They looked straight ahead, continuing down the street as if they owned it, tough brown men who had fought Bonaparte to a finish and looked capable of doing the same to the Americans. When a group of mounted officers rode by they showed the same unshakable confidence, never looking to either side, not in the least afraid to ride down the empty streets between empty silent houses.

One of the seamen, standing behind Page, cursed under his breath and then immediately apologized. But she didn't blame him; she could have cursed herself, if only to relieve the hot fierce hatred boiling up inside her.

By nightfall the town was filled with British troops. From the cracked shutter Page could see the red flames staining the sky as the enemy put the torch to Washington. They had lighted no lamps in the house, not wanting to draw any attention, but Hester Carroll's French wallpaper was as crimson as the velvet curtains, reflecting the glow from the burning town outside. Then an explosion shook the house, and another, heavy and deafening, and all through the long night the explosions rattled the windows and trembled in the very walls. But nothing was set afire within a block of the Carroll mansion, and at least they did not face a choice of being burned inside the house or going out to face the British troops.

Miss Eliza and Marie-Thérèse would not go upstairs, but tried to catch naps on the uncomfortable sofas. Page, however, stood by the window most of the night, keeping watch with MacDougall and the two grim seamen from the *Esperance*.

When dawn finally came, smoke hung listlessly in the hot sullen air, choking and dense, hiding the devastation of the night, and one of the sailors decided to slip out of the house to see what was going on in the rest of town. Having been abandoned to their fates once, the Negro servants did not trust Page to keep them safe and refused to leave the cellar until the British had left Washington, so Page and Marie-Thérèse cooked breakfast and served it in the drawing room. But none of them were very hungry, and Page after swallowing a piece of bread and butter with difficulty, pushed the rest away.

By noon the sailor returned with the news that the British had fired the Capitol, the Arsenal, the Treasury, and the War Office. The President's House and the Navy Yards were also in flames, and the great bridge over the Potomac to Virginia had been fired by the Americans on one end and the British on the other. No civilians, as yet, had been hurt; the inhabitants were ordered to stay indoors, and the British had declared that they would destroy no private property or harm any private citizen.

"Do you think they truly mean it?" Page asked.

"Maybe," the seaman said, "but damn their eyes, begging your pardon, I didn't give them a chance to show me. I was hiding behind a hedge, down close to the President's House, and saw Cockburn himself, prancing about on a big horse and grinning at the devil's work he'd done, and loaded down with plunder he'd stolen from the President's House."

Page said quietly, "It sounds very like him. Were his men plundering, too?" She paused, remembering Hampton, thinking with blank horror of what they might face if the troops were let loose upon the town to sack it. "Were they still under control?"

"Aye, I'd say they were. Most of them were mighty quiet, standing around as meek as you please. I saw a general arguing with Cockburn, and somebody said it was Ross. He didn't look too happy with the night's work."

"I should think not," Miss Eliza said. "It was a night's work that will not soon be forgotten, and I do not believe General Ross to be a man who could approve of such infamous behavior."

Page sighed and sat down on the sofa, so weary and spent and stunned that she could not think clearly about anything. The day dragged on, miserably hot and still, and even in the gloom of the drawing room with its closed shutters the heat was so breathless and sullen that they felt drugged and helpless with inertia. The only sounds drifting in from outside were an occasional shouted order, the scattered voices of the distant troops, and a jingle of horses and dragoons passing by. There were no screams, no shots, no indication of sack.

In the late afternoon the sky began to darken, and the sweltering stillness was stirred by a rising wind.

"A thunderstorm," Page said with relief. "At least it will cool the air and lay some of the dust." And put out the remaining fires, she thought, and spoil some of the fine scarlet uniforms that marched so grandly into Washington.

It was a thunderstorm of magnificent proportions, sweeping into the capital with torrents of lashing rain and a wind that roared out of the black sky with the thundering force of a cavalry charge. Lightning split the clouds and zigzagged to earth with a violent impact. Across the street a tree bent almost to the ground before the wind and finally went over with a crash of waving branches and torn roots. A wooden sign torn loose from some tavern clattered wildly down the street.

Page, who had seen a lifetime of southern thunderstorms, was not unduly frightened, but Marie-Thérèse held MacDougall's hand tightly and murmured her Hail-Mary's with closed eyes; and even Miss Eliza looked alarmed by the violence of the wind and rain.

"It will pass over in a few minutes," Page said, and smiled reassuringly. "The noise is the worst part of it. All sound and fury, signifying nothing." Then she added with sudden decision, "I think we should all be better for something to eat. Marie-Thérèse, will you help me in the kitchen?"

Called to a duty she could never refuse, Marie-Thérèse opened her eyes and ventured bravely into the kitchen with Page. Aunt Hester's larder, as always, was plentifully supplied, and in a short while Marie-Thérèse was happily basting several fat hens on their spits and preparing buttered crab. Page, enveloped in a voluminous apron, tried her inexperienced hand at pastry tarts. By the time she had them ready for the oven her face was dusted with flour and the white apron liberally stained with cherry juice.

The storm, now dying away in the darkness of night, was forgotten by Marie-Thérèse, who laughed immoderately at Page's appearance and the lopsided cherry tarts.

"You will never make a cook," she said, "unless you develop a light hand with the dough and the character not to taste the filling."

"I only ate one cherry," Page protested. "Or perhaps two."

"I saw you," Marie-Thérèse said with amusement. "Two or three or four, I think. I meant to ask you to pour the wine, but if you are a taster it would surely be unwise."

Page's laughter faded away. MacDougall stood in the kitchen doorway, looking from Page to Marie-Thérèse, and just behind him Miss Eliza, her face less tranquil than usual, gave Page a smile that was plainly intended to be reassuring.

"What is it?" Page asked uncertainly.

MacDougall hesitated. Then he straightened his shoulders, almost with resignation.

"Samuel Bradley is here," he said.

Page stared at him, her eyes widening. Then she whispered, "Papa," and made a dash for the door, passing both Miss Eliza and MacDougall without a second glance, running straight through the dining room and down the long hall to the drawing room doors.

They were closed. The two seamen stood in the front

hall, grinning widely at her, but she paid them only a cursory attention. Catching her breath unsteadily, she put her hands on the big brass handles and opened the doors.

"Papa," she began, then stopped abruptly.

Across the room, Samuel Bradley stood with his back to the fireplace, feet planted firmly apart and hands on his hips, his cloak dripping a puddle on Hester Carroll's carpet.

Beside him Hazard leaned his big shoulders against the mantel, one leg in mud-spattered buckskins and boots propped on the empty grate.

For what seemed a small eternity of time, the drawing room was incredibly still. Hazard straightened slowly and stood erect.

Page could not move or breathe during that endless moment of stunned silence. Then, gradually, the numbness of shock began to thaw, prickling at her nerves like a frost-bitten finger coming back to life. For a single panic-stricken instant her only emotion was an instinctive cowardly urge to back out of the room and close the doors again, never saying a word.

"Well," Samuel Bradley said in a thundering voice, "and what have you to say for yourself?"

Her panic instantly dissolved. Smiling radiantly, she flew across the room and fell into his arms.

"Oh, Papa," she whispered, "I feared you'd be terribly angry."

He didn't speak at once, but his arms tightened around her. Then he cleared his throat, and held her away from him.

"There, now," he said, "no need to take on about it. I'm wet enough as it is."

The words were those a man invariably uses to comfort a woman who weeps on his waistcoat, but Samuel

Bradley's voice, even when lowered to a gruff tenderness, rattled the ormolu and china figurines on the mantel.

"The devil fly away with you, I've never known anyone to plague me so." He looked down at her with his penetrating blue eyes, heavy brows drawn in a straight line across the beaked nose. "Are you well, missy? Have you had a bad time of it? Tell me the truth, now, I've no time to waste with civilities."

She smiled at him and wiped her face with the back of her hand, leaving a damp streak across the smudges of flour. She had not even glanced in Hazard's direction since that first incredulous moment, but the awareness of his presence throbbed in her blood until she thought the pounding of her pulses should be clearly audible.

"Do I look ill-used?" she answered, her voice not entirely steady. "Everyone was amazingly kind to me, Papa."

"Don't quibble," her father said severely. "As for myself, I fail to see any kindness in the shameful behavior of the British. It's a miserable state of affairs when a dab of a girl can be dragged all over the world, alone and unprotected, with no man to stand against such arrogance."

In a small unemphatic voice she said, "The British treated me with every consideration, Papa."

Samuel Bradley gave her a searching look. Then he said, "It's been an awkward business from the start, and I don't mind saying you deserve a beating for it. But never mind that now." His voice hardened. "I'd like to know, if you please, why this gentleman had the effrontery to come to Bradley's House, bold as the devil, and ask my permission to pay his addresses to you."

There was no alternative. She was forced to look at

Hazard, seeing again the dark face and remembered gray eyes and the big size of him, finally admitting the astonishing and unbelievable fact that he was, indeed, standing there in the Carrolls' Washington drawing room.

He was very grave, watching her with an expressionless face that told her nothing except that he was on his guard, and as calmly in control of himself as always.

"How did you know I was in America?" she asked carefully.

"Thanks to Miss Eliza's good offices," he said, "I've known everything about you since you left London."

She stared at him, forgetting completely, between one breath and the next, that there was anyone else in the room. After a moment she whispered, "She promised she wouldn't betray me."

A brief smile flickered across his face. "But it all depends, you see, on one's definition of betrayal."

So he had known all along, and all because of Miss Eliza. Page drew a deep breath, suddenly remembering a number of unexplained matters.

"And Daniel Mason?"

"I sent him word by Miss Eliza that I would hold him responsible for you. Did he take good care of you?" Then he added, "He might have better served me by keeping you out of Washington at this particular time."

"He had to stay with his ship for fear the British would take it as they did the *Caprice*," Page said stiffly, "but he sent two of his men to escort us, along with MacDougall. He couldn't know, after all, what the British would do to Washington."

His face was closed, unreadable, waiting for her to go on as if he already knew what she would say.

"Do you find a great deal of pleasure in the sight?" she asked bitterly. "I daresay you had a hand in planning the attack, since you did all the work of spying beforehand. Was it you who suggested burning all the federal buildings? Are you very proud of the way your troops took the capital with hardly a battle?"

"None of us are proud of the things that have happened here," he said. "Cockburn burned the buildings in retaliation for the burning of York in Canada by the Americans, but revenge is no excuse for his behavior. General Ross and his officers deeply regret the whole affair."

"I don't believe it," she said scornfully. "In any case, how would you know what they regret?"

"I spoke to General Ross," he said, "only a few minutes ago." Then he added, his face still expressionless, "He informed me that he is withdrawing his troops from Washington tonight. By late tomorrow they should be back aboard their ships."

"Why aren't you wearing your uniform?" she asked, and despised herself for being unable to go on without taking another breath. "Or are you here to spy again?"

There was a little silence. His eyes were very direct, very steady, and the tiny blaze in their gray depths might have been anger. But when he spoke his voice was patient, as if he were explaining matters to an obstinate child.

"I sold out when Bonaparte abdicated, and am no longer with the army. When Miss Eliza wrote me that you were sailing, I was able to arrange an immediate passage in a ship carrying dispatches to General Ross. Once they had landed me on the Maryland shore it was not difficult to find my way to Bradley's House, though

I was somewhat surprised not to find you there before me."

In another moment, she thought drearily, she would begin to weep. "We were not as fortunate as you," she said, "in having the protection of an armada of warships. However, it doesn't signify why or how you're here. I only hope you'll leave soon, and take your British friends with you."

"When I leave," he said coolly, "you will be with me." He added, his eyes gone as hard and light as stone, "Hate all the British in the world, if you like. But don't think you can hate me, or count me as an enemy."

Her heart gave a painful lurch. She retreated a step, then another. Suddenly she remembered her father, and turned toward him with a helpless appeal for aid.

Samuel Bradley had been listening in frowning silence, his searching gaze going from one to the other. But now, to Page's surprise, he offered her no support.

"You may as well hear him out," he said, "because he's going to say it, one way or another. I've had my share of arguing with him, the past day or so, and now it's your turn." He regarded her sternly. "I'm beginning to suspect you brought it on yourself, missy."

She could not believe that he was deserting her, leaving her to deal with the situation as best she could. "Perhaps I did," she said, close to desperation. "But I didn't know, until the very end, what he had done."

"You knew he was an Englishman," Samuel Bradley pointed out. "Did you expect him to behave like an American?" He put his hands behind him, a solid squarely-built man with an air of decision and capability as forceful as his voice. "I know what he's done," he said thoughtfully. "He told me all about it, first chance he had. But if you're thinking that it makes him less than a man, you don't know much about it."

"I only know how I feel about the war," Page said, low, "and the things that have happened."

Samuel Bradley gave her a long sober scrutiny. "Bessie always told me I was wrong to keep you so much with me, away from the other girls. But I hoped you'd learn to think for yourself, and not turn out to be the usual sort of silly peagoose."

Uncertainly, Page said, "Doesn't any of it matter to you?"

"It matters that you've gone off and gotten yourself involved with a smug, arrogant, opinionated, rascally devil of an Englishman," Samuel Bradley said forcibly, "but for the rest of it, you can't damn a man for doing his duty."

Page opened her mouth to speak, then closed it.

"You'll have to settle it between you," her father went on. "It's your answer he wants, missy, not mine. That's fair enough, Englishman or not." He turned toward the door. "And now I'd like a look at this Miss Eliza, and a word or two with a scoundrel named Mac-Dougall."

The door slammed, starting a wave of jingling and rattling on the mantel. Then even that faint noise faded away into a dangerous and formidable silence.

Hazard's level voice cut across it. "I sympathize with your distress, Page, and admire your loyalty to your country. But nothing that has happened, or will happen, can change what is between us."

He did not look very sympathetic, she thought with a rising panic; he looked big and grim and implacable, a man not easily turned aside from his purpose.

"The war has been a foolish muddle from the beginning, and it will end as foolishly. Next year, perhaps, or next month, whenever they can agree to terms. Wellington, I am convinced, thinks Britain cannot afford another lengthy war, and will advise them to sue for peace. At this point, I hardly think Mr. Madison will disagree. Nothing has been settled and nothing will be, and whatever the war has accomplished it will not be immediately apparent to anyone fighting in it."

She said nothing, and he looked down at her silently for a moment.

"Do you really believe I would allow the mistakes of a few misguided men to take you away from me?" Then he added, in a cool curt voice, "I am not asking you, Page. I am telling you that you are going to marry me, regardless of the war and all its muddling politicians."

Page drew a deep breath, but it caught in her throat. She had thought the barriers between them insurmountable, and she had put him behind her with all the resolution and courage she could muster; but it was one thing to deny herself resolutely when he was half across the world, and quite another to withstand the dangerous force of his immediate presence.

"You look very much," he said, "as if you thought I might carry you off at the point of a pistol."

She raised her eyes. "Would you?" she asked unevenly.

"I might," he replied, still in that hard decisive voice.

Involuntarily she took another step backwards.

"You couldn't run fast enough," he said provokingly, "or far enough."

His hands closed on her shoulders, lifting her off her feet. Then, while she dangled helplessly above the floor, he kissed her leisurely and thoroughly; and despite all

Jan Cox Speas

she could do, she felt her resistance draining away at the first touch of his mouth on hers.

It was a long breathless time before he raised his head. He put her down gently, but his hands still held her fast.

"You do love me," he said quietly. "I was beginning to wonder if you had changed your mind since I last saw you."

"No," she whispered. Then she asked, "If you knew I meant to sail with Daniel Mason, why did you let me leave London?"

"I was sure I could trust Mason, and I thought it would do no harm to let you play out the game in your own way. You had been among strangers for a long time, and you wanted to come home to the protection of your family." He kissed the tip of her nose, then her mouth. After a moment he went on, his voice oddly shaken, "I knew I would be just behind you, in any case, being obliged to pay my respects to your father and offer him my credentials."

Page sighed. "I can see that Papa accepted your credentials," she said, "but I have a very poor opinion of his notions of protection."

Hazard laughed. "I like your father," he said. "We got along famously together, with the exception of a heated argument or two when I feared he would call me out. In time I have great hopes of persuading him that I am not quite the rascal he thinks me."

"You know very well that he thinks nothing of the kind," Page retorted, "else you wouldn't be here." She added with some exasperation, "You have both behaved abominably."

"We have," he agreed promptly, "but admit the temptation was too great to withstand. Farley, by the way, is convinced that a sober and prudent wife should certainly be able to correct all my abominable faults."

"He can't mean me," Page said, startled.

His eyes laughed down at her. "By no stretch of the imagination," he said, "could anyone think you either sober or prudent. But since he assured my mother that he would not allow me to return without you, I suspect that the two of them have resigned themselves to my faults and would not exchange you for all the sobriety and prudence in England."

They were silent, looking at each other. Then his hands tightened on her, pulling her to him. With his face against her hair he whispered, "None of it matters, except this."

Someone knocked on the big double doors, but they did not hear it. Then the doors opened, flung back on their hinges, and they could not escape Samuel Bradley's powerful voice.

"I know you're a lucky fellow, Mac, and she's certainly a taking little thing. But I'm blessed if I'll have her in my kitchen, ruining good food with pesky French sauces and serving up frog legs and snails."

Miss Eliza said tranquilly, "I'll tell her myself, Mr. Bradley, so she will understand that such things are different in America."

"I'll thank you, ma'am, if you would be so kind," Samuel Bradley said, his roar suddenly dwindling away, his voice holding a note of surprised pleasure. "We'll be honored to have you with us at Bradley's House, and hope you'll find that things aren't all that different, you know, in America. A lovely and cultured lady, Miss Wyndham, is appreciated in any language."

Page, her eyes widening, lifted her head to meet Hazard's amused gray gaze. Then she turned, still in the circle of his arms, to face Samuel Bradley, and Miss Eliza, Duncan MacDougall and his Marie-Thérèse, and behind them, his face wearing a broad smile, that gentleman's gentleman from London, Farley.

"And to think," she said in an awed voice, "that none of it would have happened if I had not decided to go to Annapolis one dull summer's day."

Farley, with a look of great respect, bowed.

"Just so, ma'am."

*To her people
she was Sarah Wells.
To her Indian captors
she was . . .*

JAMES HOUSTON

AN EPIC NOVEL
OF RAPTURE AND SURVIVAL

"This stunning novel has everything going for it
to capture and hold the reader's imagination: exciting action and drama, convincing characteriza-
tions and ultimately, a very moving love story."
Publishers Weekly

"A powerful, totally convincing book, drumming
with action, tender and moving."
Cosmopolitan

"Impressively realized, appealing . . . an American historical novel of high quality."
Wall Street Journal

 Avon 35733 $1.95

*"The secret of the entire world
is whispered here at Eden."*

THIS OTHER EDEN

He was the last Lord of Eden Castle,
a man of brooding desire
and sudden passion.

She was his servant girl, a fiery
young beauty who would rather submit to the
cruel kiss of the whip
than suffer the lust of a man
she did not love.

He humiliated her . . . he wooed her . . .
he deceived her . . . then he became her slave.

THIS OTHER EDEN: a breathtaking epic of
torment and fulfillment on the
dark side of love.

By

MARILYN HARRIS

author of the romantic bestseller
BLEDDING SORROW

EDEN 3-78

 AVON / 36301 / $2.25

"The most important book on child-rearing to be published in a generation."

Dr. T. H. Bell,
U.S. Commissioner of Education

THE FIRST THREE YEARS OF LIFE

The famous guide to the physical, emotional, and intellectual growth of your baby by

BURTON L. WHITE

Project Director of Harvard University's world-famous Pre-school Project

Finally in paperback, the bestselling book by America's foremost expert on early childhood and host of the unique nationwide TV series "The First Three Years"

SELECTED BY 3 BOOK CLUBS

 AVON/37234/$4.95

FTY 5—78

The triumphant biography of a Queen!
The intimate story of a dynasty

MAJESTY

ELIZABETH II AND THE HOUSE OF WINDSOR

By Robert Lacey

"Highly entertaining . . . an astute blend of gossip
and uplift . . . a phrase I thought I would
never use describes it:
It is a good read."
Newsweek

"The best book on the fascinating
subject of 20th-century royalty"
Clifton Fadiman

With 32 pages of photographs

 Avon/36327/$2.25